Kore

S. L. Wideman

To my family, whom I love with all my heart
In loving memory of Laurie Wideman

Other books by S. L. Wideman

Space Station Olympus Series

Iona

Kore

Lykaios (coming 2018)

Medea (coming 2020)

Other books

Verucca Victorious

Forbidden Magic (2017)

ISBN:0692777768

ISBN-13:9780692777763

Part I:
Goddess of the
New Spring

Chapter One

The sacred home of Demeter, Level 07 of the enormous Space Station Olympus, was dedicated almost solely to farming. Vast fields of wheat and vegetables stretched as far as the eye could see, large orchards of fruit trees filled the Southern section, and tall silos towered over each field. As vast as it was, this level was not the only place growing food for the ever-expanding population of the space station. There were two more levels between the inhabited cities and Hades that produced grain, fruits, and vegetables, and personal farms could be found on nearly all other levels.

Even with all that, food was starting to become scarce. The humans prayed daily to Demeter for a bountiful harvest to feed the masses. Legends told of how Demeter blessed the mortals and the fields yielded untold edible treasures, but for the past eighteen years, Demeter barely paid the mortals any mind. All of her focus was now on her daughter, Kore, and protecting her from the dark forces Demeter knew were plotting against them.

"It's us against them," Demeter would tell Kore each day as she braided her daughter's dark, curly hair. "I'm the only person you can trust."

Kore grew under her mother's watchful eyes. Like Demeter, she heard the prayers of the humans every day. By the time Kore was eighteen, the lamentations haunted her. There was nothing Kore could do without being officially named a goddess, and Demeter seemed to no longer care. The only thing the Goddess of Grain and Harvest cared about was keeping Kore hidden and safe.

All her life, Kore never left the sanctity of her mother's home. The only people she had contact with were Demeter and her nanny, Minthe. While Demeter clung to her daughter and acted as a shield against the imagined evils of the world, Minthe delighted in pointing out how different Kore appeared. Demeter and Minthe were both pale with straight hair. Demeter was plump with hair the color of wheat and Minthe was slender with hair dyed a pale green. Kore was a mere slip of a girl with dark brown skin, frizzy black hair, and dark brown eyes that sometimes appeared to glow when she was angry.

"You do realize there is a reason why all the statues of the gods are made from alabaster," commented Minthe. "No one else looks like you."

"Maybe I'll change when I get my godhead," said Kore.

Minthe laughed. "There is no power on all of Olympus to change you. If you're lucky, you might get to hang out with the other rejects, like Hephaestus and Psyche."

At eighteen and a half, Demeter made the decision to let Kore attend Hestia's School for Girls. Hestia, Demeter's eldest sister and Goddess of the Home and Hearth, took in young girls of rich families to teach them how to care for the home. Kore was the oldest girl there, a fact that embarrassed her. All the other girls were mortals and wanted nothing to do with Kore. She quickly learned they thought she was an idiot to be going through the program at such an advanced age.

To help Kore, Hestia took to privately teaching her the importance of sticking to and making a budget, balancing financial records, and setting a schedule for housework and meals. Unlike the other girls, Kore learned how to manage a house of servants and the etiquette of the gods.

"What's the use of my learning all of this?" complained Kore one day. "Mother will never let me out on my own."

"She'll have to once you are named a goddess," Hestia said.

"When will that be?"

Hestia shrugged. "When you turn eighteen."

Kore's heart sank. Did Mother forget that she was of age? Or did the gods mark time differently than humans, and she was still a child by their reckoning?

When Kore approached her mother that night about when she'd be named a goddess, Demeter flew into a fit of hysteria.

"Why would my daughter want to leave me? Have I not provided for you? Oh, woe is me! There is no pain sharper nor more deadly than that delivered by an ungrateful child. I raised you with love, and you repay me with words of hate! I gave you food and shelter, and you now stand before me wishing to leave me! Oh, woe! Oh, woe! My own precious daughter has stabbed me through the heart with her poisoned words!" Demeter pushed past Kore to pick up a small statue of Zeus off the mantle. "Oh, my sweet Zeus, do you hear what our daughter has said? I gave her life, and now she wishes to be free of me! Where could I have gone wrong?"

"Mother -"

Demeter shoved the statue at Kore. "Who turned you against me? Who dared pour such venom into your heart?"

Frightened, Kore mumbled, "No one turned me against you..."

"Speak up! How can I get the name of my enemies if I can't hear you?"

"I said, no one turned me against you. I love you, Mother, and I am grateful for all you've done for me. It's just, Hestia mentioned -"

"Hestia! I should have known! She's always had it out for me. Did you know that Hestia took Hades' side? She did! There we were, trapped in that suffocating darkness of Cronus' stomach, and she sat by while Hades did nothing. He, that vile creature, was at home in the inky black pit. Oh, but not I! I needed the sun and air, like the gentle flower I am. When I confronted him after Zeus saved us, Hestia came to Hades' aid. 'What could he have done?' she asked me with that smug little grin." Demeter sank down on a couch, sobbing. "He could have saved us! He was our eldest brother, the one who should have been the hero. He did nothing!"

Kore knelt by her mother, taking her hand. "Mother, you were all just children at the time. Maybe he was just as frightened." She knew she'd have to calm Demeter down if she was ever going to get to discuss her becoming a goddess.

"No! Hades has always loved the dark. Why else would he now rule the Underworld where no sun shines or flowers grow? He is the vilest creature to ever exist." Demeter gasped and looked at Kore. Before the young woman could escape, Demeter snatched her up and held her tightly. "You must beware of him! I have kept you safe all these years, but he's still out there. He'll take you away from me and lock you up in a dark dungeon. You'll wither and die!"

Kore smiled gently. "I will be careful, Mother. Though, I might be able to better protect myself if I were named a goddess."

"No, no, no! That's how he'll get you! Kore, my sweet flower, have I ever told you what happened the day I presented you to the other gods? There you were, just an innocent baby, so helpless, and he tried to kidnap you! I knew I had to keep you hidden away after that. If we name you as a goddess, he'll be able to find you. I just know he's been biding his time. Oh, a curse on Hestia for her foul plot to deliver you into Hades' hands."

Kore pulled away from her mother. "I guess this means my lessons with Hestia have come to an end?"

"What? No, you'll be continuing them, my dear." Demeter got up and smoothed out the skirt of her wheat-colored chiton. "It's almost dinner time, isn't it? Come along, Kore. We should wash up."

"But, what about her being in league with Hades and my goddess status?"

Demeter waved her concern away. "As long as you remain my little Kore, nothing bad will happen to you. Hestia is family - rather misguided family, but family nonetheless. If I pull you from her classes now, she'll sense something is wrong and come here to find out what. And once she's been here, she'll be able to lure you out for Hades. That's the last thing we want! No, it's best if we just pretend none of this happened and you don't ever talk about being named a goddess ever again."

Confused, Kore followed her mother. Demeter, having seemingly forgotten the whole episode, talked gaily about some gossip she heard while in the above levels. Kore only half-listened as Demeter laughed over some mortal woman picking a mortal man over Apollo, and the mysterious Lift crash that took the lives of the newlyweds. Demeter was able to pretend that Kore was not old enough to be a goddess, but Kore couldn't ignore that fact. Demeter easily ignored the tension that brewed between herself and Hestia, changing the subject anytime Kore mentioned the goddess or asked about when she'd be named goddess.

"All right, niece of mine," said Hestia nearly a month later, "what is bothering you? You've been distant and moody for a while now."

Kore couldn't meet her eyes, keeping her head down over the document tablet she was studying. "It's my mother and my goddess status."

"I told you that you'll be a goddess once you turn eighteen."

"That's just it!" Kore slammed the tablet on the table, causing the computer screen to sputter to black. "I am eighteen. In fact, I'm nearly nineteen."

Hestia looked stunned. "You are?" Kore could see the goddess mentally count the years. "By Zeus, you're right! Why hasn't Demeter set up your Becoming Ceremony?"

Kore shrugged and turned the tablet back on. She pretended to be more interested in the various household schedules on the screen. "Mother mentioned something about if I were named goddess, Hades would take me."

Hestia's mouth opened and closed as she tried to process this. Finally, she sputtered, "That's just ridiculous! Why, as a recognized goddess, you'd have more protection. Hades might dare steal an ordinary human woman if he were the kind of man who would do such a thing, but he'd never just kidnap a goddess. It's against the laws of the gods. Demeter has done you no favors by keeping you locked up all these years."

"But, what about Hades?"

"What about him?"

"Mother is positive that he'll kidnap me."

"And I just told you that he wouldn't. Hades plays by the rules." Hestia smiled. "I'll let you in on a little secret. Of all my brothers - I daresay, of all the gods - Hades is the most noble."

Kore turned the tablet off. "Mother did say you sided with Hades."

Hestia laughed. "Your mother could never see beyond her nose. If she ever really thought about it, she'd see that Hades isn't the enemy. All he's ever done is not bow down to her. Zeus and Poseidon both adore Demeter and treat her like a little princess. She's our middle sister, but she acts like she's the youngest. Did you know that Demeter is the only lover Zeus ever had that Hera was never jealous of? She knows Demeter isn't a threat."

"Why would my mother be a threat? She's a virgin goddess." When Hestia quirked her eyebrow, Kore added, "Okay, so she had me, but Mother is practically a virgin."

"She has other kids," Hestia said. "No man, mortal or divine, can put up with Demeter's antics for long. She's worse than Aphrodite."

Kore gasped. "Please, don't say such things about my mother."

Hestia studied her niece. "Let me guess; you feel a bit torn? You want to be the perfect daughter for Demeter, but you also want to grow up and be your own person. What should you do? Stay with Demeter and be her good little girl or become the goddess you were born to be?"

"I...I do feel torn. I mean, who wouldn't? I love my mother and I want to make her happy, but I do want to be a goddess. I've been told since birth it will happen someday." She looked down at her dark skin, wondering once more if it will lighten once she was truly named a goddess.

Hestia patted Kore's arm. "What you should do is talk to Psyche. She'll know how to ease your troubled thoughts and help you pick the right path."

Chapter Two

It took Kore nearly a month to get her mother to allow her to see Psyche. Demeter just couldn't understand why Kore felt the need to discuss her problems with anyone but her.

"What can you tell her that you can't tell me," Demeter demanded. "I am your mother! You can tell me anything, Kore. There is nothing that you can tell Psyche that you can't tell me. She's not half as smart as she likes to think she is, you know."

"Please, Mother. I just need someone to talk to. Hestia suggested Psyche, and I think it's a good idea."

"Oh, of course Hestia! I should have known."

"I want to be the daughter you deserve, Mother, but I keep feeling like I'm being torn apart. I was raised being told I'd be a goddess, and I understand your reasons for wanting me to wait. But I want to fulfill my destiny, and I know that wish hurts you. That is why I want to talk to Psyche. I'm hoping someone outside our situation will help me see a solution that will benefit the both of us."

"Hestia told you to say that, didn't she?" Demeter huffed and stormed off down the hall, wailing about how her own flesh and blood betrayed her. In the end, she finally relented as long as Kore took Minthe with her. Kore did not like Minthe. The shifty-eyed maid was Demeter's spy and Kore found out the hard way that there were no secrets from her mother when Minthe was around. Minthe reported everything from what Kore ate, wore, said, and did. When, at the age of six, Kore innocently told Minthe about a dream she had involving a lovely woman with thick dark hair calling to her with a funny-looking dog with three heads by her side, Minthe ran straight to Demeter. Apparently, dreams of lovely women with three-headed dogs were not allowed.

The day Kore and Minthe left to meet with Psyche, the air was oddly cold and crisp outside of Level 07. Kore shivered, pulling the thin shawl around her shoulders as Minthe led her down the street of the Minor God's Level to the home of Eros and Psyche. "Why is it so cold? Is there something wrong with the environment system?" asked Kore.

Minthe snorted as she hurried on. "Many of the other Levels have seasons. Right now, they are experiencing the start of winter."

"Winter?"

"Yes. The Station's climate changes four times in one standard year. Spring is the thawing period in which new plant life emerges. Summer is the hot period and time to tend the crops. Autumn is a cooling period and the time of harvest. Winter is very cold and all plants die."

"I've never heard of that. Mother's home is always the same perfect temperature."

"That is because autumn and winter are despised by Lady Demeter. They are seasons of death, and thus, are not fitting for the Goddess of Grain and Harvest," Minthe said. "Lady Demeter, in her wisdom, banished those seasons from her realm. It is always perfect and only rains on the crops. As it should be."

"But, why autumn? You said it was a time of harvest, and Mother is the goddess of the harvest."

Minthe shrugged. "I believe Hades has something to

do with that. His venom toward Lady Demeter knows no bounds. It wouldn't be beyond him to devise a way to kill all her plants each year. It speaks of your mother's strength that the Station becomes green and full of life every year."

Kore couldn't help but shudder at Hades' name. Though Hestia felt there was no danger from him, he was the boogie man hiding in every shadow. "Hades is the God of the Underworld and King of the Dead, right?"

"Yes."

"Why would he have any power over the weather to kill plants? Wouldn't it make more sense to poison the ground from which the crops grow, if he were trying to hurt Mother through the plants?"

"Don't question the way things are," Minthe said. "It has always been Hades associated with the cold, and it will always be."

Kore let the subject drop and continued down the street to Psyche's home. Psyche, Goddess of the Mind, lived in a grand estate at the end of the long, cobbled road. Smaller, but just as grand-looking, homes lined the street. Signs above the doors let Kore know which minor god lived where. She never knew there were so many gods and goddesses.

The home of Psyche had probably the most beautiful gardens that Kore ever saw. The lush front garden was decorated with small temples to the main Olympian gods with a white stone path leading to each. Off to the left of the yard was a small pond with fish swimming peacefully inside. Flowering ivy climbed up the walls, though the incoming cold weather took the green from the ivy and left a tangle of brown vines. Kore knew that in the greener months the garden would be gorgeous.

Minthe marched right up to the front door and knocked. Within moments, a handsome man with curly brown hair and neatly trimmed beard answered the door.

"We are here to see Psyche," said Minthe.

"Do you have an appointment?"

"No. But we are very important people. She'll want to see us," Minthe said.

"And you are?"

"I am Minthe, faithful servant to Lady Demeter, and this is her daughter, Kore. We are here seeking Psyche's wisdom."

The man studied the two women. "I am -" he started, but Minthe cut him off.

"Just tell Psyche we're here to see her! Make it quick. We are very busy." Minthe turned to Kore. "Some servants just don't know how to treat their betters."

The man frowned. "Lady Psyche is in the back garden. Just walk around the house." He shut the door.

"How rude," huffed Minthe. "I shall have to tell Psyche about her servant's behavior."

"You weren't exactly polite, either," said Kore.

Minthe sniffed. "You will learn that there is an order to things. I am in service to Lady Demeter, who is a major goddess. That makes me higher up in the hierarchy than a servant of Psyche. He should have treated us with the respect due to Lady Demeter."

"Where do I fall in the hierarchy?"

"Above Psyche's servant, that's for sure."

Minthe and Kore walked around to the back. Kore gasped as she saw the gardens. She always thought her mother's gardens were the most beautiful, and the front gardens had been simply breathtaking. The back gardens, however, were the most exotic Kore ever seen. Even with the approaching cold, there were still flowers blooming. At first, Kore thought they were mechanical like her mother's garden, but the scents that filled the air proved that they were real. It was a rare treat to be surrounded by so many real flowers.

"How disgusting," Minthe sneered. "Look at this. They are less than perfect. This one has brown spots on the petals and this one is uneven. I would rather have mechanical flowers. Those always come out perfect."

"I don't know," said Kore. "I like these real flowers. They all have personality."

"Mechanical flowers have personality. This is just Psyche showing off her wealth."

Down the path was a man wearing coveralls, kneeling by a small, dark glass house. He was welding the panes of glass together. His face was covered by a protective mask.

"You there! Where is Psyche? We were told she was in the back." Minthe marched up to the man. "Answer me quickly! We're very busy."

The man stopped welding and lifted his protective mask. Kore's heart skipped a beat as she found herself staring in to the most gorgeous blue eyes in all of Olympus. The man's slender face held a gaunt appearance with slightly sunken cheeks and a pointed chin. Tufts of strawberry blond hair poked out from under the strap of the mask. Now that she was closer, Kore could see the fine ropey muscled body barely hidden by the baggy coveralls. This man was, in a word, perfect.

"Oh, my," muttered Minthe. "You must be Eros. I am sorry for being so brisk with you. We've just had a bad run-in with one of your servants."

The man's blue eyes twinkled. "No, I am on loan from Hephaestus. Lady Psyche requested a special plant house to be made." He stood and gave them a small bow. "Lady Psyche is currently in conference with Lord Apollo. Please, rest and enjoy the gardens while you wait."

"Thank you. I am Minthe, faithful and most beloved servant of Lady Demeter. I am her most trusted advisor and privy to her most secret of secrets."

"And the young lady next to you?"

"Oh? Yes, this is Kore, daughter of the most exalted Lady Demeter." Minthe vaguely waved her hand in Kore's direction. "Did I mention how much Lady Demeter values me? Why, I'm sure I can show you parts of the station you never knew existed."

The man stepped toward Kore and gently took her hand. He pressed his lips to her knuckles, his blue eyes staring into her brown ones. "It is an honor to meet you, Lady Kore."

Breathless, Kore asked, "What is your name?"

"It would please me if you called me Aidoneus, my lady."

"Aidoneus," Kore said slowly, testing the word out. It just flowed off her tongue.

"Why does that name sound familiar?" asked

Minthe. "Have we met before?"

"No. I assure you, I'd remember meeting two such beautiful women. Perhaps you are thinking of Adonis?"

"Yes, that must be it."

Trying to keep her balance under Aidoneus' magnetic gaze, Kore looked down at the little glass house. "What exactly is that going to be?"

Aidoneus smiled. "A kind of anti-green house, I guess. Lady Psyche's hobby is this garden and she wants to grow as many different plants as possible. This little house is going to cancel out sunlight so she can try her hand at growing asphodel from the Underworld."

Minthe gasped and pulled Kore away from the little house. "And just how will Psyche get asphodel?" Minthe demanded.

Aidoneus shrugged. "Maybe Hades himself will bring the seeds up to her, or maybe one of his servants? I'm not sure if seeds are something that can be safely transported by PortMat."

Kore felt as if someone squeezed the air from her lungs. Growing up, Hades was just a vague threat. Despite being warned that the dreaded King of the Dead could appear at any moment and drag her to the Underworld, Kore knew deep in her heart that he'd never set foot on Demeter's holy land. But now, standing in Psyche's marvelous garden, the threat of Hades became very real.

"Lady Kore?" Aidoneus gently led her to a bench. "Are you alright? You suddenly paled."

"I will be fine," Kore said softly.

Aidoneus nodded. "If you need me, I will be

working." He went back to the little house and pulled his protective mask down. In a moment, he was welding the glass walls on.

Kore couldn't help herself. She found herself watching him. Aidoneus was really one of the first men she'd ever seen. Was that why he fascinated her? Demeter and Minthe warned her that all men would hurt her, but something about Aidoneus drew her. As Kore watched the graceful way he moved, she was struck by a thought: Maybe he could protect her from Hades?

Chapter Three

Psyche was not what Kore imagined a goddess to look like. The woman who walked out to the garden did possess the regal confidence of a goddess, but her face was horribly scarred. An old scar ran down the left side of her face, pulling slightly at the corner of her mouth. She looked to be smirking all the time. Her deep red hair was pulled back in a simple braid and she wore a plain purple chiton. Compared to Demeter and Minthe, Psyche looked very humble.

Following Psyche was the second most handsome man Kore ever laid eyes on. This man was obviously a god; tall and tanned and muscular with blond hair and a face so beautiful it made Kore's heart ache. The man fairly glowed in his short golden chiton.

"I don't think you understand the hierarchy of things, Psyche," the man was saying. "When I say jump, your husband jumps. When I say bring me the twins, he gets that pesky gun of his and gets me the twins!"

"The answer is no! She's married, Apollo. Find someone else. You don't even need Eros to get women."

"She should never have left me! I thought Eros shot her and her twin nineteen years ago with a long-lasting bolt. They both should still be in my residence. When did she leave? How could she leave?"

"She left the same day as I did." Psyche sighed and pinched the bridge of her nose. "Really, Apollo, just leave her be and find someone else."

Apollo frowned. "I am Apollo, God of the Sun,

Music, Medicine, and Prophecy! I am known as the most handsome of all the gods in Space Station Olympus. When I demand a woman, she better drop her chiton so fast that it rains garments in Hades! I don't care if she's married! When I crook my finger, she comes to me! You tell that useless husband of yours to work his gun in my favor, or else!"

"Are you done with your temper tantrum? Go and find a nice unmarried maiden." Psyche noticed Kore and Minthe. "I have guests, Apollo."

Apollo turned to see the two ladies. The dark look on his perfect features lifted and he flashed a heart-stopping smile. "I do not believe I've had the pleasure of meeting you fine women."

Minthe hesitantly stepped forward. "I am Minthe, favored servant of Lady Demeter. This is her daughter, Kore."

"You're Kore?" Psyche pushed Apollo to the side. "Oh my, look at how you've grown."

"Demeter has a daughter?" Apollo asked.

"Yes. She announced Kore's birth the night before I married Eros."

Apollo snapped his fingers. "Right! Wasn't there some disturbance with Hades and one of Ares' sons?"

"We do not speak of that," said Minthe.

"That, at least, explains why Demeter has become more reclusive than normal," Apollo said. "If I had such a pretty daughter, I'd guard her just as zealously. Tell me, little cousin, are you finally joining us gods?"

Kore looked down. "I hope so. That's why I need to

talk to Psyche. I'm unsure of my path."

"Why, your path is with us gods," said Apollo. "A beauty such as you should be seated in the top of Olympus, dressed in jewels and the most luxurious silks. In fact, I'd be honored if you came to my dwelling so I could show you all you've been missing."

Apollo reached for Kore. Just as she took a step back, Aidoneus walked between the two, his protective mask down.

"I've finished, Lady Psyche. Was there anything else you needed?"

"No, thank you." Psyche turned back to the house. "Ladies, follow me."

Aidoneus kept himself between Kore and Apollo. Kore appreciated the gesture. There was something about Apollo that frightened her. He was too forward, too aware of his own allure. Apollo oozed all the dangerous promises of men, the seductive pull that lured many innocent maidens to their demise. Kore wanted adventure, but Apollo was more than she could handle.

The inside of Psyche's home was a shrine to Eros. Frolicking cherub statues could be seen in every room, the cream and pink marble gave a relaxed, loving feel, and the furniture was designed for comfort and intimate conversations. Psyche led them to a sitting room with the plushest couches Kore ever sat on and vases overflowing with flowers.

"Now, Kore, why don't you tell me what is bothering you," Psyche said as she sat on one light pink chaise.

Kore sat gingerly on a chair, demurely crossing her

ankles and folding her hands in her lap. "I am torn between two desires. Mother and I hope you can be of some assistance."

"What are these desires?"

"On one hand, I want to keep my mother happy. She wants me to stay home. I fear no one will ever even know I exist. If I follow Mother's path, I will never be named a goddess and never get to leave her home. It would be a lonely existence."

"Lady Demeter has done so much for Kore," added Minthe. "As you know, my lady raised Kore and provided her with everything she'd ever want. How can anyone be lonely in the presence of a goddess? All Lady Demeter asks of Kore is that she stay with her and remain safe."

Psyche nodded. "I am well aware of Demeter's involvement with Kore. What is the other path you see before you, Kore?"

"I want to live on my own. I dream of being a goddess and taking my rightful place in Olympus. I want a chance to meet my father, Zeus. And, maybe, get married someday."

"Blasphemy!" cried Minthe. She rose out of her chair, pointing an accusing finger at Kore. "After all my lady has done for you, and you wish to break her heart!"

"Minthe! That is enough!" Psyche stood up, crossing over to Kore. She put a hand on Kore's shoulder. "What she is feeling is perfectly normal."

"It is?" asked Kore.

Psyche nodded. "My daughter, Hedone, is going through the same thing. On one hand, she wants to stay home where everything is familiar, but on the other hand, she longs to be her own person. Of course, it probably doesn't help that she was betrothed at birth to Hypnos. Knowing that leaving the house means a wedding and a life as a wife can be just as frightening as having no place to go when you leave home."

"How is she dealing with it?" asked Kore.

"As well as can be expected. She learned how to manage a home from Hestia and is learning how to cook from her Uncle Anteros. I am also having her learn how to defend herself with her Uncle Phobos. That is really all I can do. It is the destiny of every child to eventually leave home. All a parent can do is make sure that he or she is well prepared for the world."

Kore looked down at her lap. "I learned how to manage a home from Hestia, but I have no skills beyond that. Do you think I should learn how to cook and fight?"

Psyche tapped one finger against her scar as she pondered. "I think learning some self-defense will help put Demeter's mind at ease. Showing that you are not as vulnerable may soothe the tension Demeter feels and," she nodded toward Minthe, "have you declared a goddess. That is why Demeter is so late in announcing your godhood?"

"Lady Demeter does things in her own time," Minthe huffed. "If Kore was truly ready to be a goddess, my lady would have announced her."

Psyche turned back to Kore. "Hedone is going to have her Becoming Ceremony in three months. Let me talk to Demeter and see about making it a double announcement. I will also press for you to begin self-defense lessons. I'm sure Phobos won't mind taking another pupil."

"Absolutely not!" Minthe stalked over to Psyche, trying to intimidate the goddess. "There is no way my lady should allow that traitor anywhere near Kore. Surely you remember the fiasco at Kore's Naming Ceremony?"

This was the second time her Naming Ceremony had been mentioned. "What happened?"

"We don't talk about it," Minthe said, realizing her mistake.

Psyche rolled her eyes. "It's not a huge secret. Phobos tried to take you away from Demeter, and Demeter blamed Hades for the incident. I can assure you, Phobos won't try that again."

Kore gasped. Someone really tried to kidnap her when she was a baby? No wonder Demeter was so protective of her. And Psyche wanted her to take self-defense lessons from the same man who once tried to steal her?

Psyche must have seen the look of fear on Kore's face. "If you are worried about Phobos, don't be. He had his reasons, but he will respect Demeter. He learned his lesson." To help take Kore's mind off Phobos, Psyche talked about Hedone's Becoming Ceremony. Kore was soon caught up in the various stages of the planning and was intrigued by all that she'd have to do to catch up to Hedone. Before Kore left, Hedone came home. Hedone instantly took a liking to Kore and invited the shy girl out to a party.

"Lady Demeter wants Kore home immediately," said Minthe.

"I will ask Mother. If she says it's okay, I would love to go to this party." Kore smiled. She never went to a party.

Minthe was not optimistic that Demeter would allow such a thing. Much like Demeter, Minthe could come up with the wildest possibilities as to what might happen if Kore left the safe confines of her home. Everything from contracting a deadly disease to being kidnapped and killed.

"I think you and Mother are too preoccupied with all the evils that might happen that you don't think that they might not happen," Kore said as they arrived home. "It's important for me to have friends."

"But not Hedone! Do you know where her betrothed lives? Hypnos inhabits the Underworld. He's one of Hades' minions!" Minthe wrung her hands in despair. "They're just trying to get us to drop our guard."

Kore sighed as Minthe launched into all the tortures of Hades. Demeter showed up and, upon hearing Minthe's report, added her own objections.

"What if I had a bodyguard?" Kore asked. "Surely, Mother, there must be someone you trust to keep me safe? I want to go to the party. I need to experience life outside these walls. Psyche thinks that would be good for me."

Demeter snorted. "I don't care what Psyche thinks. I'm your mother and I know what's best for you."

"Please, Mother."

"The answer is no!"

"But -" Kore started. Minthe cut her off sharply.

"Your mother has spoken. Go to your room and think about your disobedience. If this is what visiting

Psyche has wrought, I doubt Lady Demeter will let you visit her again. Oh, the shame!"

Kore left and went to her room. There was no use arguing with her mother. Demeter always won.

Kore's room was located in the highest tower of her mother's dwelling. The decor hadn't changed since Kore was a little girl, and it made her feel like a child. Stuffed animals and the color pink dominated everything. The words 'Mother Knows Best' were painted above her bed. Bars were on her windows, and Kore used to believe they were for keeping the bad guys out. Now she knew better. They were to keep her in.

She sat on her bed after pushing the small army of stuffed animals off her bed. She could feel her freedom slipping away. She'll never be named a goddess and will never be allowed to leave. Tears stung her eyes as she thought of all the things she'd miss out on.

The sky outside was starting to darken when Demeter came to Kore's room. She didn't look happy.

"I just got a call from Zeus," Demeter said. "Someone, most likely Psyche, reminded him that you are of age for your Becoming Ceremony. He was also informed about you being invited to that party by Hedone." Demeter struggled to get the next part out. "He's sending a bodyguard to take you to the party and has agreed to you and Hedone having a shared Becoming Ceremony."

"Really?" Kore jumped up and hugged her mother. "Oh, thank you!"

"Don't thank me. If I had my way, you'd stay here and be safe. That meddlesome Psyche is putting you in danger. I can only hope you come to your senses before catastrophe finds you."

Chapter Four

Kore's chaperone/bodyguard was the ever-imposing and dangerous Phobos, God of Fear. He stood at an intimidating six feet, his muscular body covered by leather armor and several sharp daggers. A blaster was holstered by his side. HIs bushy black hair was tied back and his dark eyes flashed when he saw Kore. He assured Demeter in his deep, rumbling voice that no harm would befall Kore.

"What was Zeus thinking in sending you?" Demeter demanded.

"That everyone deserves a second chance. Besides, who else would be more qualified to guard the girl?"

The party was on Dionysus' special level in a beautiful building nestled between two grape vineyards. Beautiful gods and exotic humans mingled throughout the level, and Kore felt shabby standing in their presence. She had put on her best wheat-yellow chiton, but it was far too plain when compared to the elaborate styles and jeweled embellishments around her.

When Kore took a step back, overwhelmed by the crowds, Phobos gently placed his hand on her back. "Don't show them fear," he advised. "You are worth more than all of them put together."

"I don't feel like I'm worth more," Kore whispered.

Phobos was silent for a moment. "You remind me of a person I used to know. Odessa was also very shy and very humble. Though she could outshine Aphrodite, she preferred to hide her beauty and sing the praises of the gods. But, when push came to shove, Odessa could be the bravest and most compassionate person on the whole station. She'd be intimidated by this crowd, but she'd hold her head high and march in if she had to. Believe me, Kore, you are so much like her, that I know you have that same bravery inside you."

"I'd like to meet her. Would she be here?"

"No. Odessa was murdered several years ago. I failed to save her." Kore could hear the pain in his voice.

"I'm sorry for your loss."

Phobos shrugged her words away. "It's a sad fact that, no matter what, we will outlive the humans. Though I wanted a lifetime with her, I treasure our few stolen moments. Come on. We can honor her memory by not backing down from this challenge."

Kore wanted to protest that she never heard of Odessa until now, and while she was important to Phobos, she was nothing to Kore. Yet, on the other hand, it meant something to Phobos and Kore felt oddly drawn to the gruff and imposing man.

They walked up to the front of the building. The guard at the door demanded to know their names, and then proceeded to tell Phobos only he could enter.

"This is a party for gods only. Humans must be specially invited," the guard said. "No one named Kore is on the list."

"She's a goddess," snarled Phobos.

"Never heard of her."

At that moment, Hedone showed up. She called out

Kore's name and latched on to her arm. "I'm so glad you could make it! I was worried that Demeter wouldn't let you out. Did you know Zeus called our home? Mother talked to him, but it was just so strange." Hedone tried to pull Kore into the party, but the guard stopped him.

"She's not on the list."

"She's Demeter's daughter," Hedone protested. "And she's my guest."

"She's not on the list."

Hedone huffed. "Wait here," she ordered and ran into the party. A few moments later, she returned with a short man in tow. The man wore dark purple robes with grapevines sewn into the hem. His skin was dark, almost the color of night, and he had no hair. A sleek jaguar followed meekly at his side, a crown of grapevines on its head.

"He won't let Kore inside," Hedone complained.

The man took the guard's list. "Hmm, yes? Oh! Here's Kore's name. She's right here." The man took a pen out of the guard's pocket and wrote on the list. When he turned it to the guard, Kore could see that he added her name.

"My apologies, Lord Dionysus. I must have not seen it."

"You're Dionysus?" asked Kore. She had thought all the gods would be taller, more regal, and white. Everything she was not. But, he was darker than she, and only came up to her shoulders.

"I am." Dionysus smiled and his whole face beamed. "Welcome to my humble party. Come, come! Make yourself at home."

Inside, Kore was introduced to several of the guests. Many were minor gods and goddesses while there were some privileged humans in the mix. There was no way Kore could remember everyone.

"Well, well! Hello there, little cousin!" A man with curly brown hair sidled up to Kore. He moved gracefully and Kore was surprised to notice his feet never touched the ground. He hovered a few inches in the air.

"Kore, this is Hermes," said Hedone.

"We're cousins?" asked Kore.

"All the gods are related to each other in some fashion," said Hermes. "But, yes. Zeus is my father, and he's your father."

"That actually makes us half-siblings," said Kore.

Hermes laughed. "Well, so it does! I don't know when I got in the habit of calling everyone cousin."

Hedone suddenly grabbed Kore's hand. "I see Hypnos! Come on, I want to introduce you!"

"Be careful," Hermes warned. "I saw Hades hanging around a few moments ago. Demeter would freak if you were the one to introduce Kore to Hades."

Kore felt cold. "Hades is here?"

"Yeah. Well, it didn't look like he was here to party," said Hermes. "It's unusual for him to come up from the Underworld."

"Let's go," said Kore, turning to Phobos. "I don't want to stay anymore."

"I won't let anyone hurt you," promised Phobos. "Go

and meet Hypnos, and then we'll leave. If I see Hades moving toward you, I'll come and get you."

Hesitantly, Kore allowed Hedone to drag her toward Hypnos. The God of Slumber appeared to be fairly ordinary. His skin was pale from living in the Underworld and his black hair was tied back in a long ponytail that fell below his shoulders. Hedone let go of Kore's hand to run up to him. Kore stopped and watched as Hedone, normally so boisterous, stood almost shyly in front of Hypnos as they talked. Kore felt her heart tug as Hypnos reached over and gently tucked a lock of Hedone's hair behind her ear. The love he felt for her was so obvious in his dark eyes.

Not wanting to interrupt the two, Kore took a step back, intending to melt into the crowd. However, she bumped into someone behind her. She turned, and nearly fainted on the spot. Behind her was a rail-thin man with sickly pale skin, a black chiton, and dark eyes. His lips curled up in a cruel smile.

"Hello there, Kore," he said. His voice was raspy, making Kore think of a person trying to talk around grave dirt. He raised a hand and reached for her, his long fingers looking like claws.

Kore shrieked and ran out of the party. She pushed past party-goers and hurried out into the vineyard. She kept running, not caring where she was going as long as it was far, far away from that man. She didn't dare look behind her, fearing she'd see him there.

When Kore finally slowed down, she realized she was lost. All around her, grapes grew in rows on spikes from the ground. She could faintly hear the music from the party, but she could no longer see any buildings. Worse, she had no idea where the PortMat or lifts were located.

"Kore?"

She turned to see Aidoneus standing behind her. Now that he wasn't hiding behind a protective mask, Kore could clearly see his face. He had a beauty that made the perfection of Apollo seem obscene. He still wore coveralls and had on a bulky tool belt. His strawberry-blond hair curled at the nape of his neck and framed his face in soft waves.

"Aidoneus! What brings you out here?"

"I could ask you the same thing. Did something happen at the party? You look so frightened."

"Hades was at the party. I just need to get home, but I'm lost."

Aidoneus' blue eyes widened. "Kore, I..."

"He scared me," Kore went on. "He looked just like a corpse, and his hands were like claws. It was just awful! I knew he was going to drag me away."

"Who?"

"Hades!"

Aidoneus looked confused for a second. "I'm guessing you're talking about the man who came in with Hypnos, right? Tall, skinny, dressed in black?"

"Yes."

Aidoneus laughed. "I can see how you can make that mistake. No, that man was not Hades. He's Thanatos, God of Death. Even the humans seem to mix him and Hades up at times."

"Hermes let me know that Hades was at the party. I

was so sure he was Hades."

"Most of the gods wouldn't know Hades if he was at the party. He hardly ever leaves the safety of the Underworld." Aidoneus stepped in front of her. "I promise you, Kore, despite what you may have heard, Hades will not drag you to the Underworld. Please, before you think of Hades too harshly, ask the opinions of the other gods. You'll see he's not the villain Demeter wants you to believe him to be."

The little star lights on the ceiling twinkled and the only real light came from the moon. Hidden in the vineyard, Kore felt like they were the only two people in existence.

"Why is it so important to you that I don't fear Hades?" asked Kore. "Doesn't everyone fear him?"

"No. You'll see. He's...As I said, he almost never leaves the Underworld." Aidoneus reached up and tucked a strand of Kore's dark hair behind her ear. She felt herself blush. Under the cover of darkness, she could just make out the look of adoration on his face. "You're so beautiful, Kore," Aidoneus whispered.

"We've only just met."

"I can still think of you as beautiful. Hasn't anyone else ever told you how you can outshine the stars? Or how your skin is the softest ever touched? There is a sadness in your eyes that tugs at my heart every time I see you, and all I want to do is make you smile."

He leaned in closer to her. Kore's heart beat so loud that she was sure he could hear it. His lips were so close to hers. All she had to do was close that last small distance and they'd kiss.

"Aidoneus," she whispered. She closed her eyes, waiting for the touch of his lips.

"There you are!" Phobos' deep growl broke the spell. Aidoneus jumped back and Kore felt a stab of regret and guilt. She had wanted him to kiss her! What would her mother say if she knew? Would her mother be relieved that Kore was falling in love with a man who was not in league with Hades, or would she be disappointed that Kore was enchanted by a mere mechanic?

Or, perhaps, Demeter would be angry that Kore would dare fall in love at all?

Phobos took Kore's hand. "Come on. Do you know how much trouble we'd be in if word got to Demeter that I let you meet up with him on my watch?"

"Aidoneus is just a mechanic. Mother would under-" Kore sighed. "No, Mother would not understand. You're right."

There was a slight twitch to Phobos' lips and he looked over at Aidoneus. "We'd better get going. I won't mention your little meeting with, uh, Aidoneus the mechanic, but don't let this happen again. You need to be more careful. It's bad enough that people know you gave me the slip at the party."

Kore turned her gaze to Aidoneus. He looked so uncertain and bashful under the simulated night sky. She was seized by a strong desire to kiss him. In her mind's eye, she could see herself wrapping her arms around his shoulders and pulling him to her. She wanted to know if his lips were soft and how would his hair feel through her fingers.

"By Aphrodite! You're acting like you've been shot

by Eros!" Phobos pulled Kore away, breaking her thoughts. She blushed, realizing how lustful she'd become in just one day.

Aidoneus gave a little bow. "Until next time, Lady Kore," he said.

Not wanting to just leave, Kore broke free from Phobos. Without thinking, she stepped up on tip-toe and kissed Aidoneus on the cheek. "Thank you for coming to my rescue."

Phobos made a disgusted sound. "Are you coming, or do I have to toss you over my shoulder and carry you away?"

"Coming," said Kore. Her last view of Aidoneus was him standing in the vineyard, a look of wonder on his face and his hand over the spot where she kissed him.

Phobos meant to get Kore back to her mother, but they were stopped at the PortMat by Hedone and a young woman in a short tunic. Hedone gushed over Kore, complaining that she was so worried when she turned around and Kore was nowhere to be found. When she learned that Kore had left, Hedone was in a panic. She swore she had been looking all over for Kore.

"As you can see, she's found. I'm bringing her home," said Phobos.

"Home sounds nice," said the woman. "I don't know why I let myself get dragged out to these parties. They are so boring."

"Artemis, you find anything that isn't hunting to be boring," Phobos said. With that, he quickly introduced Kore to Artemis, Goddess of the Hunt and the Moon. She was also Apollo's twin sister, though they didn't look anything alike. Where Apollo was tall and golden and impossibly handsome, Artemis was a short woman with a slightly olive cast to her skin, dark brown hair pulled up in many braids, and almond-shaped eyes that she accented with dark eyeliner.

"Oh, I met Apollo earlier today," Kore said.

"Well, that explains his interest in this party. We must have arrived just after you left."

"That means you got bored faster than normal," said Phobos.

Artemis rolled her eyes. "Drunken men are not my idea of fun. Anyway, little Hedone told me something very interesting just before you showed up, Phobos. Is it true you're teaching her self-defense?"

"Yes. As her uncle, it is my right to teach her how to shoot a gun and protect herself."

"There is nothing a man can teach that a woman can't do better," said Artemis. "There is no finesse to what you do, Phobos. Much like your father, you represent the emotional reckless rage of all males. That is why the humans pray to Athena, a woman, for wisdom before battle and not for brute strength."

"I'm teaching her how to protect herself," snarled Phobos. "As one who has been trained to fight in wars, I can teach her how to defend herself against a variety of enemies."

Artemis laughed. "Oh, look at how angry...how emotional...you become when faced with the truth. Not to mention. All of your 'varieties of enemies' are all men." Artemis turned her attention to Kore. "What about you? Are you also going to let this man teach you?"

"I haven't talked to Mother about lessons. I do need to learn how to defend myself. I believe that would help put Mother's mind at ease."

"I'll teach you," Artemis declared. She smirked at Phobos. "We can have a little contest to see which of us can train you girls best. Say, at the Becoming Ceremony?"

"You're on. Best out of three tasks wins, judged by the other gods," Phobos said. "Though I will win. I've been teaching Hedone for months now. You only have three months to get Kore up to speed."

Hedone protested. "But there is no fighting at a Becoming Ceremony! It's all niceties and meeting a new goddess."

"Even better," said Artemis. "It's about time something livened up those dull events. I will call Demeter in the morning and tell her it's decided." Kore bit back a groan. She really had no say in the matter. Once Artemis, much like Demeter, made up her mind, than nothing could change it.

Chapter Five

Just as Kore expected, Demeter was not welcoming to the idea of Artemis teaching self-defense. It meant more time away from home. Demeter also loathed the idea of Kore having a shared Becoming Ceremony, but wasn't willing to actually plan a separate one. The more time Kore spent with Hedone and Psyche, the more Demeter lamented that they were poisoning Kore against her.

"They just don't understand the dangers of the world," Demeter cried as Kore modeled a dress for the ceremony. "They stay locked away at home and never travel among the humans. I've been there, Kore. I've seen how horrible people can be to each other. Those two are filling you with lies so you'll drop your guard and let Hades drag you away!"

Kore smoothed her hands over the spring green chiton, admiring how it looked against her dark skin. After meeting Dionysus, Kore felt a new appreciation for her skin tone. Gods, she realized, didn't have to be alabaster white. "Mother, in order for Hades to kidnap me, he'd have to leave the Underworld. Everyone I've talked to has said he hardly ever leaves, only coming up to Olympus once a year. I'm safe."

"Oh, that's what they say, but it's all lies! He's sneaky and cruel and so devious. I bet he skulks around Olympus on a regular basis, hiding in the shadows so no one notices him." Demeter grabbed Kore and hugged her tightly. "I can't lose you, my darling daughter! I just know that if I don't protect you, that vile brother of mine will snatch you up. You don't know how men are, Kore. You think it's like a romance story, where the man is gallant and saves the trembling woman, but it's not. Men are like horror stories. They lie and manipulate you until they get what they want, and then they leave you. If you are unfortunate enough to find one who will stay, he will mistreat you and cheat on you. That's what all men do!"

"Mother, please! I am more in danger from the likes of Apollo than I am of Hades."

"All men, Kore! That includes Apollo."

"And my lessons with Artemis will help with that." Kore pushed away from her mother and picked up a deep red chiton from the pile. "What about this one?"

"Certainly not! You are being named the Goddess of the New Spring, not one of that bloody goddess of vengeance and war! You will wear what is appropriate!" Demeter ruffled through the pile and pulled out a very plain, white chiton. "Here, try this."

Kore quickly changed into the white chiton. "I don't know," she said, modeling it. "I think this one looks more like virgin sacrifice than New Spring."

"Well, virgin is the idea," said Demeter. "After all, you will be taking a vow of eternal chastity."

"What?! When was this decided? Why would I ever do that?"

Demeter pushed her to the changing screen with another armful of chitons. "To keep you safe from all those men. They can't touch you if you take the vow. Just ask Artemis how it's made her life a lot easier."

At her next lesson, Kore did just that. Artemis, while

happy with her decision, encouraged Kore to think it over and not make the vow lightly.

"I'm not under the vow of eternal chastity," Artemis said as she checked the guns they would be using that day. "If I ever decide to break my chastity, I have that right. But, if you swear to be a virgin eternally, you can never break it."

"My mother wants me to take the vow as part of my Becoming Ceremony."

Artemis laughed. "Oh, that's rich coming from Demeter. That woman likes to pretend she's a virgin, but the fact she's popped out a few kids belies that fact. She devotes all her time to you, ignoring all her other kids since birth. That woman is warped. You'd think she'd be happy that Despoina married Deimos, but she doesn't even remember that she's Despoina's mother! She's a mother as long as you're in the house, but the moment you move out, Demeter swears she's a virgin."

"I have a sister?"

"Oh, yes. You have a few half-siblings on Demeter's side. You're related to most of the pantheon on Zeus' side. You and I are half-sisters."

"Hermes said as much," Kore said. "He also said something about calling his siblings through Zeus' cousins?"

"It's just something he does. Most of us actually ignore the familial bonds. Otherwise, it gets a bit dizzy to think about how everyone is connected."

Impulsively, Kore hugged Artemis. "I always wanted a sister. You have no idea how lonely it was growing up."

Artemis gently pushed her off. "Yeah, well, as I said, we don't think about the whole family bond through Zeus. We may be family according to a family tree, but we are all different genetically. That way, we can marry and not have to worry. You'll see, once you get your godhead and join us, you may end up marrying a god. Being family in name only means you don't have to worry about really marrying your half-brother or uncle."

"Does that happen a lot?"

"Yes. Zeus and Hera are brother and sister, but their hosts are not related so there is no danger of really inbreeding. My brother, Apollo, has probably slept with every goddess out there, regardless of family bonds. We just ignore it and only trace the genetics of our hosts when planning marriage." Artemis beamed. "This is why my life is so easy. I choose to not marry, so I don't have to worry about it."

Kore shuddered. "Mother always warns me about men wanting only one thing from women and hounding me if I ever leave her home. Won't becoming a goddess stop that?"

"Who can say? My current host was pursued relentlessly by men before I chose her. Now, they have to leave me alone. You? I'm not so sure. The only person who can decide how much the men bother you, is you."

Artemis led Kore to one of her hunting areas on Level X. They were fitted with special vests that worked with the guns. Neither of them could be hurt by the guns, but if shot, the vest would light up and register the hit. The object of the lesson was to "hunt" a man and score more hits than him as he "hunted" them in return. Artemis explained that the purpose was to sense danger.

"These are the targets," said Artemis as two men joined them. One man was adjusting his vest while the other twirled his gun around his finger with a cocky air. Kore recognized both of them. The man twirling the gun was Apollo, while the man fixing his vest was Aidoneus.

"Well, hello beautiful Kore," Apollo said. "What a perfect day for a stroll in the woods. What do you say we lose these vests and guns and just enjoy the day? You, me, and a nice shaded spot in the forest?"

"I'm your target, brother," said Artemis. "It would not be fair for me to pair you with Kore considering your skills."

"I'd love the chance to show Kore my skills," Apollo said. Suddenly, his vest lit up. Kore turned to see Aidoneus holstering his gun.

"My bad. I was just making sure it worked," he said. He smiled. "Kore, it's an honor to be paired with you for this exercise. Please, be gentle with me."

"Aidoneus volunteered to help you," said Artemis. "The rules are simple; the man will have a five-minute head start in the woods. Then, we women will enter. As we try to hunt down our target, he will try to hunt us. After three hours, a horn will sound and the hunt ends. Not only will I look at how many hits you scored, Kore, but I will ask Aidoneus how he felt you did. Did you manage to sneak up on him? Did you sense his presence before you saw him?"

"How will this help me?" asked Kore.

"It's about sensing danger. No matter where you are, danger can appear. You need to know how to trust your gut. Now, this is a bit of a setup, since you know you are hunting and being hunted, but the idea is that it makes you more aware of your surroundings," said Aidoneus.

The game started and the men headed into the woods. Aidoneus ran while Apollo moved at a more leisurely pace. After five minutes, Artemis and Kore followed. They split up and the game was on. The woods were filled with replicas of trees and robotic animals to simulate life. Large, fake bushes offered cover for Kore to hide behind as she tried to find Aidoneus.

Twenty minutes later, Kore knelt behind a tree, using an animatronic deer as extra cover. Her eyes were trained on a bush several feet away. She was sure she saw it move. Her hand tightened on her gun.

Yes! The bush moved. Kore could see Aidoneus, but he was moving away from her. She took aim, but knew she wouldn't make a hit from her position. There was just too much in her way. Slowly, she stood up, her eyes on Aidoneus' cautiously retreating form. She took aim, intent on scoring a hit.

Before she could pull the trigger, something spun her around. Kore found herself facing Apollo.

"Hello, again, my darling Kore," Apollo said. "Fancy running into you here."

"What are you doing? You're teamed up with Artemis." Kore tried to angle her gun between them, but Apollo grabbed it and threw it into the bushes.

"My sweet sister told me of Demeter's demented plan to have you take the vow of eternal chastity. She also mentioned that you don't seem to want to take the vow."

"Yes. When did she tell you this? You two where

hunting each other. The game isn't over yet."

"We've played this game so often that Artemis gets bored after a while. Anyway, I know how you can get out of having to say the vow."

Kore's dark eyes lit up. "How? Please, tell me."

"It's very simple. In fact, it's embarrassing that no one else thought of it. No, wait. I'm sure Demeter had, but I can understand why she wouldn't tell you."

"What's the answer?"

Apollo leered at her. "Why, you can't take the vow of eternal chastity if you're not a virgin. And, since you don't want to take the vow, I'm here to help you."

Kore protested when Apollo kissed her. His hand twisted painfully in her curly hair as he mashed his lips against hers. Kore tried to pull away from him, but he was stronger. All her efforts were like a fly attacking a horse.

A beeping noise finally got Apollo's attention. He lifted his head and noticed that his vest was blinking. Someone scored a hit.

"Let her go!" Aidoneus stood a few feet from them, his gun pointed at Apollo.

Apollo laughed. "You can't hurt me with that gun."

"I don't need a gun to hurt you, Apollo. Let Kore go." Aidoneus' voice was cold and his normally gentle eyes were like ice.

"Aidoneus! Be careful," Kore cried.

"You don't scare me," Apollo snarled. "Think she'd want anything to do with you if she knew the truth."

Aidoneus fired the gun. Kore and Apollo were

shocked as the bolt seared past Apollo's hip, burning his flesh. Aidoneus smirked.

"Your gun shouldn't be able to do that! How did you manage to get it to work?" Apollo shoved Kore away, one hand closing around the wound.

"I have my ways," Aidoneus said. "Now, get far away from Kore, or my next shot goes through that thick skull of yours."

"Fine, but don't come crying to me when Demeter makes her take the vow of eternal chastity. I could have prevented that." He spat at Aidoneus and left with a slight limp.

Cautiously, Kore went and picked up her gun as Aidoneus approached her. The cold look melted away and he was his normal, gentle self.

"Are you unharmed?" he asked.

"I'm fine," Kore said. She wiped her hand over her lips. "I just can't believe that was my first kiss."

"It doesn't count," Aidoneus said. "Your first kiss should be freely given, not stolen."

"What if all kisses are that bad? Mother always says men will just take what they want. I can't imagine anyone taking and it not feeling like a violation." Kore spat on the ground. "I can still taste him."

Aidoneus holstered his gun. "If I may demonstrate," he said. He took a step toward Kore, who took a step back. For a moment, hurt clouded Adioneus' eyes. Then he held his hands up in surrender. "I'm going to let you do all the touching, Kore. Just kiss me, and I'll show you that a kiss freely given is better. I promise to not touch you. You'll be in control. We will start and stop at your command." He interlocked his fingers and placed his hands on his head.

Hesitantly, Kore walked up to him. She stood on tip-toe, moving at a very slow pace to kiss him. His lips were as soft as she imagined. When he opened his mouth slightly and his tongue swept against her lips, the world tilted and Kore found herself clinging to him to keep from falling at the sudden explosion of feelings in her body. One hand held tightly to his vest while the other curled around the back of his neck, her fingers playing with his silken hair.

When she pulled back, Kore felt like she just ran a marathon. If kissing was always like that, she knew she'd never make it as a virgin goddess. That small taste left her wanting more.

"Wow," breathed Aidoneus.

"Is it always like that?"

"That was better. I'd pledge my life to you for the promise of another kiss," Aidoneus said. He winked and took a few steps back. "I think we better continue the game." With that, he turned and walked back into the forest. Kore gave him a few minutes head start. She touched her lips and smiled. He had been right. That was her first kiss, the only one that counted.

Chapter Six

Kore thought about Aidoneus' kiss often. She knew she couldn't tell her mother. Demeter would lock her up in her room for all eternity. For a bit, Kore feared that keeping the kiss a secret would cause her to burst. She finally confided in Hedone while the two were shopping for dresses for the Becoming Ceremony. Hedone, a fashion maven compared to Kore, declared they needed something extra special when Kore showed her the virginal white chiton she was expected to wear. The pair went to the opposite side of Level X to where all the gods shopped. If one used the PortMat to reach the Level, they ended up at the homes of the minor gods, but if one used the Lifts, they were greeted by a small city of shops that catered only to the elite of Olympus.

"He kissed you," Hedone said, her voice a mixture of excitement and quiet as Minthe was trailing the two. "What was it like?"

"Wonderful. Far better than Apollo, at any rate."

"No! Apollo kissed you too?" Hedone looked scandalized.

Kore looked behind them to see if there was indication that Minthe could hear them. "Yes. He grabbed me and forced the kiss on me. He said the only way to get out of the vow of eternal chastity was for me to not be a virgin. I shudder to think of what could have happened if Aidoneus hadn't saved me." Kore sighed. "It was like someone turned the gravity off. If I didn't cling to him, I was going to float away. And he was such a gentleman. He promised to let me be in charge, and he kept that promise."

"Oh, that is what I'm hoping for with Hypnos."

"Surely you two have kissed. You're betrothed."

"Not yet. He says he's really shy." Hedone frowned. "Sometimes I wonder if he really loves me. He barely holds my hand. We're going to be married soon, and we can't even talk to each other. I mean, I really think he's cute and I'm looking forward to it, but what if we aren't compatible?"

"Believe me, Hypnos loves you. At the party, I could see how much he loves you. It made my heart ache watching you two. I can only hope that Aidoneus looks at me with half as much adoration as Hypnos looks at you."

Hedone giggled. "Well, once I kissed him on the cheek. We were kids at the time. I've known for almost all my life that we were going to be married. At the time, he was just being raised by the previous Hypnos. Anyway, I kissed him on the cheek and he turned just the cutest shade of red. I wonder if I tried that again, he'd turn just as red."

"I think so."

"Alright you two," said Minthe as she forced herself between the girls, "that's enough for one day. I must get Kore home."

"We've barely even shopped," protested Hedone. "I refuse to go home empty-handed. Just one more shop." She linked her arm through Kore's and dragged her into the nearest boutique. All around them were the most gorgeous chitons and designer dresses in every color known to man, and a few that Kore were sure only existed in the imagination of the creator. Some of the styles were off the shoulder, while other had high necks, and even others were strapless and daring.

"Oh! This is the dress!" Hedone let go of Kore as she ran over to a beautiful pale pink dress. It was designed like a chiton with an overlay of gold lace and the neck line dipped indecently down to the navel in such a way that Kore knew she'd never get away with wearing such a dress.

"I see you are admiring our newest addition." The store manager came over. He was a wiry little man with beady eyes and twitchy hands. "This was designed for Lady Aphrodite, and we are the only shop in all of Space Station Olympus to carry it."

"Do you know what Lady Aphrodite will be wearing it to?" asked Hedone.

"No special event. It was just created with her in mind."

"This dress is just perfect. How much?"

The manager quoted a price that made Kore's jaw drop but Hedone didn't bat an eye. She merely pulled out a credchip and handed it to the man. He took it and went to the back to run the chip.

"My grandmother is paying," Hedone whispered to Kore. "Don't let her know I call her grandma, though. She says it makes her feel old."

"Who's your grandmother?"

Before Hedone could answer, the manager came back. "I'm afraid there's been a mistake with your credchip."

"What kind of mistake?"

"It says it belongs to Lady Aphrodite." The man was

giving them a look of disdain. "You, little girl, are not Lady Aphrodite. I've already called the authorities."

Hedone raised one perfectly plucked eyebrow. "Really? In a level where only the gods or the families of the gods, you called the authorities?"

The manager sniffed. "They all shop under their names, not with stolen credchips."

Hedone stood there, defiantly crossing her arms until the authorities arrived. Kore was amazed as the most beautiful woman she ever laid eyes on walked in, followed by a very intimidating man who looked like an older Phobos with a bushy beard. Behind them were a few of the Olympian guards.

"Lady Aphrodite," the manager said as he quickly ran up to greet her. "I am so sorry to bother you, but this girl is trying to purchase a very expensive dress with one of your credchips."

Aphrodite twirled a lock of her blonde hair around one finger as she studied the small group. Kore trembled at the thought of being in trouble with such a woman. There was just something special about her, from her hair styled to look as if she just tumbled out of bed, to the nearly sheer tunic she wore. Aphrodite's hooded eyes finally rested on Hedone.

"That little girl," Aphrodite asked, pointing to Hedone.

"Yes, Lady Aphrodite."

Aphrodite sighed. "And the child of my son is being treated as a thief, why?"

The manager paled. "She's related to you?"

"Yes. Hedone is the daughter of my son. I gave her my credchip so she could find the perfect dress for her Becoming Ceremony. I take it you found such a dress?"

"Of course," said Hedone. She showed Aphrodite the dress she wanted and Aphrodite nodded.

"Have it sent to the home of Eros on Level X," said Aphrodite before she turned her attention on Kore and Minthe. "And what about you two?"

"We were still looking for Kore's dress," said Hedone.

"Kore?" The intimidating man next to Aphrodite suddenly seemed interested. "As in Demeter's daughter?"

"Yes, sir," said Kore.

The man studied her and then nodded as if Kore passed some test. "Come, dear, we must be off. You know how Hera gets when anyone is late."

"Whatever they want, it goes on my account," said Aphrodite. "And, Kore, do tell Demeter I said hello." The two swept out and the guards followed. The manager had to sit down; his trembling legs could no longer hold him up.

"Well, now let's find you a dress, Kore," said Hedone.

"Aphrodite said she'll pay for anything," said Minthe. "Why not add some accessories in addition to a dress?"

Hedone gave her a disgusted look. "Just because she said she'll pay for what we want doesn't mean we need to push it. A dress each will be all she's expecting. If I overcharge her, I might lose favor. And, as the future

Goddess of Pleasure, I should do all I can to not lose favor with Aphrodite."

They went looking through the store. Every dress Hedone liked, Minthe vetoed. And vice versa. Finally, Kore found the dress of her dreams. It was a shade of red that was almost the shade of blood with just a hint of blue mixed in, a high waist gown with a delicate golden chain holding the top up. Diamond chips were sewn in at the hem and along the line of the waist with gold embroidered stars between the chips. Kore held the material against her arm and marveled at how lovely the red was against her dark skin.

"No! Lady Demeter already said that colors not associated with spring are not allowed. Kore, you need something that shows the innocence of spring and the fresh buds of the reawakening nature. Does that sound pomegranate red to you?"

The manager came over, still shaking slightly from his brush with Aphrodite. "The color would look exquisite next to her skin. This dress was designed with Persephone, Dread Queen of the Dead, in mind. It represents her royal nature as the wife of Hades."

Minthe looked as if she had been slapped. "We do not say those names! How dare you foul the air by uttering them! Kore, come. We won't shop here ever again!" Minthe grabbed Kore's hand and dragged her out of the store. Hedone, left behind, looked scandalized.

"What was he talking about?" Kore demanded, trying to pull her hand free. "Minthe! Who is Persephone? Is she my sister? Artemis mentioned I have siblings from Mother. Is Persephone one of them? Please, talk to me."

"You are the only child that matters to Lady Demeter. There are no others. Artemis was mistaken. As for Persephone, she broke my lady's heart. There has never been a more ungrateful girl than she."

"Did she really marry Hades? If so, why do we have to worry so much about him coming for me if he already has a wife?"

Minthe stopped. "It's complicated, Kore. Just forget you ever heard that name. In fact, forget what Artemis said about any siblings. You are the only child of Lady Demeter. Don't worry your pretty little head over anyone else because there is no one else."

"How can I forget that I have siblings out there? What if they want to meet me? What if they think I don't want to meet them because you never told me about them?"

"It's complicated," said Minthe. Just know that we are keeping you safe. When I accepted my life as a nymph and took the name of Minthe, I vowed to serve only Demeter. I wanted only her happiness. Keeping you away from the likes of Hades and ungrateful Persephone will ensure Demeter's joy. I have seen the pain she feels when she mentions her other children, all of whom hurt her. Keeping you safe and at home keeps her happy, and that is what I intend to do."

Minthe pulled Kore to the Lifts to get them back to Level 4. Kore's mind swam with this new information. She now had the names of two siblings, and secretly planned to find both Despoina and Persephone.

At the Lift, she was surprised to see Aidoneus waiting to head down to another level. Only gods were allowed on this level, humans weren't even supposed to know it existed. Though, if Aidoneus worked for Hephaestus, wouldn't he be granted many of the rights of the gods on behalf of Hephaestus?

Kore smiled. "Aidoneus! How are you?"

"I'm doing great. How are you, Lady Kore?"

"Fine. What brings you here?"

"I'm doing a delivery." He picked up a basket at his feet and lifted a small latch. Three little black puppy heads popped up and gave the cutest tiny barks.

"How cute! I didn't know Hephaestus had dogs." Kore petted the puppies and laughed as they tried to vie for her attention. That was when she noticed that there were three puppy heads, but only one body.

"Um, this isn't for Hephaestus," Aidoneus said. He reached in the basket and lifted the puppy out. All three heads gave a tiny yip and tried to see everything at once. On head twisted and was able to lick Aidoneus' hand.

"May I hold him?" Kore asked.

Aidoneus handed the puppy over. Kore laughed as three puppy tongues licked her face. "He's so friendly."

"Just who are you taking that puppy to?" asked Minthe. She eyed the puppy warily.

Aidoneus took the puppy back and settled the dog in the crook of his arm. His bright blue eyes shifted to the floor and his cheeks blossomed with red. "This puppy has been genetically altered to give him the appearance you see. He's very rare. Only one such dog may exist at any given time."

"That doesn't answer my question," said Minthe.

"Hades. This puppy is going to live with Hades. His name is Cerebos."

Kore gasped. "You can't, Aidoneus! That's just cruel. Let me keep him. A puppy should grow up with the sun and plenty of space to play."

"I can't, Lady Kore. Believe me; this puppy will have a happy life. If you want, I'm sure you can visit him." Aidoneus gave her a small grin. "Hades won't mind if you stop by to see little Cerebos."

Minthe pushed Kore behind her. "She most certainly will not! Lady Kore will never set foot in the Underworld." She pushed past Aidoneus as the Lift doors opened and marched Kore inside.

Kore watched as Aidoneus pet the puppy. The poor creature, unaware of his fate, continued to try to cover Aidoneus' face with sloppy puppy kisses. Kore wondered if it would be worth facing Hades to see Cerebos again.

Chapter Seven

By the time the Becoming Ceremony rolled around, Kore felt like a new person. Her lessons with Artemis flourished and she could handle a gun, short sword, bow and arrow, and defend herself in most situations. Artemis taught her how to hide weapons under her clothing and several different ways to break a man's hand. What really helped was having Apollo act as the attacker. Kore honestly felt threatened by him and fought back with everything she possessed. On her last lesson, Artemis crowed that they would surely defeat Phobos and prove that women were the superior teachers.

"I really don't think you're ready for this," Minthe said as she brushed out Kore's hair. The brush caught on the tight curls and Minthe pulled harshly. Kore bit her lip to keep from crying out in pain. "Let's try this again next year."

"No! I'm ready," Kore said. Her head snapped back as Minthe tugged against a knot. "I don't want to wait another year. I'm late enough as it is."

"But you rushed into this," Minthe protested. "Most girls spend a year or more planning their Becoming Ceremony. You had only months, plus that stupid training bet between Phobos and Artemis. You're not ready. I'll let your mother know that we're holding off for another year."

"Don't you dare!" Kore leapt up from her seat and grabbed Minthe. Her dark eyes flashed as she said, "I am going to that ceremony and I'm becoming a goddess, and I'm doing it today! There is no power on this station, not

Zeus, not Hades, not my mother, that will stop me. Sit back down, Minthe, and finish fixing my hair." After all the time Kore spent fighting with her mother over the perfect dress and whether or not she'd become a goddess, Kore was not going to let Minthe's manipulation ruin her day.

Minthe clicked her tongue and reluctantly continued. Once she was done brushing out Kore's hair, which now frizzed uncontrollably, she set about braiding and pinning Kore's hair up in an elegant design. "We just don't like this," Minthe said, viciously stabbing a pin through the braid and scratching Kore's scalp. "Lady Demeter is very worried. Hypnos will be at the ceremony, and he's a denizen of the Underworld. Who knows what trash he'll bring with him? Not to mention, Psyche doesn't have a single ounce of self-preservation. She'd probably allow Hades to come, even though your mother forbade it."

"I don't think we have to worry about Hades. He's already married to Persephone, right? And why would he even have any interest in me? I honestly think you and mother worry too much."

Minthe jabbed the last pin in, stabbing Kore. "Never doubt us, Kore," she snarled. "Danger lurks everywhere. Your mother knows this better than anyone! Why, danger lurks in her family! You'll do best if you obey Demeter in all things."

Kore touched the spot that Minthe stabbed and stared at the red blood coating her fingers. "You cut me!"

"You made me," huffed Minthe. "If you want to act like a spoiled brat, fine. But you're not going to that ceremony!" Minthe got up and left the room. Kore's eyes widened as she heard the lock slide in place.

"No force on the station," muttered Kore. The first thing she did was quickly dress. The chiton she picked was duel-toned green, with a beautiful emerald color on top that darkened down to an almost black-green at the hem. Silver flowers were sewn at the hem of the skirt and top flap, matching the small crown of flowers she wore in her hair. Kore went to her window and pulled on the bars. They gave way easily, no one thinking to ever check on them since their installation when she was a kid. Demeter certainly never thought Kore would dare climb out of her window.

Kore tied her bedsheets together and anchored them to the remaining window bar. It wasn't long enough to get her safely to the ground, but she knew the risk. Once she made it to the end of her improvised rope, she jumped. She landed in a heap and had the wind knocked out of her. Kore lay there for a moment until she could breathe again.

Making her way slowly to the PortMat, Kore kept an eye out for Minthe. For the first time in her life, Kore was now in charge. It was thrilling and frightening. She wanted it to end, she wanted to run home and hide. She was more scared of being discovered by Minthe or her mother before she could make it to the PortMat than she was scared of Hades jumping out and kidnapping her.

Entering the PortMat room, Kore barely had time to duck behind a console as the PortMat flared to life. When the bright light faded, Phobos and another man were standing in the room. There was something frightening about both men, dressed in their military finest. Kore could really see how Phobos was named God of Fear.

"Psst! Phobos." Kore peeked out from behind the console. "Over here."

"Where are Demeter and Minthe? I thought we were bringing all of you down," said Phobos as he walked over to Kore.

"They're not coming. Mother and Minthe were trying that whole, 'we don't want you to do this, so we'll lock you in your room' thing that they do. I escaped. Now, come on, before they realize I'm not at home."

"I don't know about this, brother," said the other man. "You of all people should know how deep Demeter's grudges run. If she doesn't want Kore going to the Becoming Ceremony, maybe we should leave her here."

"I'll go anyway," Kore declared. "With or without you. This is my Becoming Ceremony, too. I will be a goddess or die trying."

"Demeter will be angry no matter what," said Phobos. "I really don't care if I'm back on her black list. All that matters is making sure Kore is safe, and if she means to go to that Becoming Ceremony, than we must accompany her. It's only right."

The other man grunted. "Whatever blows your hair back, Phobos."

"Kore, allow me to introduce you to my brother, Deimos, God of Dread." Phobos gestured to the man. Kore gave him a small smile. She had heard that name somewhere before.

Deimos growled. "I had plans tonight that didn't include following Demeter's spoiled daughter like a duckling. Let's get this over with."

"Don't mind him," said Phobos. "Deimos seems to think God of Dread means he has to have a dreadful attitude." He turned and quickly keyed in their new coordinates in the console.

Kore's heart thumped as she realized this was it. There would be no turning back. No one was going to stop her from becoming the Goddess of the New Spring. Today, she took her first step toward independence with her escape, and now she was about to expand on that step. Once she entered the light of the PortMat, she couldn't turn back. She could no longer merely be the daughter of Demeter, that silly girl who cowered at the thought of hurting her mother. She would be a goddess and get used to saying no to those she once revered.

"Take a deep breath. It's a whole new world after this." Phobos held out his hand as the bright light of the PortMat flared to life.

Making up her mind, Kore took his hand.

The Becoming Ceremony was held on the very top of Space Station Olympus. A large, glass dome encased the ballroom, letting the majesty of space to be seen. Only the gods were allowed in this most honored place. Not even devotees or human servants could set foot this high up. The hierarchy of the gods could clearly be observed as the lowest of the gods waited on the upper crust. Gods who were divine in name only walked around with trays of food and drink. Minor gods, such as Eros and Psyche, were just high up enough to be acknowledged, but Eros' brothers, Anteros and Himeros, as well as his friend, Zephyrus, were among the staff. If any felt slighted or upset over the arrangements, no one mentioned it during the Becoming Ceremony.

In one corner of the ballroom, a small shooting range had been set up to settle the bet between Phobos and Artemis. It was all the gods could talk about; a change in the Becoming Ceremony. This was the most attended ceremony as none of them wanted to miss the outcome. All around the room, gods and goddesses made bets and took sides.

Around Kore, the gods mingled and fairly ignored her entrance. Everyone wore their absolute best to outdo the other gods. The more elaborate the outfit, the richer the god and thus, the more worshippers he or she had. The only exception was the children of the gods, whose splendor reflected their parents' status instead.

Kore spotted Hedone by the gift table, wearing the beautiful pink dress Aphrodite purchased for her. It was easy to see where Hedone got her beauty as she talked to her parents. Though scarred, Psyche was a lovely woman and Eros, God of Love, was achingly handsome. The way Eros looked at his wife made Psyche a thousand more times beautiful, and that radiated to Hedone. Kore felt a stab of jealousy at how close they were, and wished her mother treated her more as a person and less of an object.

Next to Hedone, Aphrodite stood with a sour expression on her face. Kore wasn't sure if it was because Hedone and Aphrodite wore the same dress, or because Hephaestus stood by Aphrodite. The beautiful blonde goddess gazed openly at Ares. It was only when Dionysus went up to talk to Hephaestus did Aphrodite make her escape.

"Looks like a normal gathering to me," grumbled Deimos. "If you don't need me, I'm going to see my wife."

"Oh!" Now Kore remembered where she heard about Deimos. "Your wife is my sister, right? Or of some relation to me?"

"Yeah. Sister. Not that you'd know anything about that." Deimos turned to leave.

"I want to meet her," Kore said. "Please. I only learned I had siblings recently."

Phobos grinned. "See? I told you that Kore ignoring Despoina was not Kore's doing. Come on, Deimos. You and Despoina know that Demeter ignores all her kids, so why did you assume that Demeter ever told Kore of her brothers and sisters?"

"Maybe Despoina doesn't want to meet you. Ever think of that?" Deimos left them.

Kore turned to Phobos. "Would she want to meet me?"

Phobos shrugged. "Who knows? Despoina is rather bitter over the fact that Demeter acts as if she only has one child."

Kore started to head towards Hedone when she heard her mother. Turning, Kore spotted Demeter talking to a small group of gods. She recognized them only from their statues: Zeus, Poseidon, Hera, and Hermes.

"Yes, it's so sad that Kore decided against coming tonight," Demeter was saying. "My daughter is just too fragile. She isn't ready for all of this. Maybe next year."

Kore crept up behind her mother. "Who isn't coming tonight?"

Demeter jumped and turned. "Oh, Kore! What are you doing here? I thought you weren't coming."

"I just couldn't miss this, Mother. I've waited so long for this day. I really can't imagine where you'd get the idea that I wasn't coming."

"I think Minthe mentioned your reluctance this morning."

"Really? Speaking of Minthe, Mother, I want a new handmaid. I do not appreciate being told how I'm supposed to feel, nor do I like being locked in my room because I had the audacity to grow up. Today I become the Goddess of the New Spring, and I'd very much appreciate it if I wasn't treated like a little girl."

Demeter sniffed. "We'll see. Just because this is your Becoming Ceremony, it doesn't mean you're an adult."

Zeus cleared his throat. He had short white hair, bright blue eyes, and a boyish grin. No matter how old he was, when he smiled he looked like a bashful young man talking to his crush. "Demeter, I thought we talked about this? Kore is going to be one of us soon. You need to let her make up her own mind."

"I am. It's not my fault that she has a habit of making the wrong choices."

"I don't know what you are so worried about, but Kore can live up here on Olympus. There is nothing that would dare hurt her up here," said Zeus.

"What about Hades? You're too soft on him, Zeus. I know for a fact that he's been running around Olympus. Whatever happened to the decree that he was to stay in the Underworld? Why would I put my daughter in danger when I can keep her safe?"

Zeus rolled his eyes. "Demeter, I love you, but you need to let that go."

"I can keep Kore safe," said Poseidon. He was tall, tanned, with black hair and almond-shaped eyes. He gazed at Demeter like starving man. "I can promise that Hades would not dare to enter my realm."

"Hades is a god, just like us," snapped Zeus. "He is our brother. We owe him more loyalty than to just shove him in a dark hole and forget about him."

"What has he ever done for us?" asked Poseidon. "Nothing, that's what. He's a nobody, Zeus. I say we strike him from the list of Olympians and regulate him to a minor god. No one will miss him."

"I have the final say in this matter." Zeus' blue eyes flashed with anger and Kore could feel the air turn to static. "As your king, I say our brother remains an Olympian. I will hear no more on this matter, and you should be ashamed of yourself, Poseidon." Zeus turned and left, Hera hurrying after him.

"Well, you put your foot in that," said Hermes. He smiled at Kore. "So, little cousin, how are you enjoying the party?"

"I really just arrived."

"Come. I'll show you around. Let's leave these sourpusses." Hermes looped his arm with hers and took to introducing her to everyone. Kore was interested in meeting Flora, Goddess of Flowers, as she would be working closely with her soon. Hermes' son, Pan, made Kore laugh with bawdy stories of adventure with the nymphs. Telete, daughter of Dionysus, offered to teach

Kore how to dance.

"Father mentioned you," Telete said. "You need to cut loose and have fun once in a while."

"I will think about it," promised Kore. She watched as Telete made her way through the crowd, a tray of wine held high. Her movements were graceful and it was easy to see how she became the Goddess of Initiation to the Bacchic Rites.

All too soon, Phobos and Artemis announced it was time for the contest. Everyone crowded around, eager to witness the outcome. There would be three sections of the contest, and best two out of three won. Hedone won the marksmanship round and Kore won the archery round. A few people muttered that it was to be expected: Phobos shot guns all day and Artemis was famous with a bow and arrow. Everything came down to the self-defense round.

Hedone and Kore were paired with a child of Ares. Deimos, who was picked for Hedone, laughed at the thought.

"This will be simple. I know how Phobos thinks. There is nothing you can do that I won't predict," he declared. It took Hedone over fifteen minutes to find a way to escape him. He blocked all her attempts until she used her small stature and wiggled under his legs and ran to the safe zone. Kore hated to think ill of her friend, but it appeared that Hedone's self-defense lessons were all about running away from danger.

To Kore's horror, she was paired with Enyo. The burly woman looked more imposing than Phobos and Deimos put together. Her armor was red, which she proudly announced was so that no one would see how much Kore bled on her.

The warrior woman charged Kore, starting the match. This was nothing like her training, which consisted of scenarios of 'man grabs you from behind' or 'man grabs your hand'. This was a full-on assault. As Kore clumsily dodged Enyo's fast-paced punches, she got the feeling that this minor Goddess of War was trying to kill her. In desperation, Kore tried to remember all that Artemis taught her. All thought left Kore's mind as the terror of having Enyo's beefy fists come swinging at her head filled her very soul. Finally, an idea took root in her mind, but it was very risky. Did she dare?

Taking a deep breath, Kore weaved between Enyo's punches before dropping to the mat. She swept one leg out, knocking Enyo's feet from under her. The goddess fell back with a heavy thud.

Before Enyo could stand, Kore moved between the goddess' legs and stomped down hard on the woman's groin. Enyo howled in pain and sat up, giving Kore the perfect opportunity to kick her in the face.

"Do you yield?" asked Kore, bouncing back on the balls of her feet. Her body tensed, ready to strike once more.

"I will kill you!" Enyo struggle to get up; blood flowing from her busted nose. Kore kept her down with a well-aimed punch. Pain shot through her hand, but Enyo was back on the ground.

"Do you yield?" Kore repeated.

"When I get my hands on you, I'm going to rip that pretty little head off your shoulders! I'm going to string you up by your intestines! What's left of your dainty corpse will decorate my walls!"

"No you won't. This match is over." Ares grabbed Kore to pull her away. Still high on adrenaline, Kore flipped Ares over her shoulder.

"Oh, sorry." Kore stood down and reached out a hand to help Ares up. Suddenly, Enyo tackled Kore and straddled her. Kore struggled as Enyo wrapped her large hands around Kore's throat and squeezed.

"I said it's over!" Ares pulled Enyo off and Kore gasped for breath. "This isn't a battle, Enyo! All you were supposed to do was the assigned exercises. Go home. You're a disgrace."

Enyo spat on Kore before leaving. Artemis helped Kore up and brought her over to where Apollo was standing. The God of Healing took Kore's hand and studied it for a moment.

"If you're in pain tomorrow, come and see me," he said as he tilted her head up to look at her neck. "Oh, that'll bruise for sure. Say something, Kore."

"I really hate her," Kore croaked. It hurt to talk, to swallow, and to breathe.

"My baby!" Demeter ran over and wrapped Kore up in the circle of her protective embrace. "Are you all right? Oh, this is just horrible! We should go home right now. No more of this nasty business. You can have your Becoming Ceremony next year." She glared at Artemis. "I hope you're happy! Look at what you put my baby through. Oh, poor Kore. Your little neck is swollen. I can't believe that monster dared to lay a finger on you. And you have blood on her dress! Apollo! You must look her over to make sure she's not injured!"

"With pleasure," said Apollo.

"Mom, I'm fine," Kore rasped. "The blood is Enyo's."

"Demeter! We need to discuss the winner," called Zeus. "The girls are tied right now. This is important."

"My baby needs me!"

"I'm fine. Really. Go and talk with Zeus. I promise to stay next to Apollo, Mother."

Demeter reluctantly went to talk to Zeus. Her voice carried throughout the conversation about how none of this would have happened if everyone stopped poking their noses in Demeter's business and let her decide when Kore could have her Becoming Ceremony.

"You did great," Hedone said as she came over. "I'm glad I didn't get Enyo. I think I would have fainted from sheer fright if she came at me like that."

Kore smiled, one hand gently rubbing her neck. "I'm rather surprised I didn't faint either"

After another minute or two, Zeus finally walked over to Kore and Hedone. "We have made a decision. Though Hedone got free of Deimos quicker and followed the rules of the exercise, Kore was at a disadvantage with Enyo behaving badly. Because this challenge was self-defense, and we all agreed that the actions were of self-defense, we are awarding the winning point to Kore."

Hedone hugged her friend. "Congratulations!"

"It was just luck, not skill," said Kore. "Besides, it's not like winning means anything to us. It was all for bragging rights for Phobos or Artemis."

"You beat Enyo. That takes a lot of skill," Hedone

pointed out.

"She has her father's spirit," said Ares, slapping Kore on the back.

"She gets it from me, since I taught her," countered Artemis. The Goddess of the Hunt shot a smug look at the God of War. "Looks like women are the better teachers."

"Only in pre-arranged combat. Try your luck in a real battle, little girl?"

"Little girl? I'm older than you are!"

Ares snorted. "Oh, please. I'm the older one, and I'm the one who actually fights for a living. What do you do, Artemis, besides lounge around with your followers and pick flowers? You only hunt once in a while. Most of the time you giggle and run through the forest with your gaggle of girls."

"We're civilized! Unlike you!"

"Ha! Civilized? You preach about a woman's virtue and independence and throw a hissy fit if any of your girls look at a man. You're a child pretending to be an adult!"

Artemis was about to snap back when Zeus said, "Children." Artemis and Ares stepped back, both trying to adopt an innocent look. Zeus motioned for them to separate and Ares stomped away.

"Now that that's out of the way," said Hera, linking arms with Zeus, "why don't we move on to the real reason why we're all gathered here?"

Chapter Eight

The king and queen of the gods made their way to the center of the room. Everyone parted for them and a hush filled the ballroom.

"My fellow Olympians," said Zeus, "today is a special day. We have not one, but two new deities to welcome into our pantheon."

On cue, Psyche and Eros walked forward with Hedone. They helped Hedone kneel at Zeus' feet, ready to accept her godhead.

"Psyche, Goddess of the Mind, and Eros, God of Love, I have watched over the two of you since your wedding day," Zeus said. "Your daughter, Hedone, is the perfect merger between pleasure and self. Thus, I anoint Hedone as Goddess of Pleasure. May she lead the mortals into a greater understanding of the gift of love."

Zeus took a small vial of oil from Hera and poured it over Hedone's head. Kore watched closely, hoping to see the very moment when Hedone became a goddess. To her disappointment, there was no outward sign. Hedone stood up and that was the end of it. She was now the Goddess of Pleasure. Aphrodite went over with a towel so Hedone could wipe the oil off her head and proudly announced that Hedone was one of her special helpers.

"There is one more thing," called out Hypnos. The crowd parted and allowed him to walk to Hedone. "I, Hypnos, God of Slumber, do hereby desire to make Hedone my legal bride."

"What's going on?" whispered Kore. "I thought they were already engaged?"

"They are," Phobos whispered back. "But, he was engaged to Hedone the mortal. He must now ask for the hand-in-marriage of Hedone the goddess. If Eros or Psyche felt he was unworthy while Hedone was a mortal, they can now object on the grounds that the pairing is more even in status."

"Does that ever happen? Being denied once one has received their godhood?"

"Once in a while. But I doubt this will be the case."

Kore watched as Eros grandly welcomed Hypnos' claim on his daughter. Hedone blushed and smiled, holding out her hand to the man she loved. The gods and goddesses cheered as it was announced that Hedone would marry Hypnos. The only objection was raised by Aphrodite, who wanted to know what sleep had to do with pleasure.

"I know I always find it pleasurable to sleep," said Zeus. "Pleasure takes all forms, and slumber can be just as pleasurable as the exploits of the flesh."

Then it was Kore's turn. Seeing as Zeus was already standing up at the ceremonial spot, Phobos stood in as her male parental figure. Demeter glared at him the whole way. Phobos gave Kore's arm a reassuring squeeze as he helped her kneel, and then he took a few steps back to stay out of the ceremony.

"Kore, my dear daughter, you've grown into a lovely woman. Just as a flower needs the loving caress of the sun and gentle kiss of the rain to blossom, you've matured under the guidance of your mother, Demeter, Goddess of

Harvest. She has guided you all your life, and has reported back to me that you've a talent for plants. My Kore, you are fresh breath of spring air, and thus we name you the Goddess of the New Spring. May you encourage only the most beautiful flowers to grow after Winter's chilly snow, may only the softest grass spring forth under your feet, and may you always reawaken the life of this Station in a burst of fresh green."

Kore felt the oil pour on her hair. There was nothing out of the ordinary but the cool sensation of the oil dripping down on to her shoulders. Kore knew there was nothing outwardly to be seen, but she thought she might feel differently. In truth, she felt like the same Kore who first knelt down as she got up.

She expected to leave with Demeter, but two voices stopped her in her tracks. "I have more business with Kore," one called out while the other announced, "I wish to petition for Kore's hand."

The crowd parted and Kore first saw Apollo approaching. He smirked at her before taking her hand. "What Zeus said was true; a beautiful flower needs the sun. I, my dear, am that sun. I announce my intentions to marry Kore."

"I object!" The crowd parted again, and Kore saw Aidoneus and a small group of people coming toward her. He was dressed in a short black chiton with silver trim, a matching half cape, and a magnificent silver crown. Behind him were an assortment of lavishly dressed men, and hanging on his arm was a beautiful woman with dark skin in a ruby dress.

"I am here to petition for Kore's hand," Aidoneus

said. "I've loved her from the moment I saw her. A flower may need the sun, but a woman needs love. The sun is just as cruel as it is life-giving. Have plants not dried out from the sun? Have people not burned? Kore is not a mere flower that you can admire. She is a woman, a very special and beautiful woman, who needs love and compassion to survive. I vow, as her husband, I will do all in my power to keep her happy. I will love her with my dying breath."

Apollo snorted. "Pretty words, but what are you truly offering? I offer her a home of riches and light. What can you offer her, Hades?"

Kore gasped. "What did you call him?"

"He called him Hades," said Demeter. "What trickery is this? How dare you, Hades? It was bad enough I thought my daughter was being bamboozled by some dirty worker of Hephaestus, but now I find that it was you! You deceiver! By what right did you have to lie to my daughter?" Demeter pulled Kore back to her. "My poor, sweet flower! I should have known you'd try your best to sneak into her life. Don't worry, Kore. Mommy is here. I won't let him hurt you."

Kore shook her head, staring at Aidoneus. "No," she whispered. It couldn't be! Not the man she was falling in love with. Not the man who kissed her so sweetly and made her heart skip a beat.

"I am sorry, Kore. I didn't mean to hide my true identity from you. I just...When we met, I didn't want you to be scared of me. I didn't lie about everything, only my name. After all, who would have assumed that Hades would be building a small plant house?"

"And after that? Why didn't you tell me the truth

afterward?"

"Because I selfishly didn't want you to run away. Kore, it hurts me to see the way you look at me now. I can't stand the fear and horror in your eyes. I didn't tell you because I liked how you viewed Aidoneus as someone you could talk to and might consider a friend. I wanted you to get to know me without the stigma of knowing Hades hanging over us."

"Well, I think her choice is clear," said Apollo. "Does she choose the sun or the grave? I think the sun."

"Neither," said Demeter. "My daughter is going to be an eternal virgin. I'm sorry, Apollo, but that's what Kore wants."

"Mother, no!"

"You can't do that, Demeter," said Aidoneus - Hades! - said. "You might have had some pull before she was named a goddess, but she can now make up her own mind. You waited too long to make that little announcement. The oil was poured, Demeter. Just as you could have turned my proposal down when she was just Kore, you can't declare the path of her life now. As a full-fledged goddess, she now answers to herself. Also, in the terms of marriage, it is the father who accepts the suiter if the bride price is correct, not the mother. Zeus is the one who can now tell me yes or no."

"Hades, that's enough," said Zeus. "Demeter, I suggest you calm down. Our brother has a point."

"No! No! No!" Demeter stomped her foot on the ground. "He wasn't supposed to be here! Apollo was supposed to make the proposal so that Hades would never have a chance! Who let him in, anyway?"

"I did," Zeus said. "The naming of new goddesses should be witnessed by all gods, not just the ones who call Olympus home. And he is our brother. He is our eldest brother, in fact. It would be rude of me to bar him from this."

"Betrayer! How could you do this to me?" Demeter burst into sobs.

"Zeus, I asked for her hand first," said Apollo. "Name me her future husband. It'll stop Demeter from making that awful noise."

"Don't I have a say in this?" Kore demanded. "It's my life, after all."

"My baby is a delicate flower," wailed Demeter. "She needs the sun to bloom! She'll wither and die in the Underworld."

Hades sighed, rubbing his temples. "For the love of sanity, Demeter. I asked for her hand-in-marriage, not her head on a plate."

Demeter only wailed louder. Kore was sure she heard something about 'he wants to eat her' mixed in with her howls of despair.

"Kore," Hades said, "What do you want? You have four, maybe five, choices that I can see before you. Do you wish to marry Apollo? Do you wish to marry me? Remain single? Become a virgin goddess? Marry another person? What is it you want?"

Kore looked at her mother, sobbing uncontrollably into the hem of her chiton, and then at Apollo, who stood with confidence that he'd be the winner. She turned to Zeus, who shrugged, leaving the decision up to her. Finally, she looked at Hades, whose kind eyes watched her with sadness, so ready for rejection but hoping in vain to be her choice. No matter her answer, she would hurt someone.

There had been no feeling of change when the oil first was poured on Kore's head. She was almost certain, had this question been poised before she received her godhead, she would have caved and asked her mother what she should do. She was no longer Kore, daughter of Demeter. She was Kore, Goddess of the New Spring. As she stood there, the oil dripping down her hair, on her shoulders, and soaking into the top of her chiton, she felt a new sense of strength.

Without thinking, it was this new Kore who stepped out from under the protection of her mother's clutching hands. She passed Apollo, whose face crumpled with the first sign of doubt, and went to stand in front of Hades. With a glance, she sent the woman on his arm back a step or two.

The sound of her hand connecting with his cheek resounded in the ballroom. Demeter looked up, her tears already dry and a smile on her face.

"That," Kore said, "was for tricking me. For making me dream of a life with a sweet mechanic named Aidoneus."

"I am sorry," Hades whispered.

"That was beautiful," said the woman in red, gleefully. "Hit him again!"

Hades rubbed his cheek. "Is that your answer, Kore?"

"No. This is my answer," she said and kissed him. At first, Hades was too shocked to kiss back, but as soon as he realized what this meant, he wrapped his arms around her. She melted against him, one slender leg instinctively hooking around his waist as he dipped her. When they parted, Kore felt lightheaded with glee.

"I do have one request," said Kore, looking into Hades' eyes.

"Anything."

"If I am to be your wife, I don't want completion. Persephone can't be in the Underworld." She pointed at the woman in red.

The woman burst out laughing. "Me? Persephone? Oh, honey, no." She moved back to Hades' side and held her hand out to Kore. "Hecate, Goddess of Witches, Magic, and the Crossroads at your service. I have an unofficial title as Queen of the Underworld while Hades is single, but it's only a title. I'm more of an advisor."

"You're not Persephone? But, I heard...I mean, no one would come out and tell me about her, but it was hinted she was married to Hades."

"No. I can guarantee you that there is no Persephone in the Underworld," Hades said. "I am single, and that is why I asked for your hand-in-marriage. I assure you, Zeus would have objected to my proposal if I were already wed."

Hera snorted and muttered, "Not that being married has stopped him from playing around."

Demeter let out a fresh wail and crumpled to the ground. Several of the other goddesses rallied around her, trying to revive her. Kore rushed to Demeter's side, worried about what could have brought this on.

"You kissed him!" Demeter snatched her hand back when Kore reached for her. "How could you? My own daughter! You have betrayed me! My flesh-and-blood turned against me! Oh, just let me die here. I have nothing to live for."

"Demeter, stop with your dramatics," snapped Hera. "This isn't the time nor the place."

"What do you know, Hera? My daughter - my only reason for existence - has thrown me aside in favor of that monster! You can't comprehend the feelings of betrayal. The pain that fills me would kill a thousand gods. Oh, woe!"

Hera shot Zeus a nasty look. "She's your sister! You deal with her."

"Demeter, come on. Hades isn't that bad. He's a god and he has his own realm. Really, only Poseidon and I can say the same. Everyone else serves in one of our domains. Even you."

"The earth isn't owned by anyone," Demeter snapped. "I can claim it as my own."

"No you can't. You know that everything that grows, that comes from beneath the soil, technically belongs to Hades. His realm is far vaster than we ever give him credit. Isn't it time you two ended your silly feud?"

Hades held up his hands. "I am willing to let it lie. I have no quarrel with Demeter."

"Please, Mother, I have made my choice. At least, at the very least, give me a chance to learn more about Hades. A year. I promise to not marry anyone for a year, Mother. I only want to be my own person, to choose who I wish to marry or not. I am no longer a child."

"I can see that," snapped Demeter. "Don't think I didn't talk to Minthe. You have grown into a very disobedient girl."

"I will decide this matter." A regal-looking woman with dark skin and thick black hair walked up to them. All the gods, including Zeus, bowed to this woman as she passed them.

"Mother," Demeter sniffled, "tell them that Kore must be a virgin goddess and she can't ever marry Hades. He's going to steal my baby! You, of all gathered, knows the agony of a parent whose child has been stolen."

"Most honored Mother Rhea, who saved me from certain death, you know that there comes a time when a child must leave the home and be his or her own person," said Zeus.

Rhea turned to Hades. "My eldest son, do you love this woman?"

"With all my heart."

"Will you provide for her? Honor her wishes?"

"Yes."

"Demeter, do you want what is best for your daughter, even if it isn't what you want?"

"I always want what's best for Kore, Mother."

Rhea sighed. "That wasn't what I asked. If marriage to Hades is what is best for Kore, would you allow it?"

"No. That will never be what is best for her."

Rhea nodded and looked at Kore. "I already know your heart, my child. You are the Goddess of the New Spring. As such, you shall have your one year to decide on whether or not you will marry, and to whom. No one will force your hand; no one will make the decision for you. You will have quarters in Olympus to do your duties and room with a chaperone of Demeter's choosing. Hades will continue to abide by the normal rules of Olympus. He may only come up if invited, but Kore may meet with him on any Level below Olympus. We will reconvene in one year to hear Kore's decision."

"That solves nothing," snapped Demeter.

"Don't argue with me, Demeter. Now, Hades, it's been too long since I've last spoken with you. Come, walk me to the PortMat."

Hades took Kore's hand and kissed it. "By your leave, my lady. I will send you a message after you've a chance to settle in your new rooms. I can only pray you accept my call." He and his retinue left with Rhea.

"Well," said Hedone, "this will be a Becoming Ceremony talked about for centuries."

Chapter Nine

Although the entire space station was called Olympus, only the top three Levels were actually identified as such. Only the gods and their staff could live and work on these Levels, and on Level 4, the level of minor gods. The gods had living quarters in Olympus in addition to their private homes on their dedicated Levels. Humans were allowed to travel to the dedicated Levels by invitation or vast amounts of money only, unless they were traveling to Level 14, the sacred Level of Hermes. Hermes, being the God of Travelers, kept his Level open to all.

Kore's new living quarters were on Level 3 in the division dedicated to the Gods and Goddesses of Nature. Demeter rarely stayed in Olympus, preferring her private home on Level 7. However, Kore was certain her mother would suddenly find reasons to spend more time in Olympus.

The guest quarters were smaller than the official living rooms of the gods, but were still far bigger than anything Kore expected. Her world suddenly expanded from one small room to an entire apartment with an outdoor garden, two bedrooms, and private PortMat closet.

"You won't need that," said Minthe as she let her bags drop. It came as no surprise to Kore that her mother would assign Minthe as her chaperone. Minthe closed the door to the PortMat, and since the door didn't lock, shoved a chair in front of it.

"This place is amazing," Kore breathed. From where she stood, she could tell all the flowers in the garden were mechanical. For the first time, Kore's hands twitched to personalize the flowers. One of her duties as Goddess of the New Spring would be to design the new flowering vegetation and make sure the existing flowers blossomed with the pre-programed colors and patterns.

Minthe huffed and grabbed her bags, heading into one of the bedrooms. Kore took her time, exploring her new home. The kitchen intimidated her as Kore barely knew how to cook. Her lessons with Hestia touched on the subject, but it was mostly how to run a kitchen with servants and not cook for oneself. Without asking, Kore already knew Minthe wouldn't cook.

On the kitchen table was a welcome note from Zeus. After not seeing or hearing from her father most of her life, it was nice that he wanted to catch up on lost time. Under his note was one from Hera. Kore breathed a sigh of relief as the Queen of the Gods welcomed her in the pantheon and called her 'my most treasured niece'. Hera was well known for seeking revenge on the by-blows of Zeus' infidelities, and Kore had no disillusions that her father was still married to Hera when she was conceived.

Kore found the apartment's viewscreen. A small blinking light on the console let her know that she had a message.

"Kore, these were put in my room by mistake." Minthe walked out of the bedroom with a stack of papers in her hands. She dumped them on the kitchen table.

"I have a message," Kore said. "I was about to view it." She didn't bother asking if Minthe wanted to hear them or for Minthe to leave. She knew her mother's spy would demand to be in the room to report back anything that was said.

The first message was from Hermes, a generic welcome and walk-through of the new viewscreen system. While it was still designed to make and receive calls and view the station news, the new features allowed Kore to search the station's knowledge database, receive a gods-only channel for news that the humans had no business knowing, and an updated listing to all shopping on the station.

The second message was as from Hedone inviting her for a girls' night out. The third message was from Demeter, who sobbed hysterically as she detailed how much she missed Kore. One would think Kore moved to another universe instead of a few Levels up with the way Demeter carried on.

The final message was from Hades. Minthe moved to delete the message, but Kore stopped her. She had to know what he wanted to say.

"Kore, I'm not sure when you'll get this message. I hope it finds you well." Kore could see that he was trying to sound business-like, but his shy, boyish smile and the way he subconsciously tugged on a lock of his strawberry-blond hair gave away his nervousness. "I would love it we could have the chance to get to know each other better. All our cards on the table, no more secrets. I...I want you to know the real me. Other than my name, I held nothing back. For obvious reasons, I did keep any connection between myself and the Underworld quiet around you." He grinned and rubbed his cheek. "Lesson learned. Now that everything is in the open, I can and will answer any questions you have. If you are willing, I want to take you out to dinner. Or lunch. Lunch is just as nice."

Minthe huffed. "Not going to happen. He forgets, he's not allowed up in Olympus but once a year."

"I know I can't go to Olympus unless invited," Hades continued and Kore tried to not giggle. He thought of everything. "Many of the divine Levels are a bit iffy, but I can go to the human Levels. I won't ask you to come to the Underworld. I'm sure that will be pushing it. Please, contact me with your answer. If it makes you feel more comfortable to just talk via viewscreen, we can do that. Whatever you decide, I will abide by."

"Well, he certainly wasted no time," said Minthe. "Kore, forget about him. He's a vile, evil man who will only do you wrong. If you must feel as if you need a man, there is always Apollo. Or let Demeter pick out a suitable mate for you. Or course, it will be best if you just give in and accept your position as a virgin goddess."

Kore sighed. She just had to put up with this for one year and she'd be free. She knew the path her mother wanted for her, but every time she saw Hades, she wanted to forsake her mother. She fell in love when she thought of him as Aidoneus, and she had a feeling he wasn't much different as Hades. After all, it was only a different name, not a different person.

"Start your work," snapped Minthe. "I'm going to lie down. And you better not think about contacting Hades. I'll know if you do."

Kore sat at the kitchen table, shuffling through the papers. There were some notes from Flora, Goddess of Flowers, regarding possible colors and patterns for a new batch of flowers she wanted to unveil next spring. She found a few more welcome notes from other gods and goddesses, as well as her own credchip to go shopping. Kore had a feeling she knew why these were left in 'Minthe's Room.' With a sigh, she picked up the papers and went to her bedroom and closed the door. It was, indeed, the smaller of the two bedrooms.

Psyche barely said goodbye to Eilythe when Demeter stormed in to her house. The Goddess of the Harvest looked livid, though Psyche never saw Demeter in a good mood.

"What can I do for you, Demeter?"

Demeter's stout face was a bright red. "You traitor! You fiend of Hades! Did you think I wouldn't discover your deceit?"

Psyche raised one eyebrow, causing the scars on her face to give her a more mocking appearance. "Just tell me what you want, Demeter. I can't keep up with all your imaginary slights."

"Hades! You were the one to introduce that creature to my innocent Kore! How dare you? What have I ever done to you for you to betray me like that?"

"You're making a big deal over nothing," Psyche said. She walked past Demeter on her way to the storage room.

"Do you deny that it was here where Kore first met Hades?" Demeter followed her, determined to have her say. "Was it your idea to pretend he was a mechanic? I bet you two were just laughing at me while he tricked my sweet flower into trusting him."

"Are you asking if it was my idea for him to be a

mechanic, or say he was one? Frankly, I had nothing to do with either of those." Psyche pulled out an old crib and eyed it. "He was here helping me. We had no idea Kore would show up. It took us both by surprise."

"Why was he even here? Hades is only allowed up for the Winter Meeting. Which, in case you failed to notice, winter has not been an issue lately. And I would like to keep it that way!"

"Hades was doing what he said he was doing: making a small plant house for some new plants I wanted to grow. I haven't tried my hand at growing the plants of the Underworld, and he was being nice by helping me out." Psyche pushed the crib down the hall to an empty room. Faded pink paint and a few forgotten toys littered the floor along with cobwebs and dust bunnies. Psyche pushed the crib to the middle of the room.

"You never told me! You hid the fact that Hades was seeing my Kore on the sly!"

"I don't know where you ever got the idea that I owe you any loyalty, Demeter. I never pretended to be on your side."

"You always did before! Is this about that whole 'keeping you busy' when Aphrodite was looking for your host? That was with the human, Psyche. As a goddess, you need to drop the human grudges."

Psyche went back to the storage room and pulled out a different crib and brought it to the old nursery. As she compared the two cribs, she said, "My previous hosts may have rushed to forgive you in the rush of being a goddess, but I am no longer any of those women."

"And just what does this host think I've done that

justifies such betrayal? What is it that you can't get over?"

"Odessa."

Demeter looked confused, but then a light dawned in her memory. "Oh, really, Psyche. She was a nobody. You never met her, and the human whose body you possess barely met her. Don't tell me you are holding on to Phobos' grudge? You both need to let it go. It's unseemly for a god to care so much for one measly mortal."

"We have started wars over one measly mortal," Psyche said. "We have changed the face of creation over one measly mortal. For all we gods exist above them, we know the power held by those mortals. And, yes, I will keep my grudge. You let Odessa die to feed your ego when we both know any of your faithful servants would have been happy to hand over their children to you."

"You are not me, Psyche. You'll never understand what it means to try and keep your child safe. You, who eagerly signed your only daughter over to Hypnos, will never understand what it means to love your child and then have your worst nightmare steal her away. I should have known you were in cahoots with Hades when I found out Hedone was engaged to Hypnos. I can't wait for you to switch hosts. This one has poisoned you and turned you human."

After Demeter stormed out of her house, Psyche sat in the nursery. While it was true that, in the past, she never bothered to take sides with the other gods. Her whole focus used to be on Eros. Her memories of the past were now bitter as she remembered how her previous incarnations ignored their daughter to make it easier for her to marry and leave as a goddess, how Eros became her only world so that when he picked a new host and began her cycle, it hurt more than anything in the world. She had been a shadow among the gods, just a beautiful figure who followed Eros like a lovesick puppy.

It was this most recent host where Psyche gained her grudge against Demeter. This host held on to her subconscious and refused to fade away. She dreamed of her old life at night and wept for the lives of her host's family. She found herself sneaking down among the humans to watch from afar as those she used to know went on with their lives. In the past, any promises made by her human hosts would vanish the moment she became Psyche once more, but this one wouldn't let that happen. She took Zephyrus' place when Apollo demanded retribution because her host said she would. She went down to the Underworld for lunch with Hades and Persephone, and later held Hades' hand when Persephone entered the Stasis Chamber, practically a corpse. And, it was because of this host; she held fiercely on the memory of Odessa and carried the pain of that human's death.

Chapter Ten

Throughout the next week, Kore's life became busier than she ever imagined. Flora, Goddess of Flowers, demanded much of her time to create new flowers and perfect spring. Demeter became a regular visitor, reminding Kore of how ideal life had been and could be again if she would just come home. If Demeter was around when Hedone called to hang out, Demeter begged Kore to not go. It appeared as if Demeter's contempt for Psyche and her brood magnified since Kore was named Goddess of the New Spring.

"Psyche really isn't a good person," Demeter said after she, once again, forbid Kore from going out. Kore, once again, ignored her mother and gathered up her purse.

"I don't know what you have against Psyche or her family," Kore said. "They're good people. You should be happy that I have friends, Mother."

"Nonsense! She should realize you're busy. You can't keep dropping your work to go running out with your friends. In fact, I'm surprised that she's not busier. I heard that Aphrodite took Hedone under her wing, though what she's teaching is anyone's guess. Men are such basic creatures. There's no finesse to seducing them. Men will rut with anything and everything."

"Oh, really, Mother. That was a bit harsh."

"It's true! Just look at your father. I wager half the station has his DNA. He doesn't care who he hurts as long as his needs are satisfied."

Kore paused, halfway to the door. "I never thought about that," she admitted. "Poor Hera. No wonder she gets so mad at Zeus' offspring."

"Poor Hera? I wasn't talking about her. I was talking about me. Poor me, Kore. Zeus has hurt me!"

Kore frowned. "Hera is his wife. I would think that if anyone is hurt by his infidelity, it would be her."

"I was nearly his wife. After Zeus saved us from the dark pits of our father's stomach, Zeus and I started a wonderful love affair. We were inseparable. I was the first of us girls to discover my powers and I grew the food for Zeus' army. I was by his side when he slew our father and cast the Titans into Tartarus. He used to call me his pretty flower." Demeter sniffled. "Then Hera snatched him away. I don't know how, but she did. I know he loved me and would have married me if it weren't for her. Once she was named Queen of the Gods, her powers magnified. Who knew she was the Goddess of Marriage and Women?"

"I never heard any of this before. I'm sorry for your pain, Mother."

"He would never have cheated on me. I was the true love of his life. He's not satisfied with Hera, and that's why his eyes wander. And Hera does nothing. She's weak."

Remembering a thread of information she discovered after her Becoming Ceremony, Kore asked, "When did you hook up with Poseidon? You have a daughter with him, right? Despoina?"

"I didn't hook up with him. Poseidon always thought that since Zeus wouldn't have me, I'd settle for him. One day, while I was looking for..." Her voice trailed off. Demeter shook her head to clear the memory. "Doesn't matter who, now does it? Anyway, he pursued me and tricked me. Of course, both his kids have an affinity for horses. And don't get me started on Poseidon's brats by that hussy, Medusa! I think Amphrite only allows his dalliances because all Poseidon's kids outside of his marriage are pretty much monsters."

Kore patted her mom on the arm. "Well, um, take care. I won't be late tonight."

"Kore, please, don't go. Hedone and Psyche are in Hades' pocket. I can't have you vanish. Please, stay here and be safe."

Feeling only a little bit guilty, Kore left. She knew she had to push her independence more, or she'd always just be Demeter's daughter. Kore headed to the hallway set up for the gods and goddesses of love where Hedone was currently staying. She found Hedone in a pile of fabric as the young Goddess of Pleasure tried to pick out just the right material for her wedding dress.

"What do you think? Silk? Or a print?" Hedone held up two nearly identical swatches of white material. Kore had to look closely to notice one had swirls embroidered on.

"I'm not sure," Kore said.

"Oh, tomorrow I'm finishing my Becoming Ceremony. Apollo contacted me to say that my official godhood was ready."

"I thought we already had our ceremony," Kore said. "We were declared goddesses. Wasn't that it?"

Hedone giggled. "That was just the Naming portion. Each god and goddess has a special soul. Now that we're named as goddesses, we can receive that soul and have full access to our powers. And after that, Hypnos and I can finally be married!"

"Well, I suppose I can come," Kore said. She sat down and helped Hedone pick out just the right material for her wedding dress and then they went to dinner with Psyche. Psyche was the only one brave enough to ask if Kore had been in communication with Hades.

"I have," Kore confessed. She had to be careful. Minthe had a habit of popping up at the most unexpected of times. She couldn't use the viewscreen to talk to Hades, so she sent messages through Hermes. The God of Messengers, Travelers, Thieves, and Crossroads thought it was funny to play messenger as long as Kore or Hades paid him in food or gold. Kore had to promise to create a plant that was only Hermes'.

As it was, Kore and Hades sent long letters to each other. She learned so much about him. Like, being the King of the Underworld wasn't as lonely as others thought. He had friends who lived in the Underworld with him; Minos, Rhadamanthus, and Aeacus, the judges of the Underworld, Hecate, Thanatos, Hypnos, and Charon. He let Kore know that Cerebos, his three-headed puppy, was happy and quickly learning new tricks. He did mention that the puppy would like to see Kore again, but also put in that he could bring the puppy above ground.

That night, while Kore was going over a collection of specialty orders, she came across one from Hades. Once Minthe was in bed, she called Hades on her room's private viewscreen. Kore was worried she was calling too late at night, but then Hades answered.

"Kore? To what do I owe this honor?"

She held up the order form. "I needed to talk to you about this. I have a lot of orders right now, so it might take me a while to get to it. But I'd like to get your particulars so when I can get to it, I will know what you want."

Hades frowned slightly. "My order?" Then comprehension dawned in his blue eyes. "Oh! Oh, no! I sent that to Flora. It was supposed to be a surprise for you."

"For me?"

He nodded. "I wanted to give you a special flower on our first date. I don't know when that would be, but I am optimistic that we will get to that point."

Kore smiled. "Thank you. No one's ever done anything like that for me."

"The surprise is a bit ruined. Sorry."

"I can still make it," Kore said. "I don't mind."

"Thank you, Kore. I'll think of something else to surprise you with."

Kore took a quick look out her door toward Minthe's room. She could hear Minthe snoring in bed. "So, you mentioned something about a date? Are you still interested?"

"Very much so. I know of a great little restaurant in Athens that has the most splendid lamb stew. Or, one in Crete that has this beef dish that just melts in your mouth."

"Surprise me. I'm seeing Hedone tomorrow, but I should have time to go to dinner after," Kore said.

Hades smiled. "I think I know the best place to take you. I will send up the PortMat coordinates with Hermes."

The next morning, Kore hurried out of the apartment before her mother could arrive. Hedone's ceremony would be on Level 2, in the Transference Room. It was part of the medical wing. The walls were lined with human-sized tubes, some with bodies floating inside. Two large consoles were against the far wall with wires and piping connected to two operating tables. On one table sat Hedone and the other held the sleeping and dripping wet body of a woman. Apollo stood by Hedone, checking notes on a clipboard.

"Okay, you are ready to start," said Apollo. He made a last mark on the clipboard and smiled.

Hedone looked nervous. "Ready as I'll ever be," she said. She laid down on the table and Apollo hooked her up to an I.V. and breathing mask. As he set up for the Transference, Psyche and Eros entered the room. Psyche smiled and hugged Kore.

"We're so glad you could make it. Someday, this will happen to you," Psyche said.

"Exactly what is going to happen?" asked Kore.

"Hedone is going to become a real goddess," said Apollo. He turned to the console. "We Zyspadaden, we gods, require human hosts. It's been the arrangement between our kind and the mortals since the beginning. Your friend was named the Goddess of Pleasure, and now she will receive the soul of the Goddess of Pleasure."

"Who is the other woman?"

"That was Hedone." Apollo turned a knob and the console lit up. A hum filled the room and both women on the tables started to glow a golden color.

"But, my friend is Hedone!"

"Maybe I can explain," Psyche said. "See, that woman was Hedone. She was the daughter of my previous host, making her the previous Goddess of Pleasure. However, when my daughter was born, that Hedone went into status to preserve her godhood. Now, my Hedone will take on that godhood and be the only Goddess of Pleasure."

"Does that mean that there was a previous Kore?"

Psyche looked slightly uncomfortable. "Well, yes, but the Transference is different for everyone. Just because there was a previous Kore doesn't mean you will gain your godhood the same way Hedone is. My host, for example, had to nearly die before I could enter her. Some gods require their host to go through a test, some only require permission, and there are some who must take theirs by force. Hedone is a born host, so the only requirement is that she is my daughter and agrees to be the Goddess of Pleasure."

Apollo walked over. "Now that this is underway, I can finally say hello to my dear cousin." He smiled at Kore and reached to hug her. Kore took a step back. "Aw, Kore, don't be like that. I thought we were closer."

"Sorry, Apollo. I'm just worried about Hedone."

He huffed. "Or is it because you've been talking to Hades? You do know that your year isn't just dedicated to him. There are other gods who want to be your husband."

"Really, Apollo," said Psyche, "you are not the marriage type. I'm sure that Kore wants something more lasting then maybe a month-long lover."

"Stay out of this, Psyche. You've developed a nasty habit of butting in where you don't belong."

"Just stop trying to convince Kore that you mean marriage," said Psyche. "She can see through you, Apollo. It's just pathetic."

"Is the room getting lighter?" asked Eros. Indeed, it was. The glow from Hedone and her predecessor intensified. Kore watched as something made of light and energy passed from the comatose girl to Hedone. Hedone jerked up a few times and then lay quiet as the glow faded.

Eros and Psyche rushed to Hedone's side while Apollo checked the machines. Weakly, Hedone sat up.

"How are you feeling, my daughter?" asked Eros.

Hedone eyed her parents, her brow furrowed. "This is not how I expected to wake up," she rasped. Psyche ran to get her daughter a glass of water.

"My host's memories tell me you are my parents," she said after she drank the water. "Father, I can understand. No matter the host, you always seem to look the same. But Mother..." She paused and studied Psyche. "You are a surprise. Not only are you here for the first time, but why would Father pick a woman as ugly as you?"

Psyche's face fell. "And you shall bear a daughter who will break your heart," she whispered.

"What?" Eros looked at his wife. "Her scars are all marks of love. When I see them, I remember her bravery and how she fought to be by my side. They never bothered you before, Hedone."

"That was before. I am now truly Hedone with my rightful power and memories. The Hedone you knew is gone. I am the one who remains."

"Hedone! Don't talk to your parents like that. What's

come over you?" Kore couldn't believe her sweet friend was acting like this. If this was the final step in being a goddess, she could go without.

Hedone glared at her. "Who are you?"

"I'm Kore, your friend. We had our Becoming Ceremony together. Remember?"

"I know no such goddess named Kore." Hedone turned back to her parents, dismissing Kore. "What minor son of Zeus are you saddling me with this time?"

"You are going to marry Hypnos, God of Slumber," said Psyche. "The two of you have been courting for some time, and he formally asked for your hand during your Becoming Ceremony."

Hedone's eyes widened. "You want me to marry a denizen of the Underworld? How could you? Do you hate me so much that you would exile me to the darkest depths of the station?"

"But, you love Hypnos," Kore cried. "You told me how happy you were to be marrying him."

"Again, who are you? There is no goddess named Kore. What impostor have the gods allowed in their midst?"

Apollo spoke up, "Kore is Demeter's daughter and Goddess of the New Spring. I can vouch that she is a genuine goddess."

"That is a lie. The Goddess of the New Spring is -" Hedone stopped and grabbed her head. She screamed and crumpled on the ground. "No! I like Hypnos! Get out of my head! Stop it! Accept your fate, you little fool. No! Get out!"

"Hedone!" Psyche knelt by her daughter's side and held her as she fainted. Apollo nudged the still goddess with the toe of his sandal.

"Is she okay?" asked Eros.

"Yes. Sometimes this happens," said Apollo. "The new host and the Zyspadaden lifeform have been known to battle it out for supremacy." He looked down at Psyche. "It's not always evident who wins."

"Will she be that mean forever?" Kore asked.

Apollo shrugged. "Depends on who wins. Hedone is, traditionally, not close to her parents. After all, normally, Psyche and Eros spend their marriage staring into each other's eyes and being sickly devoted to each other. This makes Hedone very irritated with them. Nothing has been normal for a while, so I can't say how Hedone will act once this is settled."

Kore stared in horror at Psyche holding Hedone. She could only pray that the change in her friend would not be permanent.

"I don't want this," she said softly. "I don't want to find out that taking my godhood will cause me to hate my mother or Hades. Or hurt my friends. I just can't do that."

"It's for the best," said Apollo. "If it makes you feel better, not everyone changes as much. Demeter always picks hosts who think the same as she, so her personality doesn't change. And my personality never changes. Neither does Hermes. It's very rare to have a personality change. I'm sure you'll remain the same."

Apollo bent and picked up Hedone. He placed her back on the bed and hooked her up to some monitors. He informed them that she would most likely sleep for a day or two.

"Do not worry," said Psyche as she led Kore out the door. "Sometimes, the old personality wins."

Kore shivered. "I'm never going through that. I want to always remain me."

Psyche patted her arm. "It will be okay. This is the way of the gods. Every deity must go through the Transference."

"Will you let me know when she wakes up? She was my first real friend, and I would hate to lose her."

"Of course."

Kore left and started to make her way back home. Halfway there, Hermes ran into her. "There you are, Kore. Come on, I'm supposed to escort you to the PortMat."

"Oh, I nearly forgot." Hermes knew the coordinates to her date with Hades. How could she have forgotten?

Hermes cheerfully brought her to the PortMat room. When Kore told him about Hedone, he nodded. "Yeah," he said, "it's a bit of a muddled mess. Psyche and Eros were more attentive parents this time around, so I can see how that is causing some confusion. I'm sure it'll all work out."

"What was your Transference like?"

Hermes shrugged. "Pretty typical. I picked my new host, told him what the deal was, and went to the chamber after he passed a simple test. It was painless. I closed my eyes in one body and woke up in another."

"Will it be like that for me?"

"Not sure." Hermes inputted his coordinates in the PortMat. "If I had to guess," he said slowly, "I'd say it won't be as bad as you think. What are you the most scared of, Kore?"

"Losing who I am."

He smiled. "Trust me, you won't. That's all I can tell you, but you will always be you."

Chapter Eleven

The PortMat dropped Kore off in a small temple on the edge of a beautiful seaside village. Modest homes dotted the streets and fish stalls lined the docks. Beyond the docks, boats bobbed in the water. Kore knew this was located on one of the Island Levels, but she's never been to one. These levels were dangerous, as the water could leak down to the Levels below or flood in to the maintenance shafts.

Hesitantly, Kore made her way down the cobblestone road to one of the docks. The water fascinated her, the way it moved with lazy purpose. It reminded her of the way wheat waved in the wind. Kneeling down, she could see little fish dart under the dock or swim up to eat some of the algae that floated in the water.

"Hypnotic, isn't it?"

Kore looked up to see Hades standing behind her. He was dressed in a black short chiton that tied at one shoulder and ended at his knees. Under one arm was an elaborate black and silver helm. He looked like the King of the Underworld, all dark and mysterious and very, very forbidden.

"I've never seen so much water before," Kore said. "I feel like I could stare at it for hours."

"My brothers have the most mesmerizing realms; Zeus with his sky and Poseidon with his oceans." Hades sat next to her, letting his legs dangle over the edge of the dock. "I doubt anyone gives my realm a second thought."

"I happen to find the earth very interesting," said Kore. "I love how it can yield crops and minerals, of how the scenery changes due to the composition of the ground. How dull would it be if all of the Levels were nothing but flat? We have mountains and valleys, and that is very interesting."

"I was talking more about my realm of the dead, but thank you."

"Oh." Kore looked back down at the water. What could she say? Most people probably found death and anything associated with it to be too depressing.

"I promised you dinner," said Hades. He stood up and held out his hand. "Come. The restaurant is close by."

"Hades, I...I didn't mean to...What I meant was..." Kore searched for the right words. She meant to compliment his realm, but she felt like she messed up.

"Don't worry, Kore. You just put more thought into anything associated with me than most would. Yes, I am a god of the earth, but not of how it's shaped. I am ruler over what comes from the earth; such as the minerals or, to a smaller degree, the plants. People forget that and just think my realm is nothing but the dead." He shrugged. "I guess that's why Plutus lives with me. He is the God of Wealth and should have a seat on Olympus. I think I dragged him down."

Kore took Hades' arm. "No. I never got the impression Plutus wasn't happy." She only met her blind brother once, but she was sure he wasn't upset with where he lived. Maybe, someday, she would ask him to confirm that.

Hades quickly gave her a kiss on the cheek. "You

are the most precious treasure I've ever beheld."

He brought her to a small diner a street away from the docks. It was not the fancy kind of restaurant that the gods often dined in. This was a small, run-down building with broken shutters, a faded painted sign, and ancient wrought-iron tables and chairs out on the patio. A scrawny white-haired man and his robust, dour wife owned the building, the very picture of salty sea folk. When Hades asked for a private table, the wife snorted around her pipe and led them to a rickety table in the back. There was no menu, only the special of the day: fish soup.

"This place may not look like much, but the food is like ambrosia," said Hades. "I used to come here a lot in my last host. Don't let Megara's attitude get to you. She acts that way until she warms up to you, but she's a great friend to have."

"Does she know who you really are?"

Hades nodded. "Well, she did. I'm not sure if she knows it's still me."

"How did you find this place?"

"Since I'm not allowed up in Olympus, I take advantage of the fact that I can travel anywhere else in the Station. When I need a break, I pick a Level and explore. I don't have to worry about being recognized. None of my statues have been updated for centuries."

"How often do you come here?"

He shrugged. "At least one week every summer."

"I didn't know that. I always heard you never left the Underworld except to kidnap bad little girls."

Hades laughed. "I bet that was Demeter who told

you that. No, I don't go around like some boogeyman and take misbehaving children. I'd really have my hands full if I did."

"Tell me more about your kingdom. I keep picturing what you've told me so far, but I want to learn more."

"I suppose saying, 'Come and visit' is out of the question?" He smiled, tugging shyly on a lock of his strawberry-blond hair. "No, I didn't think so." He paused as their soup came out. He picked up the wooden spoon and dunked it in the bowl a few times. "It's not as gloomy as you would think," he said slowly. "The motif is dark, it's true, but there is so much life."

He folded his hands, letting his spoon dangle over the bowl of soup. He thought back on all that they've talked about already before saying, "Well, most of my subjects represent the more gloomy aspects of life. Like Death, Slumber, Night, and Souls. They are not very welcome above my realm, so we have to figure out to keep our lives productive. We entertain ourselves."

"How do you keep entertained?"

"I arrange events and encourage hobbies. Your brother, Plutus, for example, works with clay and makes the most beautiful bowls and vases. Hecate, Goddess of Crossroads, Magic, and Witchcraft, paints them. We sometimes take them up to the human levels and sell them. Thanatos, God of Death, is actually a very funny guy. He has a comedy night once a month. And my judges, Minos, Rhadamanthos, and Aeacus, have a small band." He took a spoonful of soup. "Oh, this is so good. Megara outdid herself once again."

"What kind of life will Hedone have after she

marries Hypnos?" If she marries Hypnos, Kore thought. The new Hedone that woke after the golden glow was not the kind of person she could see happily married to a sweet man like Hypnos.

"Nothing too dreary, I assure you. Hedone will likely have festivals and duties for Aphrodite that will keep her from staying in the Underworld for long. Hypnos, I suspect, will request permanent rooms on Aphrodite's hall in Olympus and split his time between there and the Underworld. As long as he does his job, I don't mind if he doesn't stay in the Underworld."

Kore stirred her soup, watching as bits of fish and vegetables swirled around. "What about you? How would marriage affect you?"

"If you're worried that marriage to me will trap you, I can assure you it won't. I would never keep you from your family or your duties, Kore. Your happiness would be paramount."

"I was more concerned about your duties." Kore blushed, realizing that he caught her thinking about them having a life together.

"A wife would actually help me out. If you will allow me to use you as an example, your duties will only take you from my side part of the year. When your duties are over, you can assist me."

"And if I don't know anything about running a kingdom?"

Hades reached across the table and took her hand. "You won't have to run my kingdom; only give me advice when you see fit. I have discovered that those around me often see a solution I would not have thought of otherwise."

Kore, who never swooned a day in her life, swooned at his words. He didn't expect her to be perfect or give up her duties. He was interested in the long term and not just in the here and now. He was too good to be true. They sat there, letting the silence stretch as they stared into each other's eyes. Hades' thumb made little circles on her wrist, sending small electrical shivers through her body.

"Kore, I meant it when I said I fell in love at first sight," he said softly. "And every time I see you, I fall more and more in love. I love how determined you were to learn self-defense. I love how your eyes light up when you talk about flowers. I love how you tuck your hair behind your ear when you're feeling shy and how you bite your lip when you're thinking naughty thoughts. I have sat in my home wishing I could tell you about my day and wondering how your day was going. I want you to be part of my life, Kore."

Kore wanted to tell him that she felt the same way. The first time they met, she felt as if she had been struck by Eros' arrow. She loved how his blue eyes brightened when he saw her and how he got this shy, unsure expression on his face. She loved hearing about his day and how she could read the pride on his features when he talked about the accomplishments of his citizens. She admired how he could stand up to her mother. She wanted nothing more than to fall asleep talking to him or wake up and see him first thing. She defied her mother for him. If that wasn't love, she wasn't sure what was.

None of that came out. Before she could utter a single syllable, a voice called out to her from across the room. Kore turned to see Minthe with a small group of men standing at the doorway.

"There you are, Lady Kore. Do you have any idea how worried your mother and I were when you didn't show up at home? Why, anything could have happened to you! And then we find out he was behind this and had you in his clutches. Oh, Lady Kore, your mother is in such a state of shock. We feared we'd get to you too late."

Everyone was now staring at Kore and Minthe. Kore wanted to sink through the floor. If a portal opened up to the Underworld, she'd take it without a second thought.

"It was just dinner," said Hades. "Really, Minthe, you're overreacting. She's perfectly fine. You should try the soup. It's really good."

One burly man from Minthe's group took a step forward. "My lady has told us what you did. You kidnapped this girl! Return her at once!"

Minthe wailed. "I shudder to think what evils have befallen you, Lady Kore! What has this monster done to you? Has he taken your innocence?"

Kore blushed. "Minthe!"

Minthe stormed over and grabbed Kore's arm. "Come along, my dear. We must get you back to your mother. Don't you worry, your nightmare is over. I have rescued you. Come and let these fine gentlemen take care of this monster."

Kore fought, but Minthe was stronger. She looked helplessly as Hades slowly stood but could not come after her. The grouping of men now swarmed around the ladies on their way to Hades.

Hades picked up his helm. "I'll talk to you later,

Kore," he said. He placed the helm on his head and instantly vanished. The men stopped and looked confused.

"Where did he go?" one bulky sailor asked.

Kore wasn't sure if he teleported or just vanished, but she could have sworn she felt him kiss her on the cheek. The door behind them opened and closed without a person assisting.

"Go after him," shrieked Minthe. "He just left! Hurry!"

The burly man squinted at Minthe. "Just what have you gotten us in to? No human can just disappear like that. Who was he?"

Megara, the dour owner, swooped in and started pushing the burly men toward the exit. "Never you mind who he was! You're disturbing my patrons. Git! Don't come back until you've found your manners! And you -" she turned to Minthe, "you owe me for two soups!"

"Me? Why I wasn't the one who ordered anything."

"I don't care. He would have paid if you hadn't interrupted. And I expect a tip." She shook the heavy wooden spoon at Minthe. "Pay up!"

Begrudgingly, Minthe paid the woman and took Kore away. "This is all your fault," Minthe groused as she dragged Kore up to the PortMat temple. "When Demeter learned you had gone to see Hades, she just about died. Is that what you want? To kill your mother?"

"Everything was fine until you showed up. All we were doing was talking. And how did you find out, anyway?"

"Apollo found you on his cameras. He's such a

compassionate man. Why, I'm sure if you gave him a chance, you'd discover that he's a much better match than Hades. You are a delicate flower, Kore, and all flowers need the sun. He'd make a much better husband. And I'm sure it would make Demeter feel better."

"I don't want Apollo. I want Hades."

"You're behaving like a child," said Minthe. She opened the temple and quickly entered the coordinates. "If you insist on acting like a child, than we shall treat you like one. You're grounded!"

Eros felt a chuckle rise in his chest. He couldn't wait to get home to tell Psyche about the current kerfuffle on Crete. Apparently, Hades was caught having dinner with Kore. Whether or not it was consensual was not discussed, but he knew that Demeter's favorite handmaid found the couple and caused a scene. It was the talk of Olympus. Poor Poseidon was having a hard time with the sudden influx of worried fishermen who believed they had angered him.

Entering his home, Eros could hear Psyche in one of the back rooms. It was the low masculine voice that caused him to stop. Who could possibly be with his wife? Normally, Eros wouldn't worry so much over anyone visiting Psyche. After all, some of his staff were men and he knew Psyche would be home alone with most of them. But, that was before, back when all they did was stare longingly into each other's eyes and knew that the other was all they needed to survive.

Psyche, at least, this version of her, was not the same romantic woman he expected. Sure, she still gazed lovingly at him and they were very much in love, but she still had interests outside of him. She continued to garden and often went on day trips to visit Hades, Hephaestus, or Pan. He had caught her going to visit the graves of her host's former family and dropping off little gifts at the house of her host's former brother-in-law. These were not the actions of a woman seduced by a love dart. She acted, almost, like an ordinary woman in ordinary love.

"Hurry up," said Psyche, her voice breathless. "I want to finish this before Eros gets home."

"Agreed." Eros now recognized the man as Phobos. "I do not want that pansy knowing I had anything to do with this."

"Really, Phobos. You know you like him."

"About as much as I like a dagger in my side."

Eros frowned. He knew his wife and his brother were close, but he just couldn't image what the two were doing together. Actually, he could imagine, and he didn't like the direction of his thoughts. Jealousy was a new emotion for him, and it gripped him hard.

"Don't forget to take that off," said Psyche.

Eros couldn't take anymore. He stormed into the room, flinging open the door. He wasn't sure what he expected, but the sight stopped him in his tracks. There was no hot bed of illicit love. Psyche and Phobos stood on opposite sides of the room, paint brushes in hand. Phobos wore a long robe to keep the paint from getting his clothes dirty, while Psyche's plain dress was covered in paint splatters. In the room were two cribs, freshly painted white, and a pile of folded linens and old toys. The walls, once pale pink, were now stripped yellow and mint.

"Oh, Eros, you're home early," Psyche said. "I wanted this to be a surprise."

"This is the old nursery," Eros said. "Why are you painting it? Don't tell me Phobos is moving in with us?"

Psyche laughed. "No, dear. Phobos was just helping me with this little surprise. I would have asked Zephyrus or Anteros, but those two are off on their honeymoon." She put her paint brush back in the bucket of yellow paint. "You did remember to send a gift to Anteros, didn't you?"

"Yeah. I sent him a new lounger." Anteros was Eros' brother and God of Unrequited Love, while Zephyrus had been Eros' faithful servant for many years. The two met when Psyche's host first came to Eros' home, and it wasn't long before they formed a deep connection. It was no surprise to either Eros or Psyche when the pair announced their intent to marry and live together. It was a private ceremony with only Eros, Psyche, and Eros' other two brothers, Himeros and Pothos, Gods of Impetuous Love and Longing.

Phobos pulled off the robe and tossed it at Eros' feet. "I need to get going. I think Dad wants to run some drills by us in the morning. There's a war brewing among some of the human levels. If we're lucky, we're talking Trojan War-size." He shrugged. "Or, maybe a squirmish. Either way, I need to be ready."

"Thanks for your help, Phobos," said Psyche.

Eros waited until his brother left before turning back to Psyche. "Exactly what are you doing with the old nursery, then?"

"Really, Eros, it's rather obvious." Psyche waited a second, but it was clear the answer wasn't coming easily to her husband. "I'm having twins. Eileithyia confirmed it. I wanted to surprise you by having the nursery all set up."

Eros blinked. "But, we rarely have children outside of Hedone."

"Rarely doesn't mean never." Psyche smiled and walked over to Eros. "Besides, with how attentive you've been lately, it would have been surprising if I hadn't gotten pregnant." She wrapped her arms around his shoulder, letting her fingers play over his wings. Eros shuddered as she leaned in and placed kisses along his jaw.

"How far along are you?"

"Two months. Only you, Eileithyia, and Phobos know the truth. I don't want to announce it for another two months. Just to be safe."

"Gods don't miscarry, Psyche." Eros pulled her arms off him. "You know, it wasn't very nice to tell Phobos before telling me."

"I wanted the nursery to be a surprise. That's all."

"Still, you know my history with Phobos. I'm not sure if I really like him hanging around the house. I tolerate it for you, Psyche."

"I'm sorry, Eros. I promise, next time I want to surprise you, I will wait until I can talk to either Anteros or Zephyrus."

"You were a very naughty girl."

Psyche frowned slightly before seeing the glint in Eros' eyes. She smiled. "I was. I'm sorry. I deserve to be punished."

Eros laughed and scooped her up in his arms. "Yes you do, wife of mine. I intend on spending the rest of the night teaching you the error of your ways."

Psyche giggled as he carried out of the room and down the hall to their private chamber.

Chapter Twelve

When Minthe returned Kore home and Demeter learned with whom her daughter spent lunch with, she grounded Kore. Nothing Kore said about being an adult or having the right to decide if she wanted to accept Hades' bid for her hand penetrated Demeter's defenses. She put Kore on house arrest, and only she or Minthe could approve of anyone Kore would speak to or see. Demeter would also have outlawed any visitors if the news hadn't reached Zeus, who reminded Demeter that Kore had a job to do.

The only good that came from her grounding was that Kore learned her job wasn't to create spring. She was the overseer. Underneath her were the goddesses Chloris and Hegemon. Chloris, much like Kore, was the personification of spring, but was of a status lower than Kore. Hegemon was the goddess who made plants bloom and fruit. They became her connection to the outside. Through them, she learned that Hedone was alright and back to being her normal self. She learned that Psyche was pregnant, though no one was supposed to officially know that and had to keep it a secret. She learned that her date with Hades caused problems on Crete and that Hades was paying restitution for it.

Two months after her imprisonment came the annual Meeting of the Gods. Not every god was to attend, only the main Olympians and a small handful of minor gods to help decide the votes and bring new solutions to the table. Kore was rather surprised to learn she would be attending as she had not been a goddess for a year and knew next to nothing about the station.

"How can I help?" asked Kore. "I've lived my whole life in isolation."

"Don't be so dramatic," snapped Minthe. "You lived in safety, not isolation."

"What kind of topics do they discuss? Maybe I can try to prepare myself."

"I wouldn't know. You'll have to ask your mother. I've never sat in on a meeting."

When Kore asked her mother, Demeter shrugged. "Who cares what they discuss? All you need to do is just vote the same as me and all will go well."

The meeting took place on the upper level of the station, just down the hall from where Kore had her Becoming Ceremony. Seated around the long oval table were the Olympians, minus Hades, and seven other minor gods. Kore recognized Eros, Phobos, Deimos, Hedone, and Hypnos. The remaining two minor gods were ones she remembered being with Hades at the Becoming Ceremony. She believed the woman's name to be Hecate, but she never remembered them mentioning the man's name. On a monitor was Hades.

"Good, everyone is here," said Zeus as Kore and Demeter took their seats. "This year's meeting we have included a few more denizens of my brother, Hades', realm."

"We all know how they'll be voting," huffed Demeter.

"Demeter, I sent up Minos, once king of Phrygian

and now one of my three judges and advisors. I'm sure you can agree that, outside of the likes of our fair Athena, you won't find anyone with more wisdom than he. I also sent up Hecate, Goddess of the Crossroads, Magic, and Witches. She has a keen insight and ability to see solutions to problems that often elude me."

"We will vote on what's best for the Station," said Hecate.

"What about Hypnos?" asked Demeter. "Isn't he one of yours, too, Hades?"

"I was invited by Aphrodite," said Hypnos.

Demeter turned to glare at Aphrodite. "Traitor!"

"He's my...relation," Aphrodite said. She refused to call him her grandson-in-law or say anything that would indicate her status as a grandparent. Only the old were grandparents, and Aphrodite was not old.

"Alright, let's begin," said Zeus. "First, a moment of silence for our fallen brethren. Countless eons ago, we Zyspadaden answered the distress call from the humans of Earth. On their third planet by that name, they were in danger of extinction. Without the resources to leave Earth 3, they were doomed. We built for them these space stations and flew to the stars. It has been far too long since we heard from any of the other Stations. Our brothers and sisters have surely perished in their pursuit for a suitable planet for the humans in their care. To those we have lost to the vastness of space, we bow our heads and mourn our loss."

Everyone bowed their heads. Kore did the same, though this was the first she ever heard of other Stations. What were they like? How did they parish? Was there another Kore out there, in space, who thought she was the only one, too?

After a moment of silence, the meeting officially started. Kore's head swam as various gods read reports on how much food and animals were produced that year, the rate of human births versus human deaths, and the shrinking supplies of wood, metal, and stone.

"What about the planet below us?" asked Hades. Around the table, several gods groaned. "Now, hear me out. We've orbited this planet for over a century. We have the reports that it can sustain life that it has seasons and fresh water, and there are wildlife of both herbivore and carnivorous nature. We need only to colonize that planet, and some of our problems will be solved."

"You know the problem with colonization," said Poseidon. "We won't have as much control over the mortals down there. What if the humans decide to rebel when they discover we can't answer their prayers?"

Athena leaned back in her seat. "That won't happen. The humans are used to us not always giving them what they want. It may take some getting used to, but we will still have our abilities. Don't forget, long before we came, the humans were used to their gods being silent and living at the whims of their planet. We can dismantle most of the Station and have just Olympus in orbit in the atmosphere. That will give them a reminder that we are here and keep them from rebelling."

"Where would we put Hade?" asked Minos.

"There are many caverns and underground labyrinths on the planet. I've charted several of them through the years," said Hades. "It won't take much to adapt one to fit my realm. The only problem I see is growing food and plants underground."

"How do we grow food and plants now?" said Kore. Before anyone could think she was being stupid, she continued, "We use UV lights. This is a space station, not a planet. That means we have as much real sunlight as you would underground. I don't see growing plants underground as a huge challenge since we've been basically doing just that."

"I vote no," said Apollo. He leaned back on the back legs of his chair, his legs crossed in front of him up on the table. "I won't have the ability to watch over everything during the day. The planet is vast. We may start off with a small colony, but the humans will strike out on their own and leave. Those that leave will eventually create their own gods, forget about us, and become their own breed. No, it's best if we keep them in the Station where we can keep an eye on them."

"We can't stay here," argued Hephaestus. "Our supplies are running low. It's getting harder and harder to keep up with repairs. So what if we lose a few humans? They were not meant to stay forever on this Station. Finding a planet and colonizing was always the plan."

"What about a small colony," said Kore. "We can start with just farming and mining community. That will get some of the humans off the Station and we can stock up on more supplies."

"You think that hasn't been proposed before," Ares scoffed. "We have this same conversation every year."

"I think there is some merit to the small colony idea," said Hades. "We need to do something and time is running out."

"Of course you side with Kore's idea," said Apollo. "If I thought I could get her bed, I'd agree with anything that came out of her mouth." He idly looked over at Kore. "Need my vote, babe? You know what I want." He blew her a kiss.

"If you lay one finger on Kore, you'll be looking for a new host," growled Hades.

"You're the one who can't lay a finger on my daughter," cried Demeter. "I'd sell her to Apollo to keep her from you."

"Don't I get any say in this?" Kore asked.

"I think," said Zeus, "that we are getting off track. The motion to have a small colony for farming and mining on the planet is on the table. Let's take a vote."

Dionysus stood. "Before we do, I want to say a few words. I think it's a good idea. It won't be easy, but humans were made to live planetside. There are too many of them on this station and a war or plague won't wipe out enough for long. Everything we have was only meant to tide us over until we found a planet. Well, we found one and it's high time we utilize it. I'm not sure how long our resources will last, but we can't wait until they run out to act."

"We need to colonize," said Hephaestus. "To answer Dionysus' question, we only have resources to last us maybe only another hundred years, if we are lucky. With the way humans breed, we can run out in maybe seventy-five years."

"A war will help," said Ares. "As it is, we are in luck. The cities of Corinth and Sparta are gearing up for war. That'll wipe out some of those pesky humans, and if we can get a few more cities involved and Levels, that means more dead humans."

"War is not the answer," Hades said. "We've tried that before. All it does is make the humans more eager to replenish what they lost. It might help in the short term, but we should focus on a long-term solution."

"I say we find a way to cull the humans," said Poseidon. "We have ultimate control here. If I want to raise the water level in Rhodes, I can do that. If I need a storm to hit between the islands on Level 36 to punish Crete, I can do that. I won't have control on the planet. A storm can destroy the ships of a king in my favor or floods ruin my reputation. Not to mention, none of you will have any control, either."

The argument went round and round as the gods all put in their opinions and tried to sway the others to their way of thinking. Those in favor saw colonization as a way to survive, while those against were worried about losing control. Finally, Zeus put an end to the discussion and called for a vote. The final tally was thirteen to eight in favor of a small colony. Demeter glared at Kore as they ended up voting on opposite sides. The motion was carried and, after another round of arguments and votes, it was decided that Hestia, Hephaestus, and Dionysus lead the project. It would take a few years to finish planning before they could start.

Kore took part in a few more votes; saying yes to planting more food, no to letting the war between Corinth and Sparta get out of hand, and yes to using the planet for breeding hunting animals before colonization. She abstained from voting from anything she didn't fully understand. All in all, Kore felt her first meeting as a goddess went well.

"Demeter? A word before you leave," Zeus said at the end of the meeting. Demeter motioned for Kore to go home.

Kore started to head down the hall to the PortMat room when Hecate stopped her. Much like the day of Kore's Becoming Ceremony, Hecate was dressed in dark red and looked magnificent. Kore felt like such a little, inexperienced girl next to this woman whose beauty rivaled Aphrodite's.

"I have a message for you from Hades," said Hecate. "My lord Hades would like to apologize for the trouble he put you through. He would like to talk to you, but understands that it may be impossible for now. He asks that, when you do have the ability to contact him of your own free will, you do."

"I want to talk to him," admitted Kore. "I miss him."

Hecate smiled. "Ah, young love. I am pleased you are interested in Hades. The two of you belong together."

"You were on his arm the first time I saw you. Is there anything going on between you two?"

"Between me and Hades?" Hecate laughed. "Oh, my no! He's a nice guy, but he's not my type. No, I have my eye on someone else. Hades and I are merely friends."

Kore breathed a sigh of relief. Hades had said basically the same thing, but she had to be sure. Just because Hades wasn't interested in Hecate, she had to know if Hecate was interested in Hades. It was a great relief to know that her path to Hades was clear.

"The moment I can safely get word to Hades, I

will," she promised.

"You should consider coming for a visit sometime," said Hecate. "Even if it's just an hour or two."

"She will do no such thing!" Demeter stormed over to the two women. Behind her, Zeus looked amused at the situation.

"This is why I must watch over her," Demeter cried. "Don't you see, Zeus? I barely turn my back and those fiends of Hades are trying to steal her! I knew it was a bad idea to allow any of those denizens of the Underworld to come up among us civilized Olympians. Oh, my poor, impressionable daughter! If I hadn't arrived when I did, they would have dragged you to the dark depths where the sun doesn't shine and the air is stale. My baby belongs in the sun, blossoming in the fields!"

"By Tartarus, Demeter," spat Hecate, "you blather all the time. I invited her to think about visiting. That is not a kidnapping attempt."

"Do not talk to me about your intent, you vile witch! I know all about you! Everyone knows you want to rule the Underworld and have your disgusting eyes on Hades. You," Demeter stabbed her finger at Hecate, "want to destroy Kore because you think she stands in your way. You know that as long as Hades has his eye on Kore, he'll never look your way."

Hecate's eyes widened. "You mean, as long as Kore is around, Hades will never love me," she asked in a high-pitched voice. She dramatically flung her hand limply over her forehead. "Oh, whatever shall I do? You have seen through my evil plans. Oh, woe is me!" Suddenly Hecate laughed. "Really, Demeter, I'm all Team Kore over here.

I'm one hundred percent behind the idea of Hades marrying her."

Demeter snatched Kore's hand and marched off. "I will see my daughter happily married to anyone but Hades!"

"Word of advice, Demeter," called Hecate. "I wouldn't follow through with your threat to sell her to Apollo. Not unless you want to start a war among the gods."

As Demeter dragged Kore away, a plan took root in her mind. She knew the dangers of actually selling Kore and would never really do that. She preferred it if Kore decided to be an eternal virgin, but barring that, she would have to find just the right husband. For that, she'd need Aphrodite's help.

Chapter Thirteen

"You want me to do what?" Aphrodite stared at Demeter as if the harvest goddess lost her mind. Aphrodite felt like she should have known Demeter would pull a stunt like this, but at the same time it was just too outlandish to even consider.

"You heard me," said Demeter. "I want you to have Eros shoot both Kore and Hades and have them fall in love with different people. It's the perfect plan. I won't lose my darling daughter that horrible man and everyone is happy."

Aphrodite sighed, leaning back in the chaise. "I can't do that, Demeter. If they truly love each other, the darts won't work. I can only cause others to fall in love with Hades and Kore, but can't change their feelings. Trust me; I've tried it on others."

"That's a lie! I happen to know you use those darts to make anyone fall in love," Demeter snapped. "You're the Goddess of Love! You can make anyone fall in love..." Demeter's face brightened, "Or out of love! Yes, that's it! Hit them with the anti-love darts."

"Demeter, no! I am the Goddess of Love, and I only play matchmaker with the humans. Gods are off-limits."

"What about Apollo?"

"He's a god." Aphrodite rolled her eyes.

"No! I mean, we all know Eros has used his darts on Apollo. What about Daphne? Or Coronis? Marpessa? Hyacinthus? Your son plays fast and loose with those darts around Apollo. It won't be too much to cause him to desire

Kore. He already has some affection for her. Why not cause her to feel the same?"

"He's the exception," Aphrodite said. "I will not let my son use his darts on Hades. Remember our last conversation like this? The darts fade, and when they do, I will not want Hades to come after me for retribution for allowing Kore to get away."

Demeter pouted. "Then can you use them on other people? Have someone else fall in love with Kore and Hades. Perhaps, with other options, they will forget this stupid forbidden love and go with the other person?"

Aphrodite tapped a perfectly manicured finger against her chin. "I suppose I can do that. What's in it for me?"

"Whatever you want."

Those were dangerous words. Many gods took advantage if a human said them, but for a god to say that to another? Aphrodite was now in position to ask for anything she desired and Demeter had to comply if she wanted this favor. Just what could she ask of Demeter? As the Goddess of Grain and Harvest, Demeter had no dominion over beautiful flowers or rare gemstones. Demeter's followers tended to be sturdy women, fit for working in the fields. Not the kind of people Aphrodite coveted.

But, Aphrodite thought, Demeter does have one thing. Connections! Everyone knew that Zeus and Poseidon adored her. She wasn't the baby of the family, but she was the most beloved. Hera was a shrew and Hestia kept to herself. Demeter was the one the gods doted on.

"I want a necklace," said Aphrodite. "Not just any necklace, but one made from the rare blood pearls that Poseidon hoards. If you get me that, I will have Eros strike two people to interrupt this love affair between Kore and Hades."

Demeter blanched. "I can't ask him for those. Anything else, Aphrodite. Please."

"He adores you, Demeter. He'll hand them over if you ask."

"Not for free. I refuse to pay his price."

Aphrodite shrugged. "No necklace, no darts. It's all the same to me."

"Can't we just redo the deal we had last time?"

"Last time we joined to keep Eros from that pathetic human," Aphrodite said. "Seeing as he is married to a goddess and you have run out of single children, I don't see how we can use that deal."

"Don't you have any more kids? They'll make a better mate for Kore than Hades. Please, Aphrodite, anything but having to face Poseidon."

This got Aphrodite's attention. "Exactly why are you so scared of Poseidon?"

Demeter wrung her hands together. "I can't tell you. I swore to not tell a long time ago."

Aphrodite sighed. "I named my price, Demeter. You're resourceful. I'm sure you can figure out how to get those pearls and not meet up with Poseidon. Hire Hermes to steal them for you, if you must."

Depressed, Demeter left. If the request had been to get something from Zeus, she would have agreed in a heartbeat. Then again, it wasn't as if Aphrodite couldn't get those pearls herself. She had every god wrapped around her little finger. The fact that Aphrodite coveted something and had not wormed it away from the owner told Demeter that Aphrodite might also fear Poseidon. Or just not like him. Or hadn't thought about those pearls until now.

Damn Poseidon! After Zeus saved his siblings from the depths of their father's gut, Demeter saw him as a hero. She was Zeus' first worshipper. For a while, Demeter believed that she would be his wife. She was very much in love with Zeus. When he married Hera, Demeter's world came crashing down. Poseidon was there to pick up the pieces, claiming to be a friendly shoulder for Demeter to cry on. None of it was out of the kindness of his heart. No, Poseidon envied Zeus and wanted all that he possessed, including Demeter's adoration.

To this day, Poseidon hounded her. She couldn't go walking into his domain and ask for those pearls. She shuddered to think what price he'd demand of her.

On her way back to the PortMat room, Demeter passed through Ares' hall of Olympus. Demeter stopped to stare at one of the blood-painted statues. Maybe she can ask Ares to help her? Or take Aphrodite's suggestion of getting Hermes? Any price they ask for couldn't be any worse.

"Mother? What are you doing here?" A woman who greatly resembled Demeter came up to her. It took Demeter a moment to remember her; Despoina, her daughter by Poseidon.

Demeter smiled as a new plan formed. Poseidon would give those pearls to his daughter, wouldn't he?

Wasn't he telling her a few days ago that he wanted to connect with Despoina?

"I was looking for you, Despoina," Demeter said. "I have a very important request."

After the Annual Meeting, Kore was finally allowed off house arrest. Given her new freedom, she went to see Hedone and very pleased to note that her friend was back to normal. There was something different, though. The air around Hedone felt off, almost electrified, the way the air crackled around many of the gods. It was the only sign that Hedone was a full-fledged goddess.

Hedone and Hypnos had a small, intimate wedding and moved to an apartment just off Aphrodite's wing of Olympus. Her neighbors were the Seasons and Graces. The apartment came pre-furnished and had none of the personality of the inhabitants. Everything was pale pink or white, with lots of frills. The atmosphere was supposed to promote a loving environment, but Hypnos said it was like living in a box of spun sugar. Despite the fact that resources, such as stone, were becoming harder to come by, Hedone was scheduled to have a statue made in her honor next week.

"When are you going to get your godhead?" asked Hedone, her eyes on Kore.

"I'm not sure. I haven't really talked about it with Mother. I mean, with everything that happened with Hades and any time I try to bring up the topic, Mother is not one to listen. I'm not even sure I want to know what the previous Kore was like. No offense, Hedone, but you scared me."

"I scared myself," said Hedone. "It's very strange having the memories of so many lives in my head. I have knowledge of things I know I never learned and I can remember all of my previous husbands. I remember how lonely all the Hedone's before me felt as my parents ignored them, and it makes me realize how lucky I am that my parents were so attentive to me. All those times I thought my mother was a bother, the previous Hedone's wish she had been like that with them. It's so weird."

Kore shuddered. "I don't think I can handle that. I want to remain me."

"You really don't have a choice," said Hypnos. "Once you are named a god that means there is a Zysadaden soul with your name. In order to remain a deity, you must go through the Transference. It's not so bad if you're a minor deity. We get to retain more of ourselves than the major gods do."

"Does it hurt?"

Hedone and Hypnos looked at each other. "It depends," said Hypnos slowly. "For some, yes, it can hurt. For most, there is no pain. It's like going to sleep in one body and waking up in another."

"That doesn't sound right," said Kore. "I mean, I'm not the one waking up."

"Well, true. But it all depends on what satisfies the Transference," explained Hedone. "Mostly, it requires that the host be willing, like I was. But some must pass a test or be forced. The unwillingness of the host can make the Transference painful."

"Your mother told me some of this," said Kore. "She didn't tell me anything about a test, though."

Hedone shrugged. "It varies. My mother had to pass a long test and it wasn't easy. From the moment she met my dad, she was being tested. If she messed up any part of the test, she could have died and another host would have been chosen. At the very end, her host most gather the beauty of Persephone and fall into a deep, comatose state to simulate death before the Transference can take place. That process causes fear because the host actually believes she's about to die."

"Is that how she..." Kore touched her face.

"Oh, no. Well, sort of. It wasn't part of the test, but that is when Mother got her scars. Once you get your godhood, you're not supposed to talk about the life of your host, but Mom told me a little bit. Apparently, it was Ares and Enyo who tortured her. I'm not a hundred percent positive, but I think Uncle Deimos had a hand in it, too. Of course, that doesn't count the scars she got after becoming a goddess. Did you know that Apollo had some grudge against Zephyrus and wanted to exact his revenge, but Mom took his place? That's unheard of! Father, naturally, doesn't see any of her scars and Mother pretends they aren't there."

Hypnos patted Kore on the arm. "Don't worry. It is rare that anyone is marked by a test. Psyche is an unusual case. Honestly, the only god ever marked is Hephaestus, and that's his trial in becoming a god."

"Soooo, Kore, tell me about your date with Hades," said Hedone.

Kore smiled at the obvious change in topics. Nothing subtle about Hedone. "Mostly it went well. He was a perfect gentleman, and I really enjoyed talking to him. Too bad Minthe found us. She could have gotten him hurt!"

"I heard," said Hypnos. "Hades said he had to use the Helm of Darkness to escape. We really try to not let the humans see our powerful artifacts. And Poseidon is still cleaning up the mess. People are going on a pilgrimage to Crete in hopes of gaining favor with the gods. They have no idea who was among them, but they know it was a god."

"Will Hades do anything to them?"

"Hades? No, he's a marshmallow. He isn't all about revenge. He's the King of the Underworld. Eventually, all must pass through his gates. He can afford to be patient."

"You two had fun," prodded Hedone. "Are you giving his proposal any thought?"

Kore blushed. "He's very tempting."

Hedone squealed and clapped her hands. "That's so romantic! You already know you like his kisses. You two make such a cute couple."

"Don't let my mother ever hear you say that. She'll lock me away in a tower and destroy the key. I know most people think she was only joking when she said she'll sell me to Apollo, but she wasn't. If it comes to it, she will give me to the highest bidder who isn't Hades."

"I have faith you'll come out of this doing the right thing," said Hypnos.

Kore sighed. "I'm not even sure what the right thing is anymore."

After two hours, in which Hedone filled Kore in on the details of her marriage and her new duties with

Aphrodite, Minthe showed up to take Kore home. She and Demeter were not taking any chances with Kore sneaking out to see Hades or any of Hades' people kidnapping her. The more Demeter and Minthe tightened their grip, the more tempting Hades became.

As they walked down the hall, Minthe and Kore bumped into Demeter and Despoina. Kore's half-sister smirked when she saw Kore and held on to Demeter's arm.

"Oh, hello dear sister," twittered Despoina. "How are you finding godhood? Have you taken that final plunge? When I did it, it was a snap. In fact, Apollo told me I was his best customer. Isn't that right, Mother? Not a whimper or hiccup with me."

"I don't think I was there," Demeter said.

"Hello, Despoina. Since you asked, I have not taken the final step, but I am very busy. There seems to be some scheduling issues with spring, but I guess that's because there is now a goddess in charge of it."

"Spring did fine without you, you know," Despoina said.

"I'm sure it did," Kore admitted. "However, if you're not busy, I'd love to get to know you better. Maybe we can do lunch, sometime?"

"I'm far too busy to plan any kind of lunch. In fact, I'm off to see my father. As Goddess of the Stables, I not only take care of all the horses belonging to the gods, but I get to work with Poseidon in creating new horses. It's a much more important job than merely looking after flowers. My job takes up my time year round."

"Despoina, don't you have someplace to be," said Demeter.

"Of course, Mother. I do as I'm told." She shot Kore a smug look and quickly walked away toward the PortMat room.

Demeter linked her arm with Kore. "How was your visit with Hedone, dear? Did that awful Hypnos try to convince you to go to the Underworld? They didn't call Hades, did they?"

"My visit was fine. Hedone and I talked about her new life, really." Kore took a look back where Despoina had gone. "Mother, what did she mean? About doing as she's told?"

"Pay her no mind. There has always been a sibling rivalry between you two. I thought raising you away from her would put a stop to it, but I was wrong. Silly, isn't it?"

"How can we have a rivalry when we only first met at my Becoming Ceremony? Do you mean the previous Kores had a rivalry with her? I don't want it to continue. I'm not them, Mother. I can make up my own mind over how I feel about people."

Demeter scoffed. "Don't worry so much, Kore. You'll get wrinkles. I'm sure it's all in Despoina's head. You're the only Kore, and I mean to keep it like that." Demeter patted Kore's hand. "Besides, she's just jealous. After all, I guess I've made it no secret you're my favorite. Don't let it bother you."

Minthe snorted. "Despoina even married that brutish Deimos to prove she's better than you. As if that would prove anything more than the fact she was desperate after Eros rejected her."

Confused, Kore said, "But I'm not married." She caught the glare Demeter sent Minthe's way. It clearly said,

'Shut up'. Just as the more Demeter tried to pull Kore away from Hades made him all the more tempting, the more she kept quiet about the previous Kores made this Kore want to learn more.

"Mother, when will I receive my godhead?" asked Kore.

"When you're ready. You don't need to jump into it, Kore. You're young. Live a little."

"What was my predecessor like?"

Demeter stopped for a moment. "She was a wicked girl," she said, continuing to walk. "After all I did for her, she broke my heart. She reveled in the pain she caused, flaunting it in my face. All those who came before her were like that. Wickedness seemed to be her legacy."

"What if I turn out to be like her? I mean, yeah, Hedone was able to fight her predecessors' anger toward her parents, but what if I'm not strong enough? Mother, I really don't want to hurt you."

Demeter grabbed Kore's face, squishing Kore's cheeks as she gazed deep in her eyes. "You will never become like them! You will always be my darling daughter. Don't you worry. I'm talking to Apollo about finding a way to let you keep your memories. And I have been talking to Aphrodite to help me, as well. I will not lose you! Not ever again!"

Chapter Fourteen

The next day, Kore was surprised to open her door to find Despoina visiting. The daughter of Poseidon barely acknowledged Kore's presence as she swept into the small apartment and looked around. With a dainty finger, Despoina checked for dust on the table and rubbed imaginary dirt off on her skirt.

"Well, I am surprised. I think this is the smallest guest suite in the whole Station. I would have thought Mother would set you up in one of the bigger suites. By Zeus, I think the stable stalls are bigger."

"This is big enough for me," said Kore. "If I find I need more, I can put in a request to move."

Despoina stuck her head in the bedrooms. "Where is Mother?"

"She's not here. She might be by later in the afternoon. I understand she's got a lot work that has to be done."

"That is odd. I would have thought she'd by glued to your side."

Kore shrugged. "It was Zeus' order, I believe. Mother is supposed to be giving me some space to grow."

"And just how are you using that space? Any boyfriends?"

"There is someone I like."

"Hades?"

"It's not a secret. Believe me; Mother grounds me

every time his name is mentioned. I know Mother wants me to find someone else, but it's rather impossible."

Despoina laughed. "You like that dark and dangerous aura of Hades', don't you?"

"Well, that's part of it. And there's the fact that Mother won't let me out of her or Minthe's sight long enough to even meet anyone."

Despoina held out a small, red velvet bag. "Here. Give these to Mother and I can promise you that there will be a date in your future."

Kore took the bag. Should she give this to her mother? What if it meant that she'd never see Hades?

"Oh, I can see your thoughts," said Despoina. "Don't fret so; I totally get the attraction to man who is dangerous. My sweet Deimos is a very dangerous man. But I had to date a few softies first. Give the bag to Mother, date the person she wants you to, and then go to Hades. If he still thrills you, I suggest you marry him."

"Why are you helping me? Mother said you hated me."

"I don't hate you. Hate is not strong enough a word for what I feel for you. The depths of my feelings makes the Underworld look shallow. I wish you were never born. Do you know what your existence means? Mother ignores the rest of us, Kore. All your other brothers and sisters...all ignored. She forgets we exist! The only time she ever remembered me, and it's so I can run an errand for you." Despoina spat at Kore's feet.

"Then why do this?"

"Because, in order for you to marry, you'll need your

godhead. And once you get that, you'll be like all the others. I have hoped that this time Mother thinks about me while you are off in the..." Despoina stopped and smiled. "No, I'm not going to ruin the surprise. Not yet."

"And if I refuse to give this bag to Mother?"

"I've already told her I was going to drop it off this morning, and I'm sure Poseidon will be calling her today to see how she liked the gift. She'll know that you had them." Despoina turned to leave. "I pray the next time we meet, it's at your wedding. If I can't be Mother's favorite, than I might as well enjoy the pain you'll bring."

With that, Despoina left. Kore debated about giving the bag to Demeter or not. She opened it and found it was full of blood-red pearls. Were these bribes to have someone date her? Or part of a spell?

In the end, Kore gave the bag to her mother. Demeter was overjoyed and cut her visit short to bring the pearls to Aphrodite. At the mention of the Goddess of Love, Kore felt dread settle over her. Was it cheating to involve Aphrodite? Maybe Kore should try pleading her case to keep herself available for Hades? Aphrodite loved stories of true love.

The next day, Demeter swept into the small apartment, interrupting Kore's meeting with Chloris and Hegemon. Demeter pushed the notes on spring off the table and placed a beautiful deep green silk chiton down.

"Tonight, you are going on a date," declared Demeter.

"I am?" Kore bent to pick up her work. Even with the messed up schedule, Kore was determined to make her first spring the best. At the moment, they were talking about whether or not to have the same flowers bloom in every Level, or have a variety bloom throughout the Station.

"Yes. Aphrodite picked out the perfect man for you. He'll be here tonight. Come! I must make you presentable."

"Mother, who is this man?"

Demeter shrugged. "Don't know. Aphrodite only said he'll be over tonight. He's someone who will share your love of plants."

"I have other interests besides just plants," muttered Kore.

"What was that, sweetie?"

"Nothing, Mother." Kore watched as her mother went to her vanity and riffled through her cosmetics.

"Oh, no, this won't do," Demeter declared. "I need you to look spectacular! This could be the man for you!"

"Let's not get ahead of ourselves," Kore protested. She rushed forward to save her meager supply of makeup and haircare from the trash. Each item Demeter picked up, she threw away as 'not right'. Snatching her products out of the bin, Kore said, "I do get the final say in who I marry and if I marry."

Demeter paid her no heed. She pushed past Kore and turned on the viewscreen. Aphrodite's face appeared and Kore could hear her mother describe Kore's dismal cosmetics. Aphrodite promised to send her girls down to fix Kore up for her date.

"You're making a big deal out of this," Kore said.

"One can never make a big deal out of love," said

Aphrodite. "Who knows how this date can go?"

Kore frowned. When Aphrodite moved to call her servants, Kore noted a flash of red around the goddess' neck. It could just be a coincidence that Demeter wanted red pearls and Aphrodite appeared to be wearing red pearls. Did she have those before? It wouldn't have surprised Kore. One of Aphrodite's signature gems was the pearl.

Aphrodite's legion of beauticians swarmed down to Kore's quarters. As they measured and poked Kore, Minthe entered the apartment humming a tune with a vacant expression on her face. When Demeter cheerfully told Minthe of Kore's date, Minthe did not seem interested.

"Oh? That's nice," Minthe said absently. "I have a date tonight, Lady Demeter." Minthe meandered into her room and shut the door.

"What is going on today?" Kore asked. She then winced as one of the beauticians pulled a brush through her tightly curled hair.

"Don't you worry, we'll fix this mess," the girl said.

Kore sat in abject torture as Aphrodite's girls yanked her hair and slathered products on in an effort to tame the wild locks. At times, she was nearly pulled off her chair by the sheer force of their ministrations. As they were finishing up, Minthe came out of her room dressed in a very short chiton, her green-dyed hair piled up in a messy bun.

"Tell us about your date," said Demeter. "Maybe you can double date with Kore?"

Minthe sighed. "It was just so sudden," she said. "It was like, there he was, and I was seeing him for the first time. How could I not have noticed how perfect he was? Oh, my Lady, do you know the joy I felt when I sent him a request for a date and he said yes? Truly, this has been blessed by Aphrodite."

"Who is he?" asked Kore. The beauticians were now on makeup, fixing Kore's eyes to hold a smoky, mysterious look.

"Just the most perfect man on the Station."

Minthe talked about the mysterious man's virtues without ever mentioning a name. Kore wondered if this man was real, or a figment of Minthe's imagination. Or, if she really did have a date. Finally, it was time to put on her dress. Kore didn't recognize herself in the mirror. Her normally curly hair was straight and the makeup on her face made her look like a different person all together. The deep green and gold brought out a beauty that Kore never noticed before.

The bell chime rang and Kore took a deep breath as one of Aphrodite's girls ran to bring in her date. Nervously, she turned to see the man Aphrodite picked out for her.

"Hades?" Kore gasped as the last person she expected to see walked in to the room. He looked magnificent in a deep red and gold short chiton. In his hands, he held the most exquisite bouquet she'd ever seen.

"You look wonderful," Hades breathed. "I, uh, brought flowers. I mean, I know you deal with flowers all the time, but I couldn't think of anything else. I should have brought chocolates or something. Wow! You are beautiful."

Kore smiled. "The flowers are perfect. Thank you." She took the flowers and instructed the nearest girl to put them in a vase. Demeter was standing in the doorway, silently watching Kore.

"I guess Aphrodite agrees that we're meant to be," said Kore. "It's surprising she picked you for my date. I was so scared that I wouldn't like my mystery date."

Hades looked confused. "Aphrodite didn't pick me. You sent me a message saying to pick you up tonight." He glanced over at Demeter. "What's going on?"

"Mother told me Aphrodite picked out the perfect man for me." Kore turned to her mother. "I second his question, Mother. What is going on?"

"It appears you both have dates set up by Aphrodite, but not with each other," said Demeter. "Oh, this worked out better than I expected! See, Kore? Your little fruitless infatuation with Hades was always doomed. Not even the Goddess of Love thinks the two of you belong together."

"Just who is my date if not Kore?" asked Hades.

"There you are, darling!" As if on cue, Minthe swept in to the room and latched herself on Hades' arm. "I just saw the flowers. How did you know roses were my favorite?"

"They were carnations," said Hades. "More specifically, a breed called Theseus' Lament, created for the funeral of Theseus' son after a misunderstanding between them."

"It doesn't matter. They're beautiful."

"They were for Kore." Hades tried to pull free, but Minthe wouldn't be deterred.

"Darling, we should go. I know it's normally the man who plans the date, but since I asked you out, I did all the reservations. I got us the best seat at Hestia's restaurant. She has a soft spot for you, you know. And after that, Aphrodite promised us a private pavilion on her Level. It's such a romantic spot. Who knows, maybe we'll even watch the sun rise?"

"I am not leaving this apartment -" Hades started, but Minthe's high-pitched squeal cut him off.

"Oh, you flirt! This is our first date. Of course we must leave the apartment. Maybe next time we'll spend the whole date in bed." She giggled and turned to a very stunned Kore and far-too-calm Demeter. "Just listen to him. So eager to be with me. I do believe he forgot his manners. Pardon us, my Lady. I may not come back tonight."

Minthe dragged Hades out of the apartment, ignoring his protests. Once they were gone, Kore turned to her mother and growled, "What did you do? And don't deny it! You and Aphrodite plotted something!"

"What makes you think we plotted anything? Apparently Hades and Minthe have a date. Face it, sweetheart, he's moved on. Now, stop frowning. You'll ruin all of that hard work to make you look presentable."

"I saw Aphrodite wearing those red pearls that Despoina dropped off for you. She warned me you were planning something. I know Minthe did not just wake up this morning and decide to date Hades!"

Demeter rolled her eyes. "Oh, please, Minthe thought Hades was handsome back when she thought he was Aidoneus. It was only his creepy attraction to you that prevented her from acting on it. Well, now that you will be with the man Aphrodite picked out, Minthe is free to act on her whims. And he accepted her request."

"He thought I was the one sending the request!"

"Details. Who cares who asked whom out? The point is, Hades is with Minthe now."

The door chimed again and Kore turned to see a man she never met being escorted into the apartment. He was tall and muscular with dark black skin, black hair pulled back in braids, and his eyes were the most memorizing aqua. He wore a short tunic the same shade of green as Kore's chiton.

He bowed to Kore. "My lady, I am Bion Megalos. Never before in my life have I beheld such beauty. I am honored to have this oppertunity to treat you to dinner. I know it is customary to bring flowers on a first date, but I figured you had your fill of them. Instead, allow me to gift you with this." He produced a small jewelry box. Inside was a single strand necklace made from cream-colored pearls and matching earrings.

"They're lovely," said Kore. She set the box on a side table. "We've never met before. Why did Aphrodite pick you?"

Bion smiled. "You are the Goddess of the New Spring, and I am an honored devotee of Hegemon, as well as part Dryad on my mother's side."

Kore decided to talk to Hegemon later about this man. He was handsome, but it took more than a pretty face to replace Hades in her heart.

"I can see why Aphrodite picked you," beamed Demeter. "Off you two go. Have fun. Don't stay out too late! Her curfew is ten."

Bion brought Kore to the same restaurant on Level 8 as Minthe and Hades. She spotted the two sitting in a corner, Minthe running her hand up and down Hades' arm and the God of the Underworld looking miserable. Bion had the hostess seat them on the other end of the room. The restaurant was popular with the gods, and there were several of the Olympians eating there that night. When Zeus spotted Kore, he came over to see how she was doing. He also voiced his surprise at seeing her and Hades out with different people.

"I think I'm going to have to talk to Aphrodite after this," said Kore.

"Ah, yes, that explains everything," Zeus said.

"Isn't it wonderful?" Bion sighed and grabbed Kore's hand. "Ours is a love match. Yes, we must thank her for everything."

When Zeus left, Bion said, "Darling, I'm not sure I liked how he was looking at you. You do know his reputation?"

"He's my father."

"Trust me, that won't stop him. I think it would be better if you didn't talk to any men like him."

"What?"

Kore listened with growing horror as Bion rattled on about how beautiful she was and how that would tempt any man. He wanted her to talk to only women, as that would keep her safe.

During their meal, Aphrodite came over to admire her handiwork. She was also ruled as someone Bion didn't want Kore talking with. She dressed too provocatively and that drew the attention of men, which meant if Kore hung around her, she'd be attracting the attention of men.

With each passing course, Bion grew more possessive of Kore. By the time dessert came around, he was actually growling at anyone who stopped by. When Phobos came over, Bion looked ready to fight him.

Bion wanted to go to a private alcove on Aphrodite's Level, but Kore complained of being tired and that her curfew was close.

"I know we just met, but you already occupy my dreams. I've been in love with you once I saw your picture. This has been a dream come true, and we are meant to be. Aphrodite has given us her blessing," Bion said as he walked her to the PortMat.

"I'm flattered, but I just don't feel the same way," said Kore.

"Of course you do. You're just shy. My heart beats only for you, Kore. Let's go back to the restaurant. Hera was there. She can officiate the wedding, or Zeus can. We can be married this very night!"

"I'm not ready to get married. Really, Bion, I just want to go home."

"Can true love really afford to wait? We are connected by fate. We belong together! People will tell our love story for the ages. We're like Zeus and Hera, Eros and Psyche, Orpheus and Eurydice, Hades and Persephone!" Bion grabbed her by the shoulders, squeezing hard into her flesh. "You belong to me, Kore. I'm not going to let you run away from destiny."

"Hades and Persephone?"

"Yes, the dreary queen of the Underworld. You're right, bad example. In fact, all of them were bad examples. Ours is the purest of love and will outshine every other love story ever."

"I really need to get home. Please, Bion, you're scaring me."

"He's scaring me, too." Phobos walked over to the group. Kore wasn't sure how much he heard, but he looked murderous. "I suggest you take your hands off of her."

"Kore is mine," Bion said.

"I don't care. I'm her bodyguard, and I will not tell you again to let her go."

When Bion refused, Phobos quickly punched him in the face. One hit was all it took to knock Bion out. Phobos dragged Bion to the PortMat room and gave the attendants the coordinates to drop the unconscious man off.

"I will have a long talk with my mother and brother after this," Phobos said. "This just reeks of love darts."

"I suspect so," Kore said. "Despoina dropped off some red pearls for Mother, and I noticed Aphrodite wearing them today. I know it's connected."

"I suggest you be careful, Kore. Next time, don't hesitate to take him down. I know you have the knowledge. Anyone who can hold their own against Enyo can surely handle that weak punk."

Kore looked down. "I didn't think it was appropriate on a first date."

Phobos snickered. "I see you're point. A

roundhouse kick is definitely second date material. Stun guns, though, are good on a first date." Turning serious, he added, "Anyone who ever touches you in a way that makes you feel not safe shouldn't be allowed to get away with it. He ever lays another hand on you, I expect you to break his bones. And, once she hears about this, I'm sure Artemis will say the same thing."

"I'll bear that in mind," promised Kore. She used the PortMat to travel home. When Demeter asked how the date was, Kore told her she never wanted to see Bion again.

"Back to the drawing board," Demeter sighed.

That night, Kore woke to voices in the main room. She peered out of her bedroom and saw that Demeter was on the viewscreen with Aphrodite and Eros. Eros had a black eye, and Kore was sure that Phobos had his little chat.

"I just don't get it," Aphrodite was saying. "Those darts are meant to make someone fall in love. Bion is a nice guy. Why would he start acting like Apollo? No, worse than Apollo."

"Sometimes these things happen," Eros said. "The formula might have gone bad. Or the feeling of love gave Bion a false sense of courage and he acted on that. I'm going to shoot him with an anti-love dart tomorrow to cancel out the love dart. We can always try someone else."

"Oh no you're not!" Kore stormed out of her room. "No more love darts! You'll fix this and then stop trying to meddle in my life. I will pick who I want without any help."

"Hades is out of the question," said Demeter.

"Minthe called me earlier. It appears that Hades has fallen for her."

"I will pick my own husband. I can't believe you did this, Mother! I'll never forgive you!" Kore went back to her room, slamming the door. She leaned against the door, and heard the last part of the conversation.

"I'll fix this with Bion," Eros said, "but Minthe got a dart with the same formula. If Hades ever finds out that I was involved, he can make my life miserable. You know he's friends with Psyche."

"But Minthe told me..."

"Minthe is under the spell of a dart," Eros said. "She might not be seeing clearly. Maybe I should cancel out her dart, as well."

"Don't you dare! If I can't get Kore to marry or declare herself a virgin goddess, then I will see to it that Hades marries someone other than her. By the River Styx, I will not lose another daughter to that monster!"

Chapter Fifteen

"I didn't know the darts would be this strong!" Eros kept a nervous watch out his window as Bion circled the front of the house once more. Behind him sat his wife and Kore, neither woman looking pleased with the situation.

"He won't leave me alone," Kore wailed. "He follows me everywhere! He not only threatens any man who comes near me, but tries to 'teach me a lesson' every time. I think I preferred Apollo to him!"

"I thought you were going to get him with an anti-love dart," Psyche said. "What happened?"

"I did shoot him! Twice! It's not cancelling out!" Eros winced. "Oh, sweetie, he just ruined that cute little garden you planted for my brothers."

"How long until the dart loses its power?" asked Psyche.

"Depends. Some are only a week, some a month, some a year." Eros shrugged. "I thought I used one designed for a week. You know, just long enough for Kore to get interested in him."

"It's been a month." Kore twisted her chiton in her hands. The stress of her ardent admirer could be seen in how her normally curled hair hung in limp strands and her chiton was wrinkled and stained. She hadn't slept in days and would cry at the smallest things.

"There is only one way to force the dart's power to fade and depart his system," Eros said slowly. "It's a bit risky."

"What is it? I'll do anything!"

"If you were no longer Kore, the dart will dissipate," Eros said. He moved away from the window. "Honey, did you remember to lock the back doors?"

"Yes, dear. Why?"

"He's heading to the back." Eros left to go guard the back door. Psyche and Kore trailed behind him.

"What do you mean if I'm not me?" asked Kore. "Are you suggesting I take on my godhood?"

"Exactly. The dart was to hone in on you specifically, so if you were no longer Kore, it wouldn't have a target." Eros smiled. "It's much like the same dart that was used on Psyche and myself. If, before her Transference, anything happened to Psyche's new host, the dart in my system would fade. But, no worries about that. We were meant to be."

"I like being me. I...I'm scared of what the previous Kore was like. She hurt Mother, and I don't want to hurt her."

"Kore, I knew the previous you," said Psyche. "She didn't hurt Demeter. All she did was follow her heart. You know your mother has a hard time letting go of grudges. That's all that happened. She loved Demeter very much. You are already like her. All you'll gain is some new memories."

Kore shook her head. "No, I saw how Hedone reacted at first. I don't want to be a whole new person."

"And Hedone is herself once more. It took some time, but she now accepts that things are different this time around. You have nothing to worry about."

"She can always go into hiding," said Eros. "And, honey, call Ares. He's tearing up your garden."

Psyche took a look out the window and gave a squeak of outrage. She turned and used the nearest viewscreen to call up Ares.

"What does my least-favorite daughter-in-law need?" asked Ares when he finally picked up.

"I would like some security at my house. That Bion fellow is ripping up my garden in his search for Kore. What? Does he think I'm hiding her under my begonias?" The last was yelled toward the back, as if that would stop Bion. "Ares, send someone or I swear I'm going to shoot him."

"And Eros can't get rid of him, why?"

"He's protecting Kore. I need someone here in five minutes, Ares." She hung up on him. It took almost thirty minutes before Phobos and two guards showed up to escort Bion off Eros' property.

"Hiding might not work," Kore said once it was safe. "I'm running out of options."

"Ever thought of hiding in the Underworld?" Eros suggested.

"Mother would kill me."

"I know of a place," said Psyche slowly. She told them of a family on Elusious, a city dedicated to Demeter on Level 19 in the Attica region. They would, of course, be devoted to Demeter, so that wouldn't be a problem. And they would protect Kore.

When Kore brought the idea to her mother, she was surprised to see Demeter agree so readily. They had to keep the plans from Minthe. Just like Bion, the love darts didn't fade in Minthe and she was so infatuated with Hades that it was feared she'd tell him where Kore went. Not to mention, Minthe was turning more and more hostile toward Kore.

The next night, while Minthe was hounding Hades in the Underworld for another date, Kore packed and met with Psyche and Phobos to travel to Elusious. The city took up a good fourth of the level, sprawling with fields of wheat, dotted with small temples to Demeter, and one large, looming factory that produced flour and grain products for half of the Station.

Psyche led them to a modest-sized home on the eastern edge of the city. They could see the back garden and there were fruit trees in the front. A small personal shrine to Demeter just off the front door, and surprisingly, a small shrine to Psyche. The home was dark. Considering the hour, it was likely everyone inside was asleep. In front of the door was an old, shaggy dog, also asleep. Psyche leaned over the dog and knocked loudly on the door. The dog perked up, but once he saw Psyche, he gave a half-hearted woof and fell back asleep.

"World's most worthless guard dog," muttered Phobos.

A light came on upstairs and Kore heard someone coming down to the door. It opened to reveal a man with slightly thinning brown hair, a slender build, and a neatly trimmed beard. His eyes widened as he saw his visitors.

"Iona! What...How...?"

"Not out here, Theron. Let us in." Psyche pushed past the man and motioned for Phobos and Kore to follow.

At the other end of the entryway stood the man's family: a wife holding a baby, a teenage daughter, and twin boys. Surely, with the house this full there would be no room for Kore.

Once Psyche was inside, the family could see her clearly. The wife gasped and paled, looking like she had seen a ghost. The two young boys ran forward and hugged Psyche, calling her "Auntie."

The man, Theron, immediately stepped forward and grabbed his sons. "Telchine! Virbius! Go stand with your mother." He gave them a shove and turned back to Psyche. His face was a mixture of anger and amazement. "How," he finally said, "can you be here?"

"It's a long story, Theron. Needless to say, I'm not here and you never spoke to me."

Theron pointed to Phobos. "How is he here?"

"Have we ever met?" asked Phobos.

"Officially, no. I'm sure he saw you a few times back when...you know." Psyche looked uncomfortable. "Theron, please. We need your help."

"There are statues of you all over the place, Iona! By Hades, I have one! Did you know that? They say the statues are of Psyche, but I know better. Even with those scars, I know it's still you."

"I am Psyche. Iona Demarchis died on a lonely road on Level 14, and I am who is left. It's the way of the gods, Theron."

"You're in dangerous territory, Psyche," Phobos warned.

"I trust them," Psyche said.

"Forgive my husband," said the woman. She gently patted the baby in her arms, keeping her distance. "It's just, you look so much like someone we used to know. Someone who has been dead for nineteen years."

Psyche sighed. "Nothing leaves this house. Anything I tell you, you will not ever repeat to anyone."

"Very dangerous territory. Best to just shoot them all and find someone who doesn't recognize you," muttered Phobos.

Psyche ignored him. "Theron, yes, I was Iona. Once upon a time, I was your sister-in-law. I was chosen to become Psyche, and on the day I did, Iona became no more. I'm breaking the laws of the gods by even admitting that, but we are in desperate need of your help."

"Did becoming a goddess mean you had to cut us all out of your life? Do you have any idea the mess you left behind? I had to stand by your parents as they held funerals for your sisters - for you! Do you know how much your mother grieved for you? Or that your father died of a broken heart, believing he was the cause of all of the destruction that followed? He thought if he never went to Delphi, none of this would ever have happened." Theron looked down. "Gods, Iona, I think of all of Hedylah's children, she mourned you the most. And to find out you were okay...That hurts the most."

"I saw, Theron. I watched her sometimes when she stopped by Aphrodite's temple in Tiryns to look at my statue. I was there the day you and Chruse married, and I was at both Mother's and Father's funerals. Try as I might, I couldn't forget. I just couldn't let you know about me."

"We are not supposed to remember our past or

contact anyone from our old lives," said Phobos. "And stop calling her Iona. She is Psyche, Goddess of the Mind and wife of Eros. Treat her with the respect she deserves."

"And just who are you?" demanded Theron.

"Phobos, God of Fear, son of Ares."

One of the boys said, "Daddy, why are you angry at Auntie Ida?"

"Auntie Ida!" Theron choked.

"Auntie Ida is the one who dropped off the medicine for Mommy when she was so sick with Lykaios," said one boy.

"And she's the one who gave us Skylos."

"Worthless dog," Theron muttered. Phobos grunted in agreement.

"Does this mean we have to call you Auntie Iona or Auntie Psyche?" asked one boy.

The teenage girl gasped. "Wait a minute! You're who I'm named after?"

Chruse nodded. "Many years ago, I served Apollo at Delphi. I met a woman named Iona Demarchis of Tiryns there. We left at the same time and she gave me some jewelry to help pay my passage. If it weren't for her, I would never have met Theron."

"When did you serve Apollo?" asked Phobos.

"During the time Eros was healing from that burn on his shoulder. Or was it the beating in the hall Deimos and Enyo gave him?"

"Fine, what is you need?" Theron said. "This can't be a pleasure trip."

"I need you to hide my friend. One of her suitors is a bit overzealous." Psyche motioned for Kore to come closer. "You'll be doing the gods a huge favor."

"Which gods? Because if this ends like last time, I'd rather not put my family in the middle of some divine family squabble."

"That's unavoidable," said Phobos.

"You'll be helping out Demeter, and since she's the patron goddess of this Level, that should be your only concern," said Psyche.

"Anyone I can expect to drop by?"

"Technically, we should say Hades," said Kore, "but I think the real danger is Bion. He's not a god. He's semi-human."

"Semi-human?" asked Theron.

Kore shrugged. "He said his mom is a Dryad."

Theron rubbed his forehead. "And should I be worried that Hades will be dropping by?"

"Oh, he's a sweetheart," said Psyche. "You'll like him."

"I've got a headache," Theron muttered. "All right, we'll keep her here. Come on." Theron motioned for Kore to follow him. Phobos went with Kore.

"How much trouble can we expect?" asked Chruse once her husband was gone.

"Remember how much pain and suffering followed me? All because I, as a mortal, was chosen to be a goddess? Well, Kore was born to be a goddess, and her destiny lies with Hades. No matter how hard you try, you won't be able to keep them apart. I'm afraid trouble will find you, but I will do my best to keep the worst of it away. This is just until Kore realizes her right path."

"And how long can that take?"

"Given how Bion's been acting, I'd say a week after he finds her."

Kore's new life with Theron and his family was much like her life growing up. She wasn't allowed to leave the house and her mother visited every day. Theron was very respectful toward her, and Kore enjoyed talking to him about his life. She found out he was a son of Apollo and had been a great athlete. He was once married to a woman named Errita, who could weave the most beautiful cloth. Their life together seemed perfect, until Theron hurt himself and had to retire while he healed. Spending more time at home made him notice things about his wife. She would disappear for hours sometimes, sneaking off the property. She never told him where she went, but he learned after her death that she had a lover on the side. Errita was greedy, loving him only for the money and fame he brought. He swore he'd return to sports once he was able to, but it wasn't soon enough.

Theron fell into a deep depression, losing all hope. It was around this time that his sister-in-law returned. She had been married off to a mysterious serpent and no one in her family had contact with her. Errita and her older sister, Philomena, were invited up to see Iona, but Errita never talked to Theron about what she saw. When Iona showed up on Theron's doorstep, she was frantic. Philomena, much like Errita, had kept her true self hidden under a mask and, upon thinking she was next in line for the riches of the gods, had murdered her husband. Iona needed Errita to help talk some sense into Philomena. However, Errita misunderstood Iona's plea and believed she was the one to really receive the lavish lifestyle of one favored by the gods.

Theron's wife died and Iona once more disappeared. He stayed with his in-laws for a while, helping them cope with their loss. Chruse found them, having been sent from Apollo's temple by Iona.

"The rest is pretty much self-explanatory," Theron said. "Chruse and I fell in love. I never returned to sports and we moved here to start a family."

The only part of Kore staying with his family that seemed to unnerve Theron was the gods who kept stopping by. Having dealt with the aftereffects of gods interfering in the lives of mortals before, Theron was wary every time one would show up. He kept his wife and children away, dealing with the deities himself.

Phobos visited nearly every other day to make sure Kore was safe. He provided a blaster and side holster for her. Artemis, not to be outdone by a man, stopped by several times to see to it that Kore practiced her self-defense skills and offered to teach young Iona. She also gifted Kore with a wristlet that transformed into a shield. The shield held the image of Medusa's head, marking it one of Artemis' personal devices.

Psyche, of course, visited when she could and told Kore the gossip that her mother didn't. Apollo and Zeus were arguing over the over-population of the Station. Because the plan to get a colony down on the planet was still in the planning stages, Apollo decided to cull the human herd. He released a plague, but it backfired. Instead of spreading among the human levels, it spread among the personal levels of the gods. Mostly on Level 14, the level dedicated to Hermes. It was getting so bad that Hermes declared quarantine on his level. For the first time that anyone could remember, the one holy level open to anyone was closed. No one was allowed in or out until the plague was dealt with.

After several days of peace and quiet, Kore started to breathe easy. Bion had not found her, and Kore prayed that he had moved on, but Psyche warned her it might not be that easy. Kore was merely out of sight, but not out of mind.

To help with her new mortal foster family, Kore took to caring for the children. When the twins, Telchine and Valbious, were off to school, Kore watched over baby Lykaios. At first, Chruse was cautious with having Kore care for the baby, but she soon grew to trust the goddess.

Kore spent her time watching Lykaios in the back garden, telling the infant the various names of the flowers. Chruse let her know that Lykaios had no idea what she was saying, but he was the most attentive baby she ever met. He watched her with wide, blue eyes and a toothless, drooling grin.

"Don't tell your mom, but I think Psyche's garden is more impressive," Kore whispered to Lykaios one afternoon. Chruse was inside; taking a nap and Kore was out in the garden. "I mean, it's really nice, but Psyche's garden puts most of the gods to shame. She even has a little dark greenhouse to grow flowers from the Underworld. I wish I had gotten a chance to see those flowers bloom."

Lykaios cooed and tried to shove his fist in his mouth.

Kore gently pulled his fist out of his mouth. "I bet those flowers are beautiful. I've never heard of flowers that grow in darkness. And they're real, not mechanical. I can create flowers that won't need light to bloom. That's easy. But real flowers are so hard. So many things can go wrong with them, and that makes them beautiful. Just think: you spend days or weeks or months cultivating a flower, and it can bloom in any number of ways. A little bit of color can be off, the petals not perfect, or maybe it blooms small. That makes it so special when it can be anything but perfect."

"And some things can't help but be perfect."

Kore stood up and looked around. She thought she heard Hades' voice, but she and Lykaios were alone in the garden.

"I'm hearing things," she said softly. She missed Hades so much; she was now imagining his voice.

"No you're not." Hades removed the Helm of Darkness, appearing to her. "Sorry to startle you like that. I had to make sure no one followed me."

Kore rushed over to him and gave him a one-armed hug, turning slightly to not crush the baby. "You have no idea how much I've missed you," she said. "I was starting to think I'd never see you again."

"I was afraid of the same thing," Hades whispered against her hair. He pulled back slightly and looked down at Lykaios. "And who is this happy fellow?"

"Lykaios. He's the son of the couple that lives here."

"You look like such a natural holding him."

Kore blushed. "I should. I mean, as the Goddess of the New Spring, I am a fertility goddess."

"Yes you are." Hades' blue eyes smoldered, causing her to duck her head shyly. His look made her feel weak in the knees.

"How - how are things going with you?" she asked.

"About the same. Minthe won't leave me alone and Bion has taken to threatening me. He thinks I'm hiding you."

"I'm so sorry." Kore sat on the garden bench. "I just wish this was all over. I don't know what scares me the most now; remaining myself and living in fear of Bion, or giving up on being me to get rid of him."

Hades sat next to her. "What do you mean giving up on being you?"

"Eros said the only way to destroy the dart's affect is to finish becoming Kore. I need to do the Transference. But I'm scared. What if I stop being me? What if I die and some stranger takes my place?"

"I promise you, Kore, that won't happen. You will always be you, even after the Transference."

"But what if I'm not? It's like death. And not in a good sense, where I could spend the rest of eternity with you. I would cease to exist."

Hades shook his head. "Trust me; I've seen your Transference before. You will always be you."

"You knew the previous Kore?"

"I did. She was a lot like you; a kind spirit who

helped those in need. She was brilliant and could always see a solution to any problem. She was happiest, I think, in her garden. I could watch her for hours as she gardened, this little smile on her face. She spoke to all her plants, gave them all names. It was very enduring."

There was something in his voice that caught Kore's attention. "You loved her," she said.

"I did. She was a very special person."

"Is that why you love me? Because I'm going to be her?"

Hades shook his head. "I love you because of who you are. She was special to me, but I have had time to mourn her. You two may share a name, but I can tell you are different people."

Kore looked down, gently bouncing Lykaios in her arms. "I should be upset that you loved the previous Kore. It hits kind of close to home." She continued to look down and asked softly, "What about Persephone?"

"What about her?"

"I heard she was your wife."

Beside her, Hades nodded absentmindedly. "You could say that, but she...passed away. She was also a lot like you." He chuckled. "I guess you're just really my type."

"You're really my type, too."

Hades took her hand. "Believe me, Kore, you are the only woman for me."

They sat in silence as Lykaios started to doze in Kore's arms. Kore thought over what she learned about her previous self, and decided she really didn't care. Her previous self was gone, as was Persephone. She was left, and if Hades said he loved her for who she was, she could live with that.

A sudden crash from the house startled them. Raised voices reached their ears and Lykaios started to cry. Kore could recognize Bion's voice yelling, "Where is she? I know she's here!"

"Here," Hades said as he jammed the Helm of Darkness down on Kore's head. "Use this to hide."

When Theron, Chruse, Bion, and Hegemon came into the garden, they found Hades. He sat patiently on the bench, watching them with a bored expression. Lykaios, who was still crying, sat in his arms.

"Who are you?" Theron demanded. Chruse ran forward to scoop up her son.

"I am Hades, God of the Underworld. You must be Theron. I've heard good things about you."

"Where is Kore? What have you done to her?" Bion stomped around the garden, ripping up the flowers to look for Kore.

"She's not under the roses," Hades said. "She's not here."

"Then why are you here? I know you came here to meet with her. She's mine! She'll be my bride. We were blessed by Aphrodite, and there is nothing you can do to break that bond."

Hades shrugged. "Maybe I came here to see Theron?"

Bion roared, storming deeper in the garden and destroying the plants.

"Oh, for Flora's sake," Hegemon said. She pulled out a blaster and fiddled with the setting knob for a second before shooting Bion. He fell to the ground, stunned. Hegemon then turned the gun on Hades, who raised his hands.

"Fix this! I want my husband back. This is not who he really is," Hegemon cried. "He used to be so kind and caring. He was never obsessive. That damned dart did this to him and I want you to fix it!"

"I'll do what I can," Hades promised. He knew what to do. All he had to do was convince Kore to follow his plan.

Part II:
Queen of Hades

Chapter Sixteen

Level 14 had always been the most crowded and highly visited of the godly levels of Space Station Olympus. As the level most holy to Hermes, it was open to all travelers. Containing the best journalistic schools, this was the level for future news messengers to train. There were rolling fields for farming and caring for animals, crossroad shrines, caves for thieves to hide, and the second-best field for track runners. The best was located on Level 10, Apollo's level.

The whole floor was always crowded with eager tourists, one reason why Apollo's plague managed to spread so quickly and easily. Most likely carried by a pilgrim, it infected mortal and demigod alike. Hermes grew furious that those under his protection were harmed and demanded that Zeus do something. A cure was out of the question. Apollo, in his diabolical genius, created the plague to last for only a certain length of time and then the virus would just die out. He pleaded that since the virus would vanish after a period of time, he should not have to work on a cure. Zeus allowed him that, but for his arrogance in releasing the plague without Zeus' permission, Apollo did receive punishment. He was sent to be a mortal's hireling for a year. Instead of a king or man of importance, as Apollo had hoped, he was sent to Level 40, one of the farming levels, for hard labor.

This did not satisfy Hermes, but there was nothing he could do. His level was quarantined until the virus died out. Travelers who once enjoyed the freedom to come and go as they pleased now needed the same passports that allowed or barred them from the other holy levels.

Psyche noticed the difference right away as she stepped out of the PortMat room. Even here there were guards, checking paperwork. To her surprise, people sent through the PortMat were being sent back. Few of the mortals who could only travel by the lifts knew of this new protocol, and even fewer of the gods cared to find out if they, too, must follow the new rules.

Cries of "But I was sent here by Helios" and "I'm on a mission from Dinlas" filled the area around the PortMat as unfortunate devotees and human servants were sent back to the upper levels.

"Papers, ma'am." A guard wearing an oxygen mask held out one gloved hand. It was the appearance of the guards that lent to the rumors that the plague was just as devastating to the gods. It wasn't just the guards that made Level 14 feel different. There was a cloud of gloom in the air.

Psyche removed her veil to show her scarred face. A few people nearby murmured amongst themselves. Her scars made her one of the more recognizable gods on the station.

"I don't have any papers," she said.

"Ma'am, I'm sorry, but even the gods need to have proper passports," the guard said. "No one is allowed on this level without their paperwork, by order of Lord Hermes himself."

"I was invited here by Hermes," Psyche said. "He did not mention that I would need my passport."

"A thousand pardons, Lady Psyche, but orders are

orders."

For a moment, Psyche felt paralyzed. If she turned and left, it would undermine the gods' powers on the station. However, if she demanded they let her through, she would not only undermine Hermes' authority on his own level, but would present herself in a negative light. Her mind quickly picked through every option she could think of, weighing each for the best possible response.

"Wait! She's with me!" A handsome satyr came bounding up to the group. His chocolate curls bounced with each step, locks falling in his dark brown eyes and around his ram's horns. His legs were also covered in the same thick curls, making it nearly impossible to notice that he was naked. A pan flute hung around his neck. Psyche smiled as she saw her friend.

"Lord Pan, she does not have her paperwork," the guard said. "By orders of Lord Hermes, everyone must present their passport and travel papers."

Pan grinned. "That's okay. Father and I invited her and I believe we forgot to mention she'd need her passport. You'll find her on the list of gods who are allowed to come and go at their leisure."

One of the guards glanced down at a tablet. Psyche saw the list that came up, and it was a rather short one. She would have wondered how they could have missed her name, but they never bothered to look. The guard grunted and nodded, allowing Psyche to pass.

"Be sure to visit the purification station on your way out," the guard said. "We need to keep this thing contained."

Psyche and Pan headed to the south end of the level

where the fields lay. This was the area where many of the nymphs and dryads congregated and Pan cared for flocks of sheep in between his personal pursuits. On the way, they passed the field where the golden sheep roamed. Psyche suppressed a shudder, remembering the last time she came across those sheep and nearly became their dinner. No one looking at those deviously innocent-appearing golden sheep would guess they were vicious meat-eaters, but Psyche knew the truth. The evidence was the ugly, crescent-shaped scar on her leg where one sheep took a bite out of her.

"I'm glad you came, Psyche. It would mean so much to Casta to know you were here," Pan said softly.

Casta, a shepardess whom Pan adored, had been a bundle of energy from the moment Psyche met her. The two formed a friendship after Psyche became a goddess. While her duties kept her from visiting for stretches of time, Psyche never forgot Casta's kindness.

"I'm just sorry it was under these circumstances," said Psyche. "Everything seems so quiet now. I wish I could have seen her smile one last time."

"She was smiling even at the end." Pan grinned, his eyes focused on the past only he could see. "I thought she would beat it, you know. There was no way any illness could defeat someone as full of life as Casta. It robbed her of her strength, but she continued to be optimistic. I swear, she didn't think she was closing her eyes for the last time. She really believed she'd open them again and we'd talk about something unimportant. Her last words were, 'let me just rest my eyes'."

"I'm sorry for your loss, Pan. Casta was a great

person."

Pan grunted. "If I ever get my hands on Apollo..." He brought his hands up and mimicked choking the sun god.

"Take a number," said Psyche. "I'm sure your father wants a piece of Apollo."

They came up to a small cottage. A lump rose in Psyche's throat as she stared at the little touches of Casta that could still be seen. Her brightly colored curtains swayed in the light breeze and sunny yellow flowers blossomed in the garden. A little white stone path wound around the cottage and Psyche knew there was a small table in the back where Casta and Pan used to sit and drink tea in the mornings. Nestled among the flowers was a small tombstone. Casta wasn't buried there. As with all the dead, her body had been expelled into space.

Psyche knelt by the tombstone. "You will be missed Casta. I don't think I ever properly thanked you for pulling me through one of the toughest times of my life. I could have fallen into such despair, but you never let me. Your smile and energetic nature were a blessing." She placed a small mechanical flower on the grave. With a touch, it opened to reveal a blossom the same bright green as Casta's eyes.

"I thought of asking Kore to make something special for the grave or the gardens," said Pan, "but I don't think she'll have the time."

"With all these deaths, I'm sure others have sent her requests. I'm not sure how much Demeter is allowing to be passed on to Kore, but I know her. She'd make time for you."

"I'm sure she would. She's a good kid. What I meant was, with her visiting Hades, she's probably too busy to make anything. All her requests have been placed on Flora, Hegemon, and Chloris." Pan grinned suggestively. "Well, she's probably too busy to make anything but babies."

"She's not with Hades. She's staying with mortal family in Elusiues."

"You're a few days behind the times. She's been in the Underworld for about three days now. Dad escorted there himself."

Psyche stood up. "Does Demeter know?"

Pan shrugged. "Not yet. She's at some grain ceremony in Athens. She won't be back for another three days."

"I need to go," Psyche said. "The family Kore was staying with are very important to me. Do you have any idea what Demeter would do to them if she thought they handed Kore over to Hades? She only holds back with the gods because of our laws. I knew this day would come, but I thought I'd be more informed."

Psyche hugged her friend and ran back to the PortMat. She allowed herself to be subjected to the purification process before teleporting down to Level 19. She had to make it to Theron's home before word spread to Demeter. And she would have a long talk with Hades about leaving the mortals to fend for themselves against the gods.

What was Hades thinking? Yes, she understood that Kore needed to go to the Underworld, but she hoped she'd have more time to prepare herself for Demeter's wrath.

Theron was surprised when he opened his door to

see Psyche standing there, out of breath and looking as frantic as she had so long ago when she came to plead with Errita to save Philomena. He thought, with Kore gone, he would have no more divine visitors.

"Did Kore leave any note when she left?" Psyche asked as she sank down on a couch.

"Not really. She said she was going to hide in the Underworld. Hades came to pick her up." Theron shrugged. "He really doesn't look the way I pictured the God of the Underworld."

"She's not in the Underworld," Psyche said. "She's staying with me."

"You ran all the way from Olympus to tell me that?"

"I'm serious, Theron. Kore is not in Underworld. She's with me."

Theron told one of his sons to get Psyche a drink. "What's going on?"

"If Demeter or any of her devotees show up asking for Kore, you need to stress she's with me. You do not mention Hades at all. In fact, you've never met him. You never talked to him. Pretend you've never heard of him. Understand?"

"You're starting to scare me, Io...Psyche."

Psyche accepted the glass of water from Telchine. "Chruse," she said, looking to where Theron's wife stood silently in a doorway, "take the boys outside. I need to talk to Theron alone."

Telchine and Virbius complained as Chruse shooed them out of the room. Psyche waited until she was alone before saying, "You are aware that this level is the pride of

Demeter. The only place she spends more time than here is her own home. That is because Eleusis is where she greets her daughter every spring."

"I'm very familiar with the stories."

"So you know who Demeter hates beyond all reason?"

"I'm going to guess Hades, seeing as he kidnapped Persephone." Theron snorted with disgust. The realization dawned in his eyes. "Oh, great! Don't tell me I just helped a god kidnap another daughter of the patron goddess of my home?"

"No. Well, not really. Kore went willingly. She had to go to the Underworld, Theron. It's her destiny. Demeter just isn't going to like it. When Demeter shows up...I mean if she shows up, send her my way. It's the only way to protect your family."

At Theron's angered glare, Psyche added, "I was actually hoping to be here when Kore left. Hades was supposed to tell me when he planned to bring her down to the Underworld. I am doing my best to shield your family from Demeter's wrath. If she thinks I'm the one who let Hades take Kore...Well, I can handle her anger."

"And my family? What if she decides to get her revenge on us?"

Psyche handed him a card. "Go to any temple of Aphrodite and have the priestess contact me. This holds my mark, so they know that you are in my graces. I will do everything my power to reverse any damages Demeter may bring. If you must, have Chruse plead with her on the grounds of motherhood. Demeter has a soft spot for mothers."

Theron agreed. By the time Psyche left, she felt as if she had done all she could to protect them. All she had to do was wait for Demeter. If luck was on her side, Demeter wouldn't come knocking until Hades had a chance to woo Kore and give her the last piece of her godhead.

Chapter Seventeen

The Underworld was both everything Kore expected and nothing like what she imagined. It was gloomy and dark, but not frightening. Nothing could be frightening with Hades at her side. He cheerfully showed her the huge mechanical Cerebos that guarded the entrance to his domain and the typical arrival point for anyone coming to the Underworld.

"I thought there was a river," said Kore, looking down at the metal floor.

"The river only appears when a mortal enters my realm and is scanned," Hades said. He pointed to several nubs in the wall. "When the heroes enter my realm, they are scanned by this holographic device and their version of the Underworld loads. For example, when Psyche came through, she was confronted by the specters of her sisters and tempted to give away her fare. Aeneas encounters a large host of monsters and shades meant to frighten him, more so than any other hero. Orpheus encounters very little since his test is in his leaving. He might run into the shade of a dead beloved friend or family member, but no one hassles him."

Kore smiled. "I thought you never let anyone leave."

"There have been exceptions." He mentally ran down the list of heroes who entered his realm. "Come to think of it, nearly all the heroes who come down here end up leaving. I think only Pirithous stayed."

"Pirithous?"

Hades nodded. "He came down here with Theseus the hero. Both men had an idea to abduct and marry beautiful daughters of Zeus. Pirithous wanted Persephone. I could have just killed them when they entered my realm. It was my right since they were there to steal my wife, but Persephone had other ideas. She had me invite them to a meal and we fused them to their seats until Hercules arrived. He freed Theseus, but Pirithous had to stay."

"When was this?"

"Oh, a few hundred years, I think. After Hercules came, I sent Pirithous to Tartarus to work for the rest of his mortal life."

Kore bit the inside of her cheek. "And Persephone?"

"Maybe I'll show you her grave while you're here?" He held out his hand. "Come, there is much more to see."

He took her to where the souls were judged. The judges, Minos, Rhadamanthus, and Aeacus, greeted her and joined them on the tour of the various sections of the Underworld. Most of it was holographic. The only part that was real was Tartarus.

"We have to utilize as much space as we can," said Minos. "People expect to see all the places, like Tartarus, the Fields of Asphodel, Elysium, and the Isle of the Blessed. Truth is, there is really no one here. We've already combined the Fields of Asphodel and Elysium, and we might get rid of the Isle of the Blessed."

"Getting rid of those areas will help free up some space for living quarters and shops," said Aeacus. "We may not be keeping souls in various fields, but we do have people who need homes and a way to make a living."

"Everyone thinks of the Underworld as just one

level, but we have two levels," Hades said proudly. "We are the smallest levels of the whole station, and right below my second level is the main engine. We keep all the schools and shops on the second level for the mortals, but we are running low on space for all my divine subjects who want to keep their families up here."

"I didn't know you had shops or mortals in the Underworld," said Kore.

"I don't mention it to anyone unless I know them really well or they'll be staying for a long period of time. None of the heroes ever saw it and I didn't tell Psyche until her fifth visit."

"Who operates the shops?"

"The mortals who live down here. Sometimes a person comes across a PortMat or angers one of the gods, and they are sent here. They haven't done anything really horrible and don't deserve Tartarus, so we keep them and give them a new life here. Through time, they naturally mingle among the other mortals, find one that they love, and start a family. Thus, we have to have the same things that the world above contains."

On the way to Hades' home, Kore got a good look at Tartarus. Various kings who angered the gods and the Danaides, the forty-nine daughters of Danaus, toiled in their torment. Many of them stopped working as Hades passed and called out for mercy. They all looked so pitiful.

"Must they always stay here?" asked Kore, her eyes falling on King Sisyphus of Corinth. His only crime was betraying Zeus to a river god while the King of the Gods hid with the river god's daughter. His punishment was to roll a boulder up a hill, but never getting to the top. Just feet from his goal, the boulder always slipped from his grasp and rolled downhill.

"Yes, they must," said Hades. "Their crimes are many and this is their punishment. What mortals know and what the gods know are worlds apart." He pointed to Sisyphus, who glared angrily by his boulder. "The only crime of his that mortal know was of his tattling on Zeus in return for the river god to cause a spring to appear in Corinth. But, that was only the last straw. His was a long line of sins, each more gruesome than the last."

"What do you mean?"

"Sisyphus plotted to kill his brother. The two were at war for most of their life thanks to their parents. They wanted only the strongest son to take over the throne, but that kind of life created consequences. Sisyphus consulted the Oracle on how to kill his brother without being punished by the gods. I still can't believe Apollo gave him the answer. Sisyphus went to his brother's home and seduced his niece. He tried to persuade her to kill her father and give him the throne. He promised her so many things and never told her that the one who killed his brother would be tortured for all eternity.

"It nearly worked, but he overstepped his bounds. Before his brainwashed bride - yes, he married his niece - could kill her father, Sisyphus gained a reputation for being a bloodthirsty man. He killed anyone who came too close to the palace. He took delight in these killings, experimenting with new ways to kill a person. He poisoned, stabbed, beheaded, burned, and tore his victims apart."

"How awful," Kore gasped.

"That's not the end of it. His niece bore him two children, but they never got to celebrate their first birthday. He killed them, not wanting anyone to challenge him for the throne. It drove his wife mad. The day he betrayed Zeus to the river god, he was out looking for more victims. He had killed a couple, leaving their son for dead. Zeus sent him here due to his betrayal, but it was his dark soul that keeps him here in Tartarus."

Kore shuddered. "Are all their tales as bloody?"

"Many are, yes."

Hades led her to his home just beyond Tartarus. Through large onyx gates lay a garden that must have once been grand. It broke Kore's heart to see the plants withering and drooping. She bent to examine them, and noted with surprise that they were all mechanical. They should not have withered.

Beyond the garden lay the doors of the great home. Towering doors carved from dark wood greeted her. Kore looked closely and noted that there little scenes of the tortures of Tartarus in the wood. The door knob was gold and gem encrusted, and appeared far too gaudy for Hades. When Kore looked back at Hades, he shrugged.

"It came with the Underworld."

The inside was tastefully done in dark tones. Moments after they entered, the puppy Cerebos came bounding up. Hades gave a happy cry and bent to scoop the puppy up, but Cerebos ran past him and jumped on Kore's legs. She laughed and picked him up, rewarded with triple puppy kisses.

"I see how it's going to be," Hades said. He gave the puppy a mock glare. "The second she comes to visit, you forget about me." He petted the dog.

"I missed him, too," Kore said. "I'm glad he's doing well. Look at how big you've gotten!" That last was to Cerebos as Kore held him high and smiled.

Hades only smiled. There was something sad in his face, and Kore almost asked him what was wrong. It was as if he weren't really seeing her.

The first thing Hades had Kore do once they reached the home was to call Zeus and let him know where Kore was staying. Kore worried that Zeus would not approve. She knew next to nothing about her father. What if he had the same mood swings as her mother? However, Zeus was ecstatic with this development.

"This will be good for you, my daughter. How long do you plan on staying with Hades?"

"Maybe two weeks or so," said Kore. "This whole mess with Bion should blow over by then."

"Will that be enough time?" asked Zeus. His eyes locked with Hades', who nodded.

"We plan on telling Demeter. In fact, she's next on our list."

"Is that wise? She'll demand you send Kore home."

"Wise or not, it's the right thing to do. I will not have Demeter accuse me of kidnapping Kore. Call it a strategy. If I keep her in the loop, she can't say I went behind her back. And I plan to let Kore talk to Demeter any time she wishes or when Demeter calls."

"It won't help," Zeus predicted. "Demeter flies off the handle the moment you look at Kore."

Hades shrugged. "I've done everything legally. Kore

is here of her own free will and can leave at any given time. I'm informing you and Demeter. I have your blessing, if we should decide to marry down here."

Zeus nodded. "It would serve Demeter well to remember that I am her king, as well as Kore's father. I know you, Hades. You will treat my daughter right and make Kore happy."

"Demeter does have her own problems." Hades smiled shyly at Kore. "We'll work around them."

After they hung up on Zeus, Kore called Demeter. Her mother did not pick up the call, so she left a message. Kore explained that she was in the Underworld of her own free will and would return to the surface in a week or two, once it was safe. Hades, for his part, let Demeter now he was giving Kore the only key to his personal PortMat room.

"There are only two PortMats to my realm," Hades said. "The key is to my personal PortMat, and only Kore can get in there. If Kore feels threatened or scared in any way, she can lock herself in the PortMat room and return to you. If she wishes to leave early for any reason, she may do so. I know, Demeter, that nothing I say can alleviate your fears, but I hope you understand I'm doing my best. I would never harm Kore. She holds all the power right now."

After the call, Hades showed Kore to her rooms. She asked if this room was once Persephone's and Hades said no. It was a wonderful room, with pale green walls and dark wooden floors. A plush, dark green rug covered most of the floor. The bed was of moderate size with overstuffed pillows and soft cotton sheets. Through a door in the back,

Kore found a room filled with photographs. Each photograph had a man and a woman. In the middle of the room was a small table with a crystal bowl. Kore looked in the bowl to see a single red seed.

"What's this?" she asked.

"A way for you to understand. I can't answer all your questions, but these will help." He smiled. "Though, to warn you, if you don't want to hear the answer, don't take the seed. Once taken, there is no going back."

"What kinds of questions will this answer?"

"Whatever you ask of it."

Kore looked down at the single red seed. That seemed like a lot to ask of something so small. She left the seed and followed Hades out of the room. While she got settled, several of the other inhabitants of the Underworld stopped by to see how she was doing. They all expressed happiness at her visit. Hecate even offered to be Kore's lady's maid while she stayed, but Kore was used to doing things for herself.

"I could use a friend more than I need a lady's maid," she said.

Hades still had to work, so Hecate took over as Kore's guide during that time. The Goddess of Magic and Crossroads often had the most interesting perspective on the dealings of the Underworld. She was the one who told Kore that the gardens in the front once belonged to Persephone.

"Why is it withering? Those are mechanical flowers. They should never die."

Hecate smiled. "That is how things work down here.

They are waiting for the touch of their next owner."

"Why doesn't Persephone take care of her garden? In fact, who is Persephone? I've heard she was Hades' wife, but no one will talk about her. If Hades was married, my mother would have said something about that. Instead, it's as if Persephone is some dark secret."

"Persephone passed away a few years ago. She is buried in the back, in the pomegranate grove." Hecate knelt and touched one of the dead flowers. "She was married to Hades, and he loved her very much. I remember the day of her passing. I thought we'd lose him, as well. He threw himself in his work and withdrew from us." She looked up at Kore. "It was a blessing the day he met you. He came back to the Underworld, talking about you. He was alive again."

"But, he still loves Persephone." Kore swallowed, feeling a sense of hopelessness. If his love for Persephone was so great, how could she compare?

"He will always love Persephone. He also loves you." Hecate stood. "I don't know what it was like in your house, Kore, but it is possible to love more than one person. Just because Hades was married once doesn't mean he won't ever love again. He loves you just as much as he loved Persephone."

Three days after Kore arrived, Psyche called. She was upset that Kore left Theron's home without anyone informing her.

"If anyone asks, you were visiting me when you decided to go with Hades," Psyche said. "Theron has nothing to do with this."

"Agreed. I am sorry, Psyche. I wasn't thinking about

Demeter exacting revenge on the mortals," Hades said, putting his arm around Kore. "Okay, if anyone asks, I stole you from under Psyche's nose."

"If Mother would hurt Theron, won't she hurt you too?" Kore wrung her hands with worry.

"There is little she can actually do to me. There are rules in place that prevent the gods from hurting each other badly. Besides, I'm pregnant. Demeter may be a lot of things, but she would never hurt a baby or an expecting mother. I can handle her."

"You know Mother carries a grudge for a long time. She may not get her revenge now, but wait until she can hurt you."

Psyche snorted. "She's not the only one who can carry a grudge. Trust me, I can handle her. I want her anger focused on me. I've seen what she can do to mortals, and I wouldn't wish that fate on anyone else."

"You mean Mother has harmed people before?"

"Yes." Psyche's eyes slid to meet Hades' for a brief moment. "If you can, go to the welcoming area and seek out a shade named Odessa. She'll be able to tell you more."

"What did Mother do?"

"I think that is for Odessa to say," said Hades. "Thank you for the call, Psyche, but we have a lot to do today. Kore is going to sit in while some of the prisoners of Tartarus try to appeal their punishment."

For the most part, Kore enjoyed her time in the Underworld. Everyone was so nice to her and she felt that she learned a lot in her first three days. One thing did trouble her: how much sway did Persephone still have on

Hades? She knew Hades went to the pomegranate grove to talk to her grave and that she was the epic love of his life. She knew Persephone was her sister and that Demeter claimed she was a horrible daughter who broke her heart. All anyone would tell her was that she had been Hades' wife and that she was now gone.

"Tell me about Persephone," she demanded, trapping Hades in his office.

"I don't think this is the time or place," Hades said.

"I think it is. I only know bits and pieces about her. Everyone tiptoes around the subject. Why?"

"That is a question I cannot answer at this time. I would say to try the seed, but you must be prepared for the answer." Hades kissed her gently on the cheek and moved her out of his way. "If you don't use the seed, then I will answer everything at the end of your two weeks. Otherwise, it could destroy the whole station."

"That's a bit dramatic."

"That's how things work." He smiled. "I will be done with this report in maybe an hour. Why don't we have a picnic lunch?"

A bit dismayed, Kore went back to her room. She went to the mysterious back room and glared at the single seed in the crystal bowl. How could a seed hold any answers? She could give it a try. No one else would answer her questions. Plutus, her brother, merely commented how wonderful it was when Persephone visited and Hecate stated that Persephone was a wonderful queen who relied on her intellect. Could she really wait until her two weeks were up to find out any information when there was a way to answer her questions sitting right in front of her?

Kore picked up the seed and ate it. For a brief moment, all she could taste was the sweet-tart juice that burst in her mouth. Then, the world faded away.

The pictures on the wall came to life. Images of the men and women swirled around her; the love the couples felt could clearly be seen. Though every couple was different, Kore had the feeling they were all the same people. It was the aura around them.

With a gasp, Kore realized that the men were Hades, his various hosts. Was the woman in each picture Persephone? Why show her this? What about Kore? Where did she fit in with all of this?

Finally, the last couple stood before Kore. The man had the same youthful grin as her Hades, though his hair was black and he had a short beard. The woman on his arm had long dark brown hair, pulled back in a braid with stalks of wheat sticking out. Her gown was very much like the ones Demeter always wanted Kore to wear.

The woman smiled. "What is your question?"

"Who is Persephone?"

"I am Persephone. Well, I was. Persephone has been reborn and we all wait the day she claims her title."

"Where does that leave me?"

"That is two questions," the woman said, "but I will allow it. You are going to wake Persephone up."

With that, the couple vanished and Kore found herself back in the room. The pictures hung on the wall, but now they changed. Instead of smiling couples, it now showed the women of each picture with a staticy-looking girl. In the bowl was another seed.

"Well, that didn't help me at all," Kore muttered. Though, if it was her destiny to awaken Persephone, where did that leave her with Hades? Would she have to give him up? What if she didn't awaken Persephone?

Chapter Eighteen

Demeter loved the Harvest Festivals. There was nothing better than the celebration of life-giving food, blessed by her. She couldn't wait to officially show it all to Kore. She had thought it would be this year after her Naming Ceremony, but then all these problems with Bion and Hades started, and Demeter knew that would make a disastrous festival. Next year, Demeter vowed.

The Harvest Festival lasted nearly two weeks, and Demeter grew anxious to see her daughter again. She loathed leaving Kore with that mortal. What did a mortal know about keeping a goddess safe? She also didn't trust Psyche. How did she know these mortals anyway? The more Demeter thought about it, the more she felt anxious. Until Kore made the vow to be a Virgin Goddess or picked anyone but Hades to be her husband, Demeter knew she could not rest. Maybe it would be best to just bring Kore home?

Demeter made her way to Eleusis and to the home of the mortal family. How Psyche knew this family, Demeter wondered. She never left Eros' side and the man's name didn't come up in any of Demeter's searches. Had Kore told her? No matter. If Demeter really wanted to know, she could go ask Apollo.

When the man, Theron, answered the door, he appeared very nervous. Demeter would have thought he was awe-struck, but he never stumbled over his words with her before.

"Kore isn't here." It took him five tries to get the

words out.

Demeter narrowed her eyes. "What do you mean, she's not here?"

"She, um, she..." Theron looked back into the house and motioned for his wife to join them. The wife, a rather dumpy blonde, thought Demeter, carried her youngest child on her hip.

"Lady Demeter, welcome to our humble home," the wife said. "We are so honored by your visit."

"Where is my daughter?" Demeter demanded.

"She, um, she's not here," the wife said.

"So I've heard! Where is she?"

The pathetic fake smile slid right off the wife's face. "Kore is with Psyche," she said. "She said she wanted to go visit Psyche and left a few days ago."

Demeter frowned for a moment before smiling. "Well, I guess that explains it. I suppose I can't fault her for wanting to be around her own kind. I can see why you were so scared. Oh, poor mortals. You must have thought I'd want you to restrain my daughter. It's of no matter. She belongs among the gods. After all, what do you do that we can't do better?"

Demeter turned and left. Though she was glad that Kore was safe in Olympus, she thought it was odd that Kore wouldn't tell her when she was leaving. No, wait, it wasn't so odd. Ever since she made friends with that horrible Psyche and Hedone, Kore had been acting out. This was just the sort of defiance Demeter would have expected from any of the other brats of the gods, but not her sweet Kore! As soon as she got Kore back to the safety of her home - not that apartment set up by Zeus. No! Her real home - Demeter planned to unbrainwash her child. No more of this silly rebellious nature, no more sneaking behind Demeter's back, and no more Hades! She would not lose this Kore!

Psyche sighed and rolled her shoulders as Demeter stormed into her garden. Putting her trowel away, she stood to face the fuming Goddess of the Grain.

"Where is my daughter?" Demeter demanded.

"Which daughter?" asked Psyche dryly.

"Don't you play games with me, Psyche! You know which daughter: Kore!"

Psyche looked around her garden. "She's not here." She went back to weeding her flowers.

Demeter grabbed Psyche by her hair and pulled her up. "Where is she? That human said she was visiting you. Where are you hiding my daughter? Tell me, or I'll go get Zeus!"

Psyche jabbed Demeter with her trowel, causing the goddess to let go of her hair. "She's with Hades."

Demeter blinked as the words sank in. "I must have misheard you," she said slowly. "Did you just say she was in Hades?"

"Or he's in her." Psyche shrugged.

There was just one more minute of peace as Demeter fully took in Psyche's words before she started to wail. "You traitor! You handed my beautiful daughter over to Hades! Oh, fie, you snake, you black-hearted villain! My heart! You have stabbed me deep with your treachery!

You demon of the deepest pits! How could you betray me so? Doesn't loyalty among the gods mean anything to you?"

Psyche rolled her eyes and went back to gardening. "She went of her own free will, Demeter. Haven't you checked your messages?"

"Viper! Oh, deceitful daughter of a coward. You baby-stealing fiend of Hades! You, who claim to be a mother, gave my darling, innocent daughter right into the hands of my enemy! Why, Psyche, why? What have I ever done to deserve such betrayal and hatred? What ill could I have wrought to cause you to stab me thusly in the heart?" Demeter crumpled on the ground and started to sob in a bush. Several Anemerians, tiny blue ant-men, scattered from under the bush and took shelter in a nearby potted azalea.

"Really, Demeter. It's not as bad as you make it out to seem," Psyche said. "She went for a little visit and will return shortly. Just call her. You'll see."

"A little visit? That's how it starts! First, he lures her into his clutches with sugary sweet words and promises of a fantastic Underworld. And once she's down below, he keeps her! Oh! Oh! My poor baby must be so frightened. I can hear her now, weeping into that dark prison Hades has surely tossed her."

Psyche hoisted Demeter up. "Come on. Stop crying in my plants. If you really must, go and talk to Zeus. I know Kore has been contact with him."

Without warning, Demeter raked her nails down Psyche's face. Several angry welts and bloody scratches appeared on her already scarred face.

"I will talk to Zeus, and I will tell him of your treachery. Mark my words, Psyche; I will see to it that you end up in that foul pit right alongside Hades. It's the only pace you belong." Demeter turned with a 'humph' and marched out of the garden.

"Psycho." Psyche gently touched her new wounds and hissed in pain before angrily grabbing her gardening tools and heading into her house.

Chapter Nineteen

Kore shivered. It felt as if someone dumped ice down her back. Looking around, she saw no one. If she didn't know better, it was the same feeling she used to get moments before her mother found out of whatever mischief she'd gotten herself into. But, that was impossible. She knew she was relatively safe down here in the Underworld with Hades. No one would dare trespass in Hades' kingdom.

"Something wrong?" Melonia, Goddess of Ghosts and a computer-generated daughter of Persephone and Hades, sat next to Kore. She and the strange girl were walking in Persephone's garden. Kore decided that, before she left, she'd bring the garden back to life. It would be a nice gesture to show Hades that there was no grudge between her and his past wife.

That, and Kore hoped that by working in the garden, she'd come to know Persephone better. If she was to be the one who would wake Persephone, she might as well learn all she could.

"Nothing's wrong," Kore said. "I'm probably just paranoid. I've never been this long without hearing from my mother. I kind of expect her to pop out of the shadows at any moment and drag me home."

"She sounds terrifying," said Melonia. For a moment, static sputtered through the image and then Melonia became solid-looking again. She was a strange girl with dark hair, large eyes, and gray-ish skin. Her arms and legs started off solid but became transparent down to her hands and feet. Little ghosts followed her everywhere, some begging for attention at her feet.

Kore smiled at the thought of one of the most terrifying goddesses ever being scared of Demeter. "She can be. Mother has always been...zealous in her attempts to keep me safe. She means well, but she has a problem with knowing when to stop."

"My mother always gave me freedom. I am the Goddess of Ghosts, and she allowed me to be myself." Melonia bent to pet a closed rose. "One time, I tried to be just like her, but that wasn't me. She told me, no matter what, I should always be myself. She said, the stars shine brightest with their own light. It took me years to really understand what she meant."

Kore wondered how a computer program could act like anything but the program, but she didn't say anything. Instead, she looked down at the garden. "I think I have everything," she said. "It should really only take me a few days to get this place in order. I'll have the garden blooming in no time."

"That's good. I miss the flowers. I can't wait to see Mother working in her garden again."

"What?" Kore frowned slightly. "I thought everyone told me Persephone passed away. Do you mean when the new Persephone is awakened?"

Melinoe smiled. "You'll see." She flickered out of existence.

Kore shook her head and went to work on the garden. The first thing she needed to do was get the power flowing again. When she found it, she discovered the generator for the garden was an old model, one she never saw before. Sighing, she left to find Hades to ask if he knew how to work it.

After looking around the large mansion, she found Hades in his office with Hecate, Minos, Rhadamanthus, Aeacus, and Plutus. They were all in a meeting with Hephaestus, who glared down larger than life from Viewscreen.

"I just can't do it, Hades," Hephaestus was saying. "We are running low on materials as it is. I had to put a block on all unnecessary repairs for a reason. Have you seen the list of things I need to get done in the next ten years? Not to mention all the work that has to go into making a terraform pod for our first colony down on the planet."

"So," said Hades slowly, "that's a no?"

"That is most definitely a no. You'll just have to find another way to fix your hologram system."

Hades sighed. "What do we have to work with," he asked. "We keep cutting back on my kingdom's spare areas, but I don't think we can cut back anymore."

"What about Melinoe? You don't really need a Goddess of Ghosts. Hecate can do double duty with that," suggested Hephaestus.

"No! She's my daughter!" Hades stood up, glaring at Hephaestus.

"She's a computer program. No one will miss her."

"How about we save up on energy by getting rid of some of the Cupids? We can keep Eros, and maybe Anteros, but the other two? Come on, Hephaestus, no one remembers that Pathos and Himeros exist. How much energy and resources can we save on with two less minor gods to worry about?"

"I would say point taken, but they are flesh and blood, not machine. I don't use them to rebuild the station"

Kore coughed slightly and everyone turned toward her. "I'm sorry to interrupt, but what needs to be repaired?"

"The front hologram system," said Hades. "Come on in, Kore. I should have let you know that we had a meeting with Hephaestus."

"Yes, you should have." Hecate smacked him upside his head.

"Um, well, what hologram systems are really necessary?" Kore took a seat at the edge of the group

"Our welcome system, of course," said Minos. "That's the one that needs to be repaired. We also have the systems that create the Isle of the Blessed and the Elysian Fields. We've already combined the Elysian Fields and the Asphodel Fields since they were rather similar and used the spare hologram system to fix things around here, but we've run out of parts."

Rhadamanthus looked thoughtful. "Although, if we are honest with ourselves, it's rare that anyone sees the Isle of the Blessed. I can't remember the last time a hero even looked back there. We can dismantle that machine for parts."

"We can also shorten the Elysian Fields," said Aeacus. "It's just basically a backdrop."

"There," said Hephaestus, "that wasn't so hard."

Minos nodded. "I'm sure we would have come to this conclusion soon enough. We always figure it out."

"How soon," asked Hephaestus. "We've been arguing over whether or not you have the materials lying around for nearly an hour now, not to mention the previous discussions that went nowhere. And all it took was one small question from Kore to get you to think this through."

"I really didn't do anything," Kore protested.

"You did ask the question that helped us think," said Minos. "We've been running in circles because we didn't think of what we actually needed."

"Really, I didn't do anything important."

Hephaestus rolled his shoulders. "Moving on. How are you, Kore? Are they treating you right?"

"Yes. Everyone has been so nice to me."

"That's good. Cherish the peace. It won't last long."

Hades groaned. "Oh, no. You mean..."

"Yes. Demeter has discovered that Kore's here. She already yelled at Psyche in her garden and is now on her way up to Zeus as we speak."

"Oh, no! Psyche didn't get into too much trouble, did she?" asked Kore. "Mother wasn't too hard on her, was she?"

"No. It was just an epic hissy fit by Demeter with some empty threats. To be honest, for Demeter, it was pretty tame," said Hephaestus. "I think she's just tired from the festival. When she's had a chance to rest and recover, she'll be her normal, terrorizing self again."

"I should call Mother and soothe things over. I don't know why she waited this long to get upset, though. I did call her and left a message when I first arrived."

Hades cleared his throat. "Knowing Demeter, she probably ignored it since the sender would appear to be me. So, she's just now hearing about you being down here." He looked thoughtful. "However, it really shouldn't be that big of a surprise. This is the only place you'd be safe from Bion."

"Demeter should be in Zeus' waiting room right now," said Hephaestus. "Try calling there."

Kore rushed out of the office to make the call from her room. When she connected to Zeus' waiting room, it was not her mother who answered. Minthe stood in front of the screen, looking frazzled. Her green-dyed hair was as snarled as a bird's nest, there were bags under her eyes, and her chiton was stained.

"Kore! Where have you been? You mother is beside herself with worry. Do you have any idea what you've done? She returns from the festival believing you to be safe with some mortal and finds out you ran away to Hades! You've escaped, right? That's why you're calling here. Someone must have told you how terribly upset Lady Demeter is, and you knew you had to call and beg forgiveness. Now that you're out of the Underworld, we can start planning your wedding to Bion."

"I'm still visiting Hades," said Kore. "I sent Mother a message that I'm going to be here for two weeks. She should stop pestering Father and just relax. I'll be home when my visit is up."

"Your mother received no such message."

"Hades informed me that since I sent it from his Viewscreen, it would have his name attached to it."

Minthe scoffed. "Well, that explains it, then. There

is no reason for Lady Demeter to look at any message that comes from the Underworld."

"Tell Mother to review her messages. Of course any message from me would come from the Underworld while I'm here. For the next two weeks, she needs to stop ignoring them."

"Don't worry, Kore. You won't be in the Underworld for two weeks. Your mother will save you. In fact, she's in with Zeus right now to demand your return. We'll have you up in the sunlight before you know it. Where you belong. With your mother."

"I'm staying. Tell Mother that. I came here of my own violation and I will stay. I've actually got work to do here, and I refuse to leave until my job is done."

Minthe gave a cry. "He's making you work? Oh, you poor delicate flower!"

"He's not making me do anything. I came across a dying garden here, and I wanted to make it better. I'm doing this to thank Hades for allowing me the safety of the Underworld."

Minthe's eyes widened. "Oh, I know what has happened to you. He's brainwashed you into liking him. Curse the seductive powers of that handsome man. He must have swayed you to his side in his nefarious plot to destroy your mother. Oh! Oh, cruel Aphrodite! If any of us should have been whisked to the Underworld in Hades' strong arms, it should have been me. If either of us should have been the one to warm his cold bed at night, I should be that woman. I am the one he really loves! Oh, fie on his plans to bring ruin to Demeter. He is only using you, Kore. It was really me he wanted. Come home and let me take your place."

Kore sighed. "Goodbye Minthe. Just tell Mother I'm fine." She signed off the Viewscreen. Kore hoped that Zeus knew how to calm her mother down and explain the situation to her. The last thing Kore wanted was for her mother to storm into the Underworld, snatch her away, and force her to back into that dreary life she used to live.

She sat on her bed, thinking her options over. Everyone knew she was here. It wasn't a secret. It wouldn't be long before she was back in the upper levels, living under her mother's thumb. Unless Kore took matters into her own hands, she was doomed. She loved Hades and wanted to remain by his side. It already tore her apart knowing she might have to step aside for Persephone.

Could she convince Hades to marry her? Did he have to be with Persephone? Kore was an adult, thus legally able to make adult decisions with her life. She knew that, as the wife of Hades, Demeter would not be able to drag her back topside.

But, there was Persephone to consider. How did she fall into the grand scheme of things?

Kore got up and headed to the seed room. She needed some answers before she planned her next step.

"There is nothing I can do, Demeter," Zeus said. He felt like he'd been repeating himself for the past hour. Demeter stood before him, beautiful in her fury, but inconsolable. "Hades asked my permission to have Kore stay in the Underworld for a few days. Kore went with him of her own free will. I cannot just order Hades to send her up when she's not a prisoner. She's doing fine, Demeter.

I've spoken to her and she's not been harmed in any way."

"What if he tries to marry her? Zeus! He's got her down there and is probably using all his skills to convince Kore that she wants to stay. She belongs up here with me!"

"If Hades marries Kore, it would be Kore's decision," Zeus said. "Though, I wouldn't be surprised if he proposed while she's down there. They are so very besotted with each other."

"I can't allow that to happen! He stole my daughter! You're the King of the Gods; you can order him to return Kore this instant!"

Zeus sighed, rubbing his temples. "If I thought Kore was in danger, I'd order her back up, but she's perfectly safe."

"She's not safe! The Underworld is filled with peril! There are monsters and all sorts of unsavory people all over that place! And don't forget that you had the Titans locked down there! What if one of them got ahold of Kore? Or, what about the tortures of Tartarus? Not only is that unfitting for my baby to see, but what if one of those humans holds a grudge against the gods and tries to use her as leverage? Or kills her? She's not a full goddess, Zeus, no matter how much you and Psyche try to pretend she is. She can still die!"

"She's fine, Demeter. As your king, I am ordering you to stand down. As your brother, I am asking you to allow Kore her two weeks with Hades. You know, the more you push, the more you'll only lose her. Haven't you learned your lesson from all the others?"

For a full minute, Demeter stood there, her mouth opening and closing as she tried to find the right words to convince Zeus to come to his senses and bring Kore home. When none came, she gave a strangled cry and stormed out of the office. Minthe, seeing her mistress so distressed, ran to keep up with her.

"My lady, what did he say?" asked Minthe as they headed to the PortMat room.

"He refuses to save Kore! For years, he ignored her, leaving me to raise our daughter alone. And now, when she needs him the most, he refuses to help! Why must all men be so difficult?"

"What can we do?"

Demeter was silent for a moment and then a grin formed on her face. Her delight sent a warning shiver down Minthe's spine. "We will do the only thing we can do," she said. They reached the PortMat room and Demeter quickly shooed the technicians out of the way. "You, Minthe, will travel to the Underworld and make sure that Kore does not fall into the clutches of Hades. I will continue to forge my battle here and force Zeus to do the right thing."

"Mistress," cried Minthe, "I do not wish to go to the Underworld! It is an evil place and far too dangerous. Why can't we send Ares or one of his sons?"

Demeter snorted. "Ares? A man? No, he has no control and will probably hurt Kore. As for his sons, I don't trust that Phobos as far as I can spit. No, you're best suited for this task. After all, I'm sure you'd rather Hades fall in love with you than with Kore. Why take the chance he'll forget your charms?"

That seemed to do it. Minthe stood up straight, her eyes flashing. "You're right," she said. "Hades is mine and will always be mine. I will see to it that Kore doesn't forget that. By the time I'm through, she'll be ready to marry Bion and be your dutiful daughter once more."

Demeter entered the coordinates in the PortMat and smiled as the bright light flared to life. It caused shadows to dance over her face, giving her a very eerie appearance. "Hurry now. We have just less than two weeks. Do not come back until Hades has married you."

Minthe left and Demeter sighed as the PortMat beam faded. She would hate to lose her most trusted servant, but once Minthe successfully ensnared Hades, Demeter could no longer allow Minthe to work for her. Oh, well. She could always find another Minthe.

Chapter Twenty

Kore stared down at the new seed in the bowl. Two seeds down, and what has she learned? Not a whole lot, really. The second seed she hoped would answer her question on whether or not Hades had to marry Persephone. She was bombarded by images of a loving marriage and the voices of the previous Persephone's telling her to go for it. Was that message really meant for her? Did she really have Persephone's blessing to marry Hades?

She left the room before she was tempted to pick up the next seed. How many did she have, anyway? Kore didn't want to use up her questions and then really need them.

Walking down the hall of the large mansion, Kore ran into Hecate. As always, the goddess was dressed beautifully and looked too sexy for Kore's comfort. In her arms was a bundle of clothing.

"There you are, Kore. I wanted to thank you for your help today," Hecate said.

"I really didn't do anything."

"You may feel that way, but trust me, those men can be stubborn. Sometimes, it's saying the right sequence of words to get them to think differently. I know Hephaestus kept hinting that we had systems we could go without, but none of them caught on. It was either they figured out the solution on their own, or you phrased it in a way that jogged their minds."

Kore looked down. "I guess if you say so."

"Anyway, I thought you might like some more appropriate clothing. I noticed all you brought with you are the very childish and innocent clothing your mother bought for you. You're an adult. Live it up a little." Hecate shoved the clothing bundle in Kore's arms. "Here, I think these will fit you."

"Oh, I can't wear any of this," Kore said. "I mean, what if Mother comes down here? She'll kill me."

Hecate snorted. "Demeter would never come down here. Trust me on that." She leaned in close to Kore. "Besides, you want to catch Hades' eye, right? I know he adores you, but let's turn up the heat a bit."

Kore gingerly looked through the bundle. "These would look better on you."

"Come on, let's try them on. Just wear one to dinner tonight, and I won't mention it ever again. Believe me; Hades will swallow his tongue when he sees you."

Hecate gently led Kore back to her room, where Kore tried on each of the dresses before picking one. By the time they were done, things had slightly changed in the Underworld.

The Underworld was not what Minthe imagined. The PortMat did not drop her off in front of Hades' home or by the River Styx or anything she might recognize. Instead, she found herself standing in a large open room. She could make out a door on the far end, but it was too far to walk. She called out to see if anyone was present. No one answered her, but red lasers from the wall scanned her.

Instantly, the room changed and Minthe found herself in a huge cavern at the banks of an underground river. Where the door once stood were now craggy rocks and the shadow of the enormous Cerebos loomed to the left. All around her, meandering aimlessly, were shades of people who died without proper burial. Minthe thought she recognized a few, but paid them no mind. What did the affairs of humans - dead or alive - matter to a goddess?

Minthe squinted and noticed a small boat leaving the far side of the shore. It had to be Charon, coming to take the newly dead or those who waited their hundred years over to Hades. At that moment, Minthe realized she had not brought payment for the boat ride. Would it matter? She was Minthe, most beloved of Demeter and official nanny to Kore. Surely they would waive the ritual payment for her.

Charon, Minthe decided, was taking his sweet time to get over to the shore. The boat moved slowly, thought there didn't appear to be anything in its way. Frustrated, Minthe started pacing on the shore. She weaved between several of the shades, keeping to herself.

As she paced the shore, she saw a shade heading her way. At first, Minthe paid it no mind, until the shade was nearly on top of her. With a start, Minthe realized she recognized the shade. She knew that dark-skinned woman with the three scars down her face. The last time she saw that woman, the woman was dying and begging with her last breath to see her child.

"Odessa?"

The woman fixed her glare on Minthe. "You," she snarled. "What are you doing here?"

"My business is none of yours," Minthe said.

"Are you here on her business? Are you here to further the goals of that murderess?"

Minthe frowned. "Don't speak of Lady Demeter like that. She did not murder you."

"Oh, but she did. What kind of goddess locks away her own servant and starves her, ties her to a bed, and keeps her weak so that when she gives birth, she passes away? Demeter killed me as surely as if she had stabbed me. She stole my baby! And all you did was watch. What happened to you, Euryale? We used to be such good friends. Why did you betray me to Demeter?"

"I found my true calling. If you hadn't wanted to betray my Lady Demeter, I never would have been forced to tell her. You and that disgusting Phobos, plotting to leave Demeter...I couldn't let that happen. Not when my lady needed a child. You should have volunteered, Odessa. It would have been so much easier on you. Besides, my name is no longer Euryale. I am Minthe, devoted right hand to Demeter."

Odessa laughed. "You think Minthe is devoted to Demeter? You stupid fool! You're being set up. Demeter doesn't care about you at all."

"What do you know? Being dead must have addled your mind."

"I am dead because of you. Tell me, what happened to my child?"

"Lady Demeter raised her. She used to be as calm and loving as any devoted daughter, but lately she's become more like you; defiant and untrustworthy."

"And her father?"

"We've tried to keep Phobos away from her, but he has had contact this past year. No more. Once I get Kore out of the Underworld, she'll go back to being a good child." Minthe spat at Odessa. "Your influence and his will never taint her. Lady Demeter won't lose this one."

Again, Odessa laughed. "You have much to learn. She is my daughter, and she is her father's daughter. There is no way she'll ever be some meek puppet for Demeter."

Minthe heard the boat reach the shore. She turned and walked quickly to it, not wanting Odessa to see how upset the conversation made her. She could remember their childhood, of how excited they both were to be working for Demeter. But, that all changed when Odessa fell in love with Phobos. Suddenly, working for a goddess wasn't enough. Odessa had to be married to a god.

That was when Demeter came to her. "Help me get Odessa, and I will place you above all my devotees," she said. "You will be like a goddess."

Minthe did her lady's bidding. She watched from the shadows as Odessa wasted away, barely kept alive throughout her pregnancy. It was Minthe, then Euryale, who shut the door in Phobos' face each time he came looking for Odessa. When Odessa breathed her last, Demeter brought Minthe into a small chamber of the grand house and released a beautiful light from a box. The light smelled of mint leaves and Euryale, when touched by the light, became Minthe.

If she had to do it all over again, she wouldn't change a thing.

To Minthe's surprise, Charon was not alone in the

boat. Kore sat next to him, dressed in black. Anger coursed through Minthe. Just what was Kore up to? Was she trying to get Hades' attention by looking the part of the Queen of the Underworld?

"Minthe! What are you doing here?" asked Kore. She reached out her hand to help Minthe in the boat, but Odessa pushed Minthe back.

"Don't touch her! You have no right to touch her," Odessa cried. "You have already tainted her with your vile ways."

Kore shrank back. "Who are you?"

"I was Odessa, devotee to Demeter. That woman betrayed me and brought about my death." Odessa moved toward Kore. "Listen to me. Don't trust her. She will betray you, too."

"Don't listen to her, Kore," Minthe snapped. "She's one of the dead. All they do is lie."

"Do you even know what Kore means," said Odessa softly. "Do you know how each Kore has been procured? Look at me. You know in your heart who I am." She held her hand out to Kore. "I am your real mother."

Kore stared at her. All her life, she searched her mother's face for some kind of semblance and never found it. Here, with this stranger, she could finally see pieces of herself. This woman had the same nose and same hair. Her unsure smile was the same as the one Kore saw in the mirror almost every day.

"If you're my mother," Kore said, "who is my father?"

Odessa opened her mouth to answer and vanished.

The cavern returned to its natural, open room state. The river became a floor, the shades disappeared, and only the living was left. Charon got out of the boat and motioned for Kore to do the same.

"Come on, we need to push this thing back to the other side," he said. "No sense in wasting all that theatrics for some henchwoman of Demeter's."

Minthe sniffed. "I'm not some henchwoman. I am her devoted right hand."

Kore got out of the boat and helped push it to the other side. "Minthe, who was that woman?"

"What woman?"

"The shade. The one who said she was my real mother."

"Don't you worry about her. She was just a computer program," Minthe said. "The landing area of Hades is supposed to test you, see how gullible you are. All they say is lies."

Kore remained silent. She wasn't sure if that was the truth or not. Minthe was not above lying to her if she felt that Kore didn't need to know the information.

The walk back to Hades' home was not as silent as Kore would have wished. Minthe found something to say about everything they encountered. She didn't like being tested at the landing area, she found the distance to be too much, she didn't like seeing the tortures of Tartarus, and she thought everything was just too gloomy.

"When I'm queen, I'll see to it all of this is changed," Minthe declared as they passed between the torments of Tantalus and Sisyphus. "Why in the world would anyone want to see such misery?"

"I'm sure Hades knows what's he's doing," said Kore.

"He doesn't know anything," snapped Sisyphus. Kore turned to see the man leaning against the boulder, taking a break.

"He knows enough to keep criminals locked up," Kore said.

Sisyphus snorted. "Little girl, you are out of your mind. Hades doesn't deal in justice. None of us really did what we are punished for."

"You -" Kore started, but he cut her off.

"Oh, I know what he told you, but maybe you should find the truth out for yourself. Ask Tantalus about his crime. He's got something really interesting you should hear."

Minthe, having heard enough, grabbed Kore and pulled her away. They left with Sisyphus' mocking laughter still ringing in their ears.

"Don't listen to the likes of him," said Minthe. "He's a killer. Everyone knows you can't trust a killer."

When they reached Hades' home, the God of the Underworld reluctantly greeted Minthe. He showed her to a guest chamber, the furthest from his room as he could find. Minthe demanded one closer, as she felt the guest room was too tiny for one as important as she.

"This is the best I can offer you," Hades said. "You did show up unannounced. I will see to placing you somewhere else if you are determined to stay for the rest of Kore's two weeks."

"Maybe Kore should have this room," Minthe said. "After all, it's more fitting for one of her station."

"Then you should love it," said Hades. "If this room is fit for a goddess, then why are you complaining?"

For a few seconds, Minthe looked stunned. "Well, um, that is...Anyway, I will also need clothes. I rushed down here so fast; I didn't take the time to pack."

"You'll find clothes in the wardrobe. You're not the first Minthe to stay in my kingdom."

As Minthe got situated in her room, Kore followed Hades down the hall. "What do you mean; she's not the first Minthe to stay here?"

"Just what I said. There always seems to be a Minthe when there is a Kore. Sometimes, she's your nurse and comes here to protect you. That room is always set aside for her."

"And the other times? When she's not my nurse?"

Hades shrugged. "There are times when Minthe thinks she can get between us. I heard you had a long day. Try to rest up before dinner. I have a feeling we're all going to be feeling a little more stressed after today."

Kore went back to her room. This was all becoming so confusing for her. Every day seemed to bring a new mystery. Who was Odessa? Was she really Kore's mother? If so, what did that mean? Could Kore still be a goddess?

She knew that there were other Kores before her, other Goddesses of Spring. But, the way Hades talked, it was as if she wasn't the first to come down to the Underworld. What happened to the other Kores?

Kore's eyes slid to the seed room. She felt so

tempted to try another seed. It was so much easier to get answers that way than to try and wiggle them out of the people down here in the Underworld. But, what if there was a price to using the seeds too much?

Then again, there was that tip to talk to Tantalus. Could she trust the words of a criminal?

Kore stood there, chewing on her lip as she thought over her options. Finally, she made a decision. She grabbed a shawl for her head and headed out. She'd risk talking to Tantalus.

Kore crept out of the large mansion, avoiding any of the inhabitants. She would have thought that a home that size, it would be easy to stay away from anyone, but everyone seemed to need to talk or walk in a way that meant she'd run into them if she weren't careful. She left by way of a side door and hurried through the dead gardens. For the briefest moment, she paused as she found herself near the path that would take her to the pomegranate grove. Back there was supposed to be the body of Persephone. Someday, Kore knew she'd head down that path, but today was not that day.

She made it to Tantalus just as Sisyphus came sliding back down his hill. She ignored the murderer and knelt next to Tantalus. He was buried with a small pool of water around him, just barely touching his chin, and a small tree planted next to him. One branch hung over him, the fruit just out of his reach. His hands were tied at his sides so he could not reach up.

"Is it true that you have information for me?" she asked.

"True," he croaked. "But I need water."

"Isn't it your punishment to not receive any water?"

"I can't talk without it." His voice came out so raspy that it hurt Kore's throat to hear it.

She dipped her hands in the pool and scooped up a small amount of water. She held her hands to his lips and watched as he drank. "Now, tell me what you know."

"I am going to die soon," said Tantalus. "You coming here signals my end and the start of the next Tantalus."

"What do you mean?"

"Kore goes missing, Demeter gets upset. To take her mind off of things, Zeus picks some unsuspecting king to host a party. That king is overcome by madness and kills his son to serve the gods. That man becomes me and is punished for all time."

"I don't understand."

"More water and I will tell."

Kore quickly gave him more water. Tantalus drank and smiled. "Thank you. You are not the first Kore to come here, nor will you be the last. It is always you who starts the change in the Underworld. Soon, a new queen will be crowned." He tried to get closer to Kore. "Have you eaten any pomegranates?"

"A few seeds, I think."

"Beware the pomegranate. That's how he traps you."

"Why did you kill your son?"

"I didn't want to. When I found out I was being called on to serve the gods, I was ecstatic. Then, a golden light filled my room. I thought it was one of the gods and went to greet it, but it suddenly entered me. I knew the pain of a thousand other Tantalases. I watched myself as I killed my son and served him, as Hades came to my home and dragged me here. I knew my fate as they hooked me up to this contraption. I was kept alive by the power of that golden light, but it recently left. I know what that means. Another Tantalus has been picked because you are here. Demeter is in mourning and will need to be cheered up. She will be distraught and actually eat the flesh of the sacrificed child, sending her into her own spiral of madness."

"Is there anything I can do to stop this?"

"Nothing. If you try to save your mother, you doom the whole ship. We need you to take your rightful place by Hades' side. But, promise me, you will be kinder to the next Tantalus. He didn't mean to kill anyone. This punishment is too cruel for the crime."

Kore dipped her hands in the water for a third time. Before she could give Tantalus a drink, she was pulled back by a person standing behind her. She turned to see Minos. The Judge of the Underworld looked furious as he gripped Kore's hand.

"Just what do you think you're doing?" he demanded. "Do you have any idea what you've done?"

"I was just trying to help," Kore said. "I didn't mean any harm."

Minos pulled her away from Tantalus and dragged her all the way back to Hades' home. He brought her all the way to Hades' office and shoved her down in front of the God of the Underworld. For the first time, Kore was truly frightened of Hades.

"I found her with Tantalus," Minos said. "She was giving him water."

Hades sighed. "I was afraid that would happen. Minos, leave us. I need to talk to Kore in private."

Once Minos left, Hades helped Kore up. "I didn't mean any harm," Kore said. "I...He looked so thirsty and I thought a little bit of water would be okay."

"I know," said Hades. "What did he tell you?"

At first, Kore wanted to deny that she talked to Tantalus. What was said was for her ears only. Hades was the one who kept Tantalus prisoner, punishing him far beyond any reason. But, as she looked at Hades, she realized this was not a secret worth keeping. He already knew Tantalus talked to her. Denying it might ruin what peace they found.

"He told me he was dying soon. There will be a new Tantalus soon, all because I am here."

Hades nodded. "That is true. Don't worry yourself about it. It's just the way things are done here."

"Why? If what he told me is true, he's being unfairly punished. Something entered him and turned him into a killer. Why punish a human for the crimes of a spirit?"

"It's not really the crimes of a spirit. He's one of us. When you come to the Underworld, the Zyspadaden spirit of Tantalus finds his next host. The crime must be committed and then he must be punished."

"But that's not fair. The Zyspadaden makes him do it. If left to his own devices, he'd never kill his child."

"I know it's not fair, but we are not the ones who came up with this," Hades said. "Long before we became the gods, the humans had stories about us. The fate of Tantalus was described in the history of their first earth, and we must abide by it."

"But, what if these roles are outdated? Do we really need a Tantalus? Or Sisyphus? Or any of them?"

For a moment, Hades looked sad. "For now, Kore, please, let it go." He kissed her cheek. "Come on. It's time for dinner."

Chapter Twenty-One

Demeter sighed dramatically, draping herself over Aphrodite's couch. When Aphrodite did it, she looked graceful. Demeter, however, looked awkward. She even laid one pudgy hand over her forehead, glancing back at where Aphrodite sat. The Goddess of Love ignored her guest, trying her hardest to focus on the reports in front of her.

Demeter sighed again. She added more *oomph* to it when she saw that Aphrodite wasn't paying attention.

Aphrodite growled. "You are more annoying than Ares! What do you want, Demeter?"

"My baby is in the Underworld," Demeter sniffed.

"Yes, I know. We all know." Aphrodite went back to looking over her reports. She felt like her numbers were off. She just knew she had more devotees than what was showing up. Artemis had better not be trying to undermine her again.

"I need to get Kore back," Demeter said. "You have to help me, Aphrodite. We're friends. Friends help each other."

Aphrodite turned back to Demeter. The words, 'we are not friends' were on her tongue, but one look at how pathetic Demeter appeared, she wisely chose to not say the words. This was the first time Aphrodite witnessed Demeter in the throes of mourning when Kore went to the Underworld. In the past, Demeter almost always headed immediately into her pilgrimage. The only time Aphrodite would see her would be at the big banquet Zeus always scheduled to cheer up Demeter.

Aphrodite smiled. She knew just what had to be done. "Wait here, Demeter," she said. "I'll go talk to Zeus."

Demeter perked up. "That's good. He'll listen to you. I don't know why, but he never listens to me about Hades."

Aphrodite hurried away to speak with Zeus. When she told him her plan, he quickly agreed. The only problem came when trying to convince Demeter to go along.

"No! I need Kore back, not dinner!" Demeter jumped off the couch and glared at Aphrodite and Zeus. "What in the world will a dinner do to ease my anguish? My little girl is being held captive by the vilest Hades, and none of you will listen to me. I want her back! That's all I want!"

"What you need to do is to allow this to take its course. Kore will be back in just over a week," Zeus said.

"How do you know that? Hades can very well keep her! He won't give her back! He's never given her back!"

"That's because Kore chooses to stay and become the goddess she was meant to be," said Aphrodite. "Stop fighting this, Demeter and come with us. Zeus has a mortal friend - a king - who will help you forget your troubles for a few hours."

"I don't want to go! I want Kore back!"

Zeus sighed and rubbed his temples. "Okay, how about this? If you come with us, I will think about asking Hades to release Kore early."

Demeter thought it over. "Alright. If this is the only

way I can get you to do the right thing."

Zeus took Demeter down to the kingdom of Nemea. There, King Nikos greeted the gods as old friends. It wasn't only Demeter, Aphrodite, and Zeus who showed up. Almost all the Olympian gods came to the dinner despite the short notice. Demeter frowned, feeling as if she had been set up.

"I had this meal specially prepared for you," Nikos said as his guests were seated. "I never dreamed that the gods would pick my humble home to visit. Please, enjoy yourselves."

The servants first brought out plates of fruit, honey, and nuts. Goblets of wine were poured and musicians played only the most popular songs. The gods seemed to enjoy themselves. Apollo, on a break from serving his punishment for the plague, got up to teach the musicians a new song while Hera gave advise about men and marriage to Nikos' five daughters.

As the main dish, a lion stew, was served, Zeus looked around the room. "Nikos, I notice your daughters in attendance, but I do not see your son and heir. I am surprised that he has not joined us by now."

"My son is closer than you think, oh Great Zeus. I assure you, he would not miss this."

The hot bowls were set before the gods. Zeus picked up his spoon when he noticed a flash of golden light around Nikos. As one, all the gods but Demeter dropped their spoons. Demeter, still mumbling to herself about wanting Kore back, took a bite of her stew.

"Demeter! Don't eat that!" cried Apollo. "That's not lion!"

Demeter looked up grumpily. "What are you yammering about?"

"That is not lion meat," said Zeus. "Nikos! Explain yourself! How dare you serve this blasphemy to us?"

The mortals around the table all looked confused. They, too, set down their utensils. Many of them had already taken a bite of the food and noticed nothing amiss, but they were not gods.

Nikos stood. "I had to know if you were the real deal. There have been rumors of fake gods walking around the Station, and I had to know if you were the real Zeus," Nikos said. "I knew if you were real, you'd see through my ruse. I am deeply honored to have the real Zeus in my household."

"You murdered your son to test me?" At his announcement, the people around the tables gasped. One of Nikos' daughters fainted. His wife turned pale and looked as if she might drop at any second.

"I had to," Nikos said. "I was ordered to. You sent me a golden light to tell me of your coming and how to test you." Nikos looked confused. "I did what you told me to do."

"I sent no such light and I never would have told you to kill your son."

Zeus had them gather all the bowls of soup and as he spread his hands over them, a golden light came up from the bowls. The light mingled in the air and slowly formed a young man. They could see the bones forming first, and Demeter gasped as she saw that the shoulder was missing. That was the part she ate.

Zeus created a solid gold shoulder bone for the

young man. Once he was created and the glow faded, Nikos could see that his son had been brought back from the dead. The queen hugged her child and ushered him as far from his father as she could.

"You have killed your own kin," said Zeus. "For this crime, I sentence you to the tortures of Tartarus."

"But I did what you asked of me," Nikos protested. "I swear, the idea came from your messenger!"

"Speak no more! Human, you have committed a sin so grave it sickens me. You are stripped of your name and rank. From this day forward, you shall be known as Tantalus, the kin-slayer."

Hermes set a portable PortMat on the floor and signaled for Hades. In a few moments, the PortMat flared to life and the God of the Underworld stood before them. For once, Demeter did not fly into a rage upon seeing him. She stood in the background, almost as if she didn't realize what was going on.

"Hades, take this criminal away," Zeus ordered. "I want him far from my sight. I have read his crimes and sentenced him. Take Tantalus and punish him as he deserves."

"As you wish, my brother." Hades grabbed the newly-named Tantalus by the arm and dragged him over to the PortMat. The poor man protested the entire time. After he vanished, his wife finally broke down in tears and mourned the husband she thought she knew.

"Do not cry, Mother," said her son. "Father may have betrayed us, but we mustn't let his actions overshadow us. I will be the king my father couldn't be."

In the human confusion, the gods took their leave.

Most of them went back home, leaving Zeus and Demeter to talk.

"You never talked to Hades," Demeter accused.

"There was so much going on," Zeus said. "I'll do it in the morning when we aren't busy."

Demeter pouted. "You're not going to talk to him at all, are you? What did he promise you for you to allow him to keep Kore? I want my daughter back, Zeus! You will return her to me, or else!"

"My sister, don't threaten me. I would do anything for you, but we both know this is how it is meant to be. Kore will be Hades' bride and rule the Underworld. That is her destiny. Why fight it?"

"I fight it because we both know it is wrong. Kore isn't meant for the dark of the Underworld. She is meant for the sun. The longer you allow her to remain with Hades, the more he hurts her. My daughter is never the same after she stays in the Underworld. Why do you keep allowing her to be changed?"

"We need Persephone," Zeus said. "Who knows what would happen if Kore doesn't follow her destiny? It might mess up our season. What if allowing one path to falter is how our brothers and sisters fell? This is how we've existed for countless centuries, and how we'll continue to survive."

"We'll see about that," Demeter spat. "Our seasons are made through a computer. We are not the gods of the first earth, Zeus. We don't need to follow a script to keep the balance. I can keep Kore and nothing bad will happen."

"Don't mess with this, Demeter. Just wait for Kore to return to you. You know she always does."

Demeter huffed and left. If Zeus wasn't going to see reason, she'd force him to. All he cared about was the old stories and how to keep up with the myths of the first earth. She was a goddess and she did not need to live her life by the rules of some primitive race. She'll get Kore back, and Zeus will see that there are no ill effects.

Her first stop was to the computer room that ran the climate controls. She used her special code to lock the climate into winter settings. She smiled. Let's see how fast Zeus changed his mind when his precious humans died of starvation.

Down in the depths of the Underworld, Hades led Tantalus to his place of punishment. The previous Tantalus had been removed earlier that night and the pit now sat empty. Tantalus protested his innocence and struggled, but Hades was stronger. His judges came to help him, and they had to work quickly. This was a process of the Underworld none of them wanted Kore to witness. It would be best for this dark side to wait until she accepted her godhead.

What they didn't know was that Kore was already watching them. From behind Sisyphus' boulder, she watched as the new Tantalus screamed when the catheters were placed in him to remove waste and the IVs inserted to keep him hydrated. He was placed in the hole and the pool filled in.

"Tantalus, you are hereby subjected to an everlasting torment of hunger and thirst," said Hades gravely. "For your crime of killing your own kin and serving the body in a stew to the gods, you will never know the sweet relief of food or water. If you try to drink from the pool, the water will forever shy away from your lips. The food above you will always be just out of reach."

"I swear, I did nothing wrong! The gods asked me to make that sacrifice! Why won't anyone believe me?" Tantalus started to cry.

"I do believe you," Hades said, "but I can do nothing about it. You are now Tantalus and must serve his punishment until the next comes alone. So, it is with all my subjects until the end of time." Hades and his judges left him there, a confused mortal with the memories of previous lifetimes of torment.

"Are these really the people you think are telling you the truth?" asked Sisyphus, looking down at Kore.

Kore sighed. "I'm not sure anymore."

Chapter Twenty-Two

Coldness crept into the Levels overnight. In the farming levels, frost settled on the crops and slowly killed them off. The humans began to panic. They cried out to Demeter to fix their crops and give them a bountiful harvest, but their prayers fell on deaf ears. Demeter no longer cared about their needs. Someone needed to be punished for her losing her daughter, and the humans were as good a target as any.

Through the frost-filled day, Demeter made her way to the home of the mortal, Theron. He was supposed to have kept Kore safe, but he let her slip through his fingers. Her mind filled with possible avenues of revenge. Maybe she would make his crops fail for generations. Or, she could curse his family with bad luck until the end of time. He cost her a child, so she might take one of his. Oh, the things she could do.

At the door, a tired mutt looked sleepily up at her and gave a half-hearted woof before going back to sleep. Feeling like a servant, Demeter knocked on the door and waited for Theron to answer. To her surprise, it was the wife who opened the door. Held at her hip was a young baby, barely a year old.

"Yes, can I help you?"

Demeter bristled at the thought they didn't recognize her. She opened her mouth to tell this mortal woman to respect her betters, but was horrified as an ancient-sounding voice issued forth. "I am Metanira. I was wondering if you had any work an old woman such as myself could take on?"

The woman studied her. "Well, we can use a nanny. We can't pay much, but can offer you room and board. Money is a little tight and I need to start working to bring in an extra income, and can use a nanny to take care of my son, Lykaios, while I'm away. I have two other boys and a teenaged daughter, but they will be in school during the day."

"Oh, I can take care of the little dear. I've raised my own children."

"Very well. Come on in. I'm Chruse. My husband, Theron, will be home shortly. I'll introduce you to the other children."

Demeter smiled as she was led in. This would be perfect. She would gain their trust and destroy them from the inside. After meeting the kids, Demeter figured it was very obvious they had some connection to Psyche. The daughter was even named after Psyche's host. Who were these people?

The husband, Theron, seemed surprised that they now had a nanny, but didn't fight it. Demeter seemed trustworthy as Metanira. And when she got a good look at herself in a mirror, she realized why no one recognized her. In her worry over Kore, Demeter aged several years. Her brown hair was now gray and she had wrinkles. She looked like a grandmother.

The first night as Metanira, she rocked the baby to sleep. Staring down at the innocent babe, Demeter made a decision. She knew Kore was lost. Deep down, she knew it was a losing battle. But, this tiny baby didn't have a destiny. Demeter could take it back with her to Olympus and raise it as a god. This child would be the one to obey her and not break her heart. Yes, this little Lykaios would be all that Kore wasn't.

The next day, Demeter left for the market. She bought what Chruse asked her to buy and then went to her temple. Inside, she took a vial of ambrosia oil from a secret spot known only to her. She needed the oil to turn Lykaios immortal. With visions of a perfect child that Hades would not take floating in her head, she went back to the house.

"This will be the last one. I swear it." Kore stared down at the third seed. She knew she needed to know the truth, but could she trust what the seeds told her. Minthe had already warned her from eating pomegranate seeds, but what was the harm? And if she learned the answers to her questions, could it really be that bad? Not only that, but who could she trust? Could she trust Hades, whom she loved and wanted to spend the rest of her life with, but who also just stuffed an innocent man into a torture device for the rest of his natural life? Could she trust any of his citizens who adored him beyond a shadow of a doubt?

She could always try calling her mother, but she knew Demeter's thoughts on Hades. She loved her mother, but could she get the truth from her? And the same went for Minthe. Would Minthe ever tell her the truth?

Taking a deep breath, Kore took the seed and ate it. The bittersweet juice exploded over her tongue and she closed her eyes, thinking as hard as she could on her first question: *Am I really the daughter of Demeter and Zeus?*

She felt the room spin around her. When she opened her eyes, Melinoe stood before her in an empty room. This was not what she expected.

"What was your question?" asked Melinoe.

"I recently met a shade named Odessa. She said she was my real mother, that Demeter did not birth me. If that is true, who am I? Can I still marry Hades if I am not Demeter's child?"

Melinoe smiled and crackled with static. "Is that what worries you? None of the gods are who they claim to be."

"I know we hold a Zyspadaden inside us, but we are the gods we say we are."

"No, you're not." Melinoe waved her hand and Kore was presented with a scene of Aphrodite fussing over an injured Eros. His shoulder was bandaged and he looked forlornly out the window.

"Eros is the son of Aphrodite, but she didn't birth him," said Melinoe. "He finds a host and is, genetically speaking, that host. The powers of the gods can't change our DNA."

"But Eros will always be Aphrodite's son, no matter what he looks like."

"Exactly." Melinoe waved her hand again and the scene changed to show Artemis and Apollo talking about the advantages of different bows and hunting guns. Apollo, in his handsome golden glory, reached out and ruffled the dark hair of his sister. Her almond-shaped eyes narrowed and she pushed his hand off her.

"Artemis and Apollo are twins," said Melinoe, "but their hosts are not. Does that make a difference in who they truly are?"

"No."

"Kore, you are the daughter of Demeter and Zeus. Do you know what that makes you and Hades?"

Her heart sank. "That makes him my uncle."

"Only in terms of who the gods are," said Melinoe. "Genetically, you two are strangers. Hades has no DNA linked to Demeter or Zeus. That is how you two can marry. If we kept going just by what the genetics of the gods dictate, we would wear out our hosts and have nothing."

Kore sat on the floor. "So, I get that our hosts allow us to interact the way we are meant to, but what does that have to do with me not being the daughter of Demeter?"

"I'm saying, it doesn't matter where you actually came from. All that matters is who you become."

"And Odessa? If I'm her daughter, what does that mean to her? How did I end up becoming Demeter's daughter?"

Melinoe sighed. "That is another question. I can answer that for you, but you will need to eat another seed."

Without hesitation, Kore held out her hand for a seed. Melinoe placed it in Kore's hand and waited until she ate it.

"It is a sad story about how Odessa's daughter became the daughter of Demeter. Are you sure you want to hear it or would you rather ask another question?"

"I already ate the seed. Tell me about Odessa."

Melinoe nodded. "Odessa grew up in the shadow of Demeter's temples in Eleusis. She and her best friend, Euryale, eagerly became devotees and were called to work on Demeter's holy level. For them, it was a dream come true."

"Is that where she met my father?"

"Yes and no. Odessa was a devotee, but your father wasn't. Odessa was at a festival for Demeter in Athens when she met the only man she ever loved. At first, they refused to admit they were attracted to each other. Odessa thought him crude and brutish, and he thought her a simpleton. In a fit of anger, they fought each other, but anger is just another form of passion. By the end, they were wrapped in each other's arms and admitting their love.

"Your father tried to get Eros to ensure that Odessa loved him, but Eros could do nothing to Odessa. She was truly in love, and thus the darts would not work. It wasn't long after that Odessa realized she was pregnant. She told Euryale, thinking her friend would be excited for her. Euryale saw it as betrayal and went to Demeter. At that time, Demeter was looking to have a child, and this was just the blessing she wanted."

"Did Odessa give me to Demeter?"

Melinoe shook her head. "It would have been so much easier if that were the case. No, Kore. Odessa didn't want to give up her child, not even to her goddess. Demeter took with force, killing Odessa in the process."

"And my father?"

"Found Odessa too late. He had been sent on a wild goose chase by Demeter and there were other obligations that kept him from Odessa's side. He tried to take you back, but Demeter already claimed you."

"Is my father still alive?"

"Yes. And he still loves you, Kore."

With that, Melinoe faded and the room changed back to normal. A new seed sat innocently in the bowl, but Kore didn't see it. Her eyes stung with tears as she thought of how deep Demeter's betrayal ran. How could Hades love her knowing she was raised by a woman who would kill to get what she wanted? Kore may biologically be Odessa's daughter, but Demeter raised her. How much of Kore was now the product of Demeter?

She sat on the floor and cried, wishing she never ate that pomegranate seed. Hades had been right. Melinoe had been right. Some questions she didn't want to know the answer to.

Chapter Twenty-Three

Demeter sighed as she watched the skylights dim to simulate night fall. The large air conditioning vents kicked on and a cold winter wind blew through the whole level of Eleusis. She shivered, feeling the temperature drop. Demeter always hated winter. It was too cold, too bleak - too dead. Winter was the time of year she lost her daughter and the whole station mourned with her. Demeter could almost hear the plants dying in the ground, withering from the cold. It was ridiculous. She only caused the systems to bring winter a day or so ago. Not long enough to cause any real damage. The humans probably hadn't even noticed.

A noise in the corner of her room caused her to jerk with a start. Demeter turned to see Chruse, the lady of the house, lighting a fire in the small, corner fireplace. Instantly, the room started to heat back up as the cheery glow from the flames danced over the walls. Shadows mingled merrily, moving across various knickknacks and furniture. Demeter's eyes were drawn to the crib on the far side of the room. One tiny hand reached up to play with the movement on the walls.

"It feels colder this year," Chruse muttered as she stepped away from the fire. "If I didn't know better, I'd swear winter came early this year. It's supposed to be spring. The flowers just started to bloom and now they're all closed up."

"You can blame Hades for the early frost," said Demeter bitterly.

Chruse looked up at her. "What do you mean?"

"Everyone knows winter is caused by Hades claiming his bride. He must not be satisfied with his looted six months and kidnapped her early this year."

"Maybe they needed to work on some issues? Or maybe Persephone missed her husband?" Chruse saw the look Demeter gave her and held her hands up in surrender. "I don't know the ways of the gods. I'm sure if Hades took Persephone early, he had a reason. They'll work it out and then everything can go back to normal."

"Would you really say that if it were your daughter? How would you feel to lose your daughter for half a year to a man you despised?"

"I suppose I wouldn't like it," Chruse said. "I'm just glad my Iona's only suitor is someone we approve of. I can't imagine the fights that would come about if she wanted someone we felt was wrong for her." With a thoughtful look, Chruse added, "I guess I can understand how Demeter feels."

Demeter folded her arms against the night air. "About that," she said. "Your daughter has a very unusual name. I don't think I've heard it before."

"Really? It was quite popular for a while before she was born," said Chruse. "Do you remember the huge uproar about twenty years ago? People felt that Aphrodite came down as a mortal and walked among us. There were many girls named Aphrodite-in-the-flesh, and my husband's sister-in-law, Iona Demarchis, was one of them."

"Interesting. Can I meet this Iona?"

"No. She died. That poor family. I think they must have been cursed. They lost all their daughters in a matter of months; two of them in a single day." Chruse smiled as she checked in on her baby. "I met Iona at Apollo's temple. She helped me out and I promised to name my firstborn daughter after her. It was because of her that I met Theron."

Demeter pursed her lips. "You're sure she died?"

"Positive. Theron and I go down to visit her grave at least once a year in Tiryns." Chruse finished tucking her baby in. "Have a good night, Metanira. We'll see you in the morning."

Demeter nodded, almost forgetting the false name she was using. When was the last time she used a fake name? It had to have been that horrible day, oh so long ago, when her last daughter was lost to Hades. Curse that man! What was his obsession with her daughters? Once one was used up, he went on to the next.

Well, no matter. Demeter glanced at baby Lykaios in the crib. She was through with daughters. A son would cheer her up. Demeter made sure the fire continued to blaze and kept the room toasty while she waited for the house to settle and the other inhabitants to sleep. Once it was time, she took Lykaios from his crib and held him close.

"Don't you worry," she whispered. "Soon, all the problems of a mortal life will fade away and you will be a god. There is no way Hades will want you. Yes, I will raise you as my own and you will be the new God of the Plow or God of the Fields. You will only know happiness and safety."

She took the ambrosia oil and slathered it over the boy's body, making sure to cover every inch. When she was done, she placed him in the fireplace. When the fire didn't burn him, Lykaios fell asleep. Demeter smiled as the first stage of her plan worked.

"I'm worried about Kore." Hades paced his office, making a circuit from his desk to a painting of his realm, crossing in front of his loyal subjects as he moved to peer out the window, and back to his desk "She was rather distant last night and has been crying all day. She won't open her door. I've tried everything. She's not eating, either. All the food I've left out for her hasn't been touched."

"Maybe she's upset over Tantalus," asked Minos. "I would hate to be the one to explain to her why he's changed after how much the previous one bothered her."

"She was also a bit upset over meeting Odessa," said Hecate. "I wonder if she found out any more about Odessa."

"She wouldn't have from Minthe," Aeacus said. "I don't understand why Minthe is here. She claims it's to protect Kore, but she hasn't been anywhere near Kore since her arrival. Did you notice during dinner that Minthe ignored Kore?"

"I noticed Minthe's outfit," Hecate scoffed. "Or rather, her lack of one."

Rhadamon grinned. "Yeah, I noticed that, too."

"None of this is helping." Hades headed to the door. "I'm going to try and talk to Kore again."

"Wait!" Hecate started forward. "Let me talk to her. Sometimes, a woman needs another woman. There are just some things we can't tell a man."

"Such as? We're going to be married. I want her to feel like she can confide everything in me."

"That will come later. For now, she's still a frightened girl who is in way over her head." Hecate passed him. "Leave this to me."

Hecate didn't want to admit it, but she was worried about Kore, too. The girl had proven herself as far as Hecate was concerned the first time she laid eyes on Kore. That slap across Hades' face for lying to her was perfect! Kore was no shrinking violet, of that Hecate was certain. And Kore's determination to win Hades had been evident in the past.

So, what happened? Minthe showed up and suddenly Kore is in her room crying. It wasn't even like Minthe was any kind of competition! Anyone with eyes could see that Hades loved Kore. He only looked to her, he truly cared what she had to say, and the way his face lit up at the mere sound of her voice...the boy was head over heels for Kore. And Kore was head over heels for Hades.

Hecate knocked on Kore's door. "Hey, it's me. Can I come in for a moment?" She heard muffled sobs from inside that quieted before footsteps padded over to the door. Kore looked a mess with red-rimmed, puffy eyes and tangled hair. Hecate took her opening the door as an invite to enter and gently pushed past Kore.

"You look a fright," she said. "Let's get you cleaned up."

"I don't think I can do this," Kore said softly. Her voice wavered under the threat of unshed tears.

"Of course you can." Hecate led her to the bathroom and ran a cloth under cool water. "What don't you think you can do?"

"Marry Hades."

"What brought this on? It wasn't that Minthe woman, was it? You do know there is no way Hades would ever even think of picking her."

Kore patted her face with the cloth. "No. It's just...you know about the seeds in the side room, right?"

Hecate nodded. She knew about them. Not every Kore who entered this realm ate them, but not each had a reason to. What those seeds revealed wasn't always pleasant and more than one Kore spent hours crying after learning the truth of some situation. If Hecate knew that Hades set them up for this Kore, she would have warned the girl not to take them.

"I used one to ask about Odessa," Kore continued. "I just had to know and...and..." She burst into fresh tears.

"What's upset you so much?"

"Demeter isn't my birth mother," Kore confessed. "I'm not really the daughter of a goddess. I'm a fraud!"

"No you're not, Kore. I'm about to tell you a huge secret. It's one you're not supposed to learn about until after your visit here, assuming it goes as we all hope."

"What do you mean, 'as you all hope'?"

"Meaning you marry Hades. I told Demeter I want to see that happen. I'm all for you and Hades marrying and ruling the Underworld together. Anyway, the truth is that Demeter very rarely actually births any of her children. I think in the whole time we've been on this station, she's birthed only a handful, and that was in the beginning. And there have been literally hundreds of children. You know you're not the first Kore, that others have borne your name. Well, there have been as many Plutuses and Despoinas and so on. All of them are the sons and daughters of Demeter, but none of them are actually born to her."

Kore shook her head. "That's different. You don't know what Demeter did to become my mother. I can't face Hades knowing the truth. What will he think of me when Odessa makes it here?"

"Honey, the shades in the welcome area aren't real. They are computer generated memories. Odessa is dead, yes, but she'll never come here unless you recreate her shade here."

Kore ran the cloth under cold water again and dabbed her face. "That still doesn't excuse what Demeter did."

"What did she do? Murder Odessa? Won't be the first time." Kore looked up at Hecate in shock. Hecate patted Kore's arm. "Remember how I said that Demeter very rarely births her own children? Almost all of them come from other sources. Many times, those sources are willing to give up their child to their goddess, but there have been times one refuses. Plutus' father is always called Iason. He's the only man, besides Zeus, Demeter loves, but he is always killed for sleeping with Demeter. His son - and he always has a son - is groomed to be the next Plutus. The fact that Demeter is the cause of Iason's death never causes Plutus any guilt.

"And take Despoina. She, much like you, comes from a mother who is normally willing to give up her daughter. But, in the instance when we need a Despoina and the surrogate doesn't want to give up her child,

Demeter takes matters in her own hands. Many women have met their demise from Demeter."

"That's awful," Kore whispered.

Hecate shrugged. "That's life. It sounds horrible, but that's the way things have been for eons. We've even cannibalized our own to keep our status quo."

"How?" Kore shook her head and held up a hand. "No, wait, don't answer that. Anyway, Hades won't want me once he realizes what Demeter did. I mean, she raised me, Hecate. What if I'm just like her? What if I'm capable of killing another for her child?"

"You're not." Hades stepped into the room. Kore took one look at him and started crying once more. Hecate shot him a disapproving glare, but he waved her off.

"Kore, you are nothing like Demeter. Look at you. Look at how sickened you are at the mere thought of hurting another like that. You could never hurt anyone." Hades walked up to her and gently moved the cloth down from her face.

"How can you be so sure? People change over time. What if we marry and I become so desperate for a child that I follow Demeter's example?"

"You won't. Kore, if there is any reason why we can't have a child of our own and you desire one, we can always adopt. There is no need to harm another for a child." He used the cloth to wipe away her tears. "I know what Demeter did to Odessa is terrible, and I'm not excusing Demeter, but she doesn't always get her children through trickery and bloodshed. I am so sorry it happened when you were born, but I'm glad you're here. And, she wasn't the worst mother you could have had, now was she?

A bit overprotective, maybe, but until yesterday, you had no other complaints about Demeter. Right?"

Kore sniffled. "I guess not." she smiled slightly, roughly wiping away a stray tear and wincing at the feel against her sensitive skin. "I must be dreaming for you to be praising Moth- I mean, Demeter."

"She's still your mother, Kore," Hades said. "And she's still my sister. I don't hate her; even after all she's done. How can I hate the woman who is destined to raise my one true love?" He took Kore's hand and held it to his chest. "Do you feel my heart? It beats only for you, no matter who birthed you. You have always been Kore. It doesn't matter to me if Demeter raised you or not because you are Kore, Goddess of Spring. And, I hope someday you'll be my wife."

"R-really? You still want to marry me?"

Hades knelt on the bathroom floor. "Kore, you are my sun, my moon, the very breath in my body. I fell in love when I first saw you, so innocent and shy in Psyche's garden. I dreamed of living my life with you, of hearing about your day over the dinner table or snuggling together in bed. Whenever I took Cerebos out to train him, I pictured how much you'd enjoy his antics and I ran home to tell you, only to realize you were still up in Olympus. I can only pray you feel the same. Please, Kore, say you'll marry me."

For a long moment, Kore stood there. Hecate leaned forward and hissed, "Say something." Finally, Kore nodded.

"Yes! I'll marry you!"

Hades stood and swept her up in his arms. He kissed

away her doubts and this time she cried tears of joy. Hecate quickly left the bathroom, giving the lovebirds some privacy.

Chapter Twenty-four

Chruse sat up in bed, watching the faint line of light under the door. This was the third night in a row that she could feel the heat from the fireplace in the nursery. She didn't mind that the new nanny, Metanira, kept the fire stoked all night instead of letting it smolder, but she let it blaze so high that the whole house could feel it.

Next to her, Theron stirred. He rolled over, flinging one arm out to drape over her. Encountering her sitting form, he woke up. "What's wrong," he asked, his voice thick with sleep.

"She has the heat too high," said Chruse.

Theron yawned and stretched. "She's an old woman, Chruse. They get cold in the winter."

"But it's spring."

"It still gets cold out at night."

"That kind of heat can't be good for the baby. He must be so uncomfortable." Chruse climbed out of the bed. "I'm going to bring Lykaios here for the night."

Theron settled back in bed. "You do that. I'll talk to Metanira tomorrow about the fireplace." He rolled away from her and was back to sleep in moments.

Chruse made her way down the hall. She wasn't sure why she felt so anxious. She wasn't a first-time mother. In fact, she really wasn't sure why she hired a nanny. Iona and the twins were old enough to help her care for Lykaios when they got home from school, and she had no problems taking care of him during the day. Her plans to find a job were slow moving, and they really couldn't afford a nanny at this moment.

It was just, Metanira looked so lost when she showed up at the front door. Chruse saw her own mother reflected in the woman, and that caused her heart to break. Who knew how many households had turned the old woman down? With an early - extremely early - winter cresting, a woman of Metanira's age could die outside.

Maybe Theron was right. Maybe Metanira was only cold due to her advanced age. They could supply her with more blankets so she didn't need to use the fireplace so vigorously.

Chruse opened the nursery door, and it took her a moment to fully comprehend what she was seeing. Metanira sat in front of the fireplace, rocking back and forth on her heels. Her gaze was fixed on something in the middle of the fire. Something, Chruse realized, was just not shaped like a log.

She walked closer to the old woman, her eyes now on the fire as well. Slowly, the shape came into focus, though it still didn't make sense. When it moved, Chruse gasped and lunged forward.

"What is wrong with you?!" Chruse snatched Lykaios out of the fire and immediately started looking him over for any burn marks or signs of injury. Lykaios, either frightened by his mother's scream or the sudden shock of cold air, started to cry.

Metanira stood. "What have you done? Why did you stop me?"

'You were trying to kill my son! Why wouldn't I

stop you?"

"I was trying to heal him. You've ruined everything!"

Chruse held Lykaios to her chest. "He doesn't need healing. He's not sick."

"Yes he is. He has the worst kind of disease," Metanira hissed. "Mortality."

"Killing him isn't the answer!"

At that moment, the nursery door swung open and Theron ran into the room. Behind him were Iona and the twins. Everyone looked confused.

"I was making him a god," Metanira said. "I would have taken away all the pain and suffering of a human life and raised him in Olympus. He would have been great, but you ruined it. If he stayed in the fire until sunrise, the last of his mortality would have burned away and he would have been perfect. Now, he's lost to the gods forever."

"Maybe we don't want our son to be a god," Chruse snapped. "Ever think of that?"

"You are a fool," Metanira said. She started to glow, causing Chruse to shrink back and seek refuge behind her husband. "You supreme fool!" The glow faded and it was no longer an old woman standing before them. Theron let out a groan as they all recognized the plump brunette goddess.

"Listen, Lady Demeter," Theron said, "we are really appreciative of what you planned on doing for Lykaios, but I think becoming a god should be a decision made later in life. He's just a baby."

"Oh, no, you don't," Demeter growled. "You have

vexed me for the last time. First, you fail to protect Kore, and now you take the boy away from me. You stupid mortals have stood between me and my children for the last time!"

"But Lykaios isn't yours," Telchine cried. "He's our brother!" Theron tried to shush his son, but the damage seemed to already been done.

Demeter's eyes flashed. "Oh, so he's your brother, eh? Well, then, he can suffer with you!" She pointed at Lykaios. "Because you all made a mockery of my suffering, he shall know my misery. Someday, one he loves will be lost to Hades, and there is nothing any of you can do about it!" With that, she vanished in a burst of golden light.

Chruse held Lykaios tightly. "What do we do now," she whispered.

Demeter appeared in her main temple on Eleusis. She sank to her knees as her energy left her. Once upon a time, so many lifetimes ago, the Zyspadaden could Port themselves at will, but it took a lot out of them. Fearing they would destroy themselves, they created the PortMats. Porting herself as she had done could destroy her if she tried going any further. Had she known she would need to Port away from the house, she would have brought a portable PortMat.

She got shakily to her feet. Making her way slowly to the wall, she started to notice something strange about her temple. Where were her priestesses and devotees? Where were her worshippers or followers who cared for her mysteries and cult? This temple should have been hoping with life, especially with the summer harvest coming up.

Demeter made her way carefully along the wall, keeping an ear out for life in her temple. She finally found a priestess in the very back, sitting on a couch and reading some smutty novel by a devotee of Aphrodite. When the woman saw her, she dropped her book and ran over to help Demeter.

"My lady, what happened to you?"

"Where is everyone?" asked Demeter. "Why are my temples so empty?"

The priestess looked guilty. "My lady, it is not my place to chastise the gods, but many of us have felt neglected these many years. With the dwindling harvests and unanswered prayers, many have moved on to other levels where you deem them to thrive. We have wondered what we did wrong for you to so reject us for nearly twenty years. And now this cold snap is destroying what little product we've managed to grow."

For a moment, Demeter gaped at her. Had she ignored them? Well, yes, she probably did, but Kore was so much more important. Those twenty years she spent raising her daughter were now wasted since Kore was in the clutches of Hades. Now, her temples were empty and the humans had left her. Demeter knew who was to blame for all of this.

Hades!

"Do not fear," Demeter said. "All will be set to right soon. Help me to my private rooms."

The priestess guided Demeter to living quarters located in the highest section of the temple. She only went there when Kore was stuck in the Underworld. Ideally, when Zeus ordered Kore's release, her daughter was supposed to appear here, but the last couple of times, Kore went straight to Olympus. Not that any of it would matter. This time, Demeter was sure she wouldn't lose her daughter to Hades.

Once the priestess left, Demeter groaned as she let herself collapse into a plush couch. She still felt weak from Porting, but her strength would soon return. Using her disheveled and fragile state to her best advantage, she turned on the Viewscreen and called Zeus.

"Demeter? What happened to you?" Zeus asked.

"It's my worry over my daughter," Demeter said. When Zeus rolled his eyes, she cried out, "It's killing me, Zeus! I can't live while my daughter is trapped in the Underworld. Bring her back to me. I will wither away without her. No plants will grow until she is returned. The humans will suffer and die. My wrath will freeze this whole station! Give me my daughter!"

"Demeter," said Zeus slowly, "Kore still has a few days left with Hades. Have you tried calling her and talking to her? She's perfectly fine. You are worrying over nothing."

"Am I? Need I remind you that he always tricks her into eating pomegranate seeds so she'll be trapped forever down with him?"

"It's not forever, Demeter. It's not wrong for a husband and wife to want to spend time together. She only stays with him for half the year."

"That's six months too long. Kore is a little girl. She should stay with me."

"She's an adult. I have it on good authority that she accepted Hades' proposal. You should just stop interfering and let her live her life."

Demeter squeaked in outrage. "Pull her out of there! Now! He can't have her!"

"She will be allowed to stay her final days with Hades. If she's accepted the pomegranate seeds, she will, of course, spend six months with him every year."

"I refuse!"

"You have no say in the matter, Demeter. Hades did everything legally. He asked me for permission to marry her, he asked her to marry him, and that is all there is. Kore is happy with Hades. Why can't you be happy, too?"

"Enjoy your human icicles. There will be no spring or summer as long as Hades has my daughter." Demeter hung up on him and quickly called Ares. If there was anyone on this station who would jump at the chance to go guns blazing into the Underworld, it would be Ares.

To Demeter's surprise, Ares turned her down. "There is no reason for me to go get your daughter. She's not being held against her will, and I have no quarrel with Hades. She'll be back soon. Just relax, Demeter."

Unable to think, Demeter sat back and wept. There was nothing to be done. Her daughter was lost to her forever.

Her Viewscreen beeped and Demeter was going to ignore the call when she saw who it was. Curious, Demeter answered and Enyo's face appeared on the screen.

"I hear you need someone to rescue Kore," the Goddess of War and Bloodshed said.

"News travels fast," Demeter muttered.

"I can help you out," said Enyo. "In fact, I would love to go get Kore for you. And, for maybe a little incentive, I might just accidentally kill Hades, too."

"What kind of incentive?"

Enyo rolled her eyes. "Money, Demeter. I want money."

"How much?"

Enyo seemed to think this over before quoting a price to Demeter. Demeter's eyes widened in shock. It was just a little under what Aphrodite spent on dresses and jewelry in a month.

"It may take some time to get the money together," Demeter said.

"Oh, come off it. I know you have it. You never spend any of the money that comes your way. You just let it sit and grow. Well, now you have something to spend it on. Pay me, Demeter, or I'll let Hades have your daughter."

Demeter sighed in defeat. "Okay, I'll start the transfer. Just save my daughter."

Chapter Twenty-five

"I can't believe you got this dress." Kore held the deep red fancy chiton against her body. She twirled in front of the mirror, admiring how the rich color looked against her skin. It felt like a lifetime ago that she saw this dress while shopping with Hedone.

"It was made for you," Hedone said. She sat on Kore's bed with Hecate, both ladies taking notes on the upcoming wedding ceremony. Kore went back and forth on whether or not to marry now or wait until after she saw her mother again. Spread around them was pages of notes on everything from what to wear, what to eat, and where to hold the ceremony. Tucked under Hecate's crossed legs was a guest list with names crossed out and added back in.

"No," said Kore. "It was made for Persephone. That's what the shop owner said."

Hecate made a noise in the back of her throat. "That's your dress. Trust me."

Kore put the dress back on her bed. As beautiful as it was, she foresaw a huge obstacle in her wearing it. Demeter. There was no way Demeter would ever allow her to wear that dress.

What was she thinking? Kore was a goddess! She was marrying a god! She didn't need permission from her mother anymore.

"Maybe we should get married now," Kore said softly. Hedone sighed and added a tick mark on a scoreboard. Marrying now was winning by three points.

"I'll let Hades know," said Hecate. She started to get up, sending a bolt of panic through Kore.

"No! Wait! I'm not sure." She sat on the bed. "What am I going to do about Moth- Demeter?"

"Do what you want," advised Hedone. "Your union has already been blessed by Zeus. There is nothing she can do. Besides, once you are married, you'll have extra protection from Hades. You'll be Queen of the Underworld."

Kore looked confused. "I haven't even told Zeus of Hades' proposal. When did he bless our union?"

Hedone shrugged. "I think we all knew Hades wanted to marry you. This was his second proposal, after all. Zeus gave his blessings a while ago."

Yes, that was right. Kore smiled slightly as she remembered how sweet Hades looked at her Becoming Ceremony. He had proposed to her then. That was part of what started off the whole drama that led to the Bion fiasco. If only she accepted at that moment. Kore frowned. She had accepted. She remembered now, she accepted his proposal, but because of Demeter's hysterics, she stepped back and allowed that ridiculous one-year decision to be made.

At least she was fixing that now.

"To be honest," said Hedone, "the only problem I see with the wedding happening now is Minthe. She's just as bad as Demeter."

"What about me?" Everyone turned to see Minthe walking in the room. She wore a clingy mint-green dress that matched her hair. On slightly closer inspection, Kore noted that the dress was slightly damp, creating a semitransparent effect to the clingy material.

"I thought I locked the door," said Hecate.

"You did. However, I have not spent the last nineteen years or so raising Kore to not know how to pick a lock," said Minthe. Her gaze swept over the dresses and notes on the bed. "What's all this?"

"Nothing for you to worry about," Kore said. She reached to hide the dress, but Minthe got to it first.

"I hope this is something Hecate was planning on wearing." Minthe sniffed indignantly. "There is no way a lady such as yourself would wear anything this scandalous."

"You mean, like your outfit," asked Hecate. She snatched the dress back. There was nothing scandalous about it beyond the color. In fact, given how freely Hecate, Hedone, and Minthe wore chitons of sheer or low-cut natures, the red dress was very modest.

"This is for my wedding," said Kore. She stiffened, ready for the onslaught of tears, dramatics, and denial from Minthe.

Minthe perked up. "Oh, you're going to marry Bion? That's good. Still, something more modest should be worn. I'm sure your mother has something more suitable. Maybe in a nice light green or virgin white."

"I'm not marrying Bion. I'm marrying Hades."

For a brief moment, Minthe looked shocked. Her expressions swiftly changed from anger to amusement before she settled on indignation. "You're not marrying Hades. I'm marrying Hades! He loves me! In fact, when I just left him, he was packing a romantic picnic lunch for the two of us. You need to really grow up, Kore. You're not a little girl anymore who can live in her daydreams. Hades is a man, and he needs a woman like me. What could he possibly want a childlike yourself?"

Hecate snorted. "Do you have any idea how messed up you sound? Hades proposed to Kore. I was there. He wants her, and she's a woman. You don't even really love Hades, Minthe. You were struck by a love dart."

"You lie!" Minthe's face turned red. "I have loved him for a long time. There are no darts involved. And he loves me!"

Kore wanted to argue, but she knew Minthe wouldn't listen. Minthe never listened. Luckily, she was saved when there came a knocking at the door. Relieved, Kore swept past Minthe. The door had been left slightly ajar from when Minthe picked the lock. Kore opened the door the rest of the way, surprised to find Psyche, Phobos, and Hades, guns drawn and held at their sides, waiting just outside the room.

"Mother? What's going on?" asked Hedone as soon as she noticed Psyche.

"We have a problem," said Psyche. "Demeter hired Enyo to fetch Kore, and she's bringing Deimos. We need to get everyone to safety."

"If Lady Demeter hired someone, the best course of action would be to hand Kore over," said Minthe.

Hades frowned. "Didn't you hear what she said? Demeter hired Enyo! This will not be a peaceful extraction."

"Lady Demeter knows best."

"Not to mention," added Phobos, "Demeter paid extra for Enyo to kill Hades."

Kore and Minthe gasped. Kore rushed up to Hades, wrapping her arms around his waist. "She can't," Kore cried. "She can't kill you."

"Don't worry, my love. No one is killing me." Hades placed a kiss on the tip of Kore's nose. "My only fear is that Enyo allows her own bloodlust to get the better of her. You embarrassed her at your Becoming Ceremony. Enyo never forgets nor does she forgive."

Minthe pushed Kore out of the way. "What do we do, darling? You'll protect me, right?"

"At the moment, we plan to send everyone up to Zeus," said Hades.

"What about you?" asked Kore.

Phobos raised his gun. "We will protect Hades." He looked over at Psyche and shrugged. "Well, I'm protecting Hades. Psyche will make sure you all get to safety."

"I can fight," Psyche said.

"You're pregnant. As much as it pains me to say this, Eros will kill me if I let anything happen to you."

Kore wanted to protest, to say that she could take care of herself. She knew in her heart that Demeter wanted Hades dead. It really shouldn't have surprised her that Demeter hired someone to kill him. It just made her feel very disappointed in Demeter.

Hecate and Hedone got up off the bed and were moving toward Psyche when an explosion shook the halls. Phobos cursed and held his gun at the ready. He quickly peered out the door, his body tensed. After a moment, he leaned back in the room.

"It's Eros," he said. "He doesn't look good."

Psyche and Hedone took off down the hall. Moments later, the three of them reentered the room. Eros was limping and one of his wings was burnt. A large, bloody gash still oozed over his left eye and his face and torso were covered in cuts and bruises.

"What happened?" asked Hades.

"They blew the PortMat," said Eros. Psyche helped him sit in a chair. "I got most of the people out, but we may have lost a nymph or two."

"This leaves only the PortMat at the welcome area," said Hecate.

Hades' face hardened. "We need to come up with a better plan. We know where they will attack, so we can set a trap." He motioned for Phobos to join him. The two men went out of the room and Kore could hear the low buzz of their conversation. After a moment, Phobos returned to the room.

"Okay, new plan. We need to hide Kore at the furthest point from the welcome area there is. Psyche will take you to the pomegranate grove. Those of us who can fight, will. The rest will need to hide."

"Where do we hide?" whined Minthe. "Why can't Hades protect me?"

Over the intercom, Hades' voice boomed. "To all personnel, by order of Hades, you need to go to the lower level. This is not a drill. Please proceed to the lower level now."

Minthe looked confused. "What lower level?"

"That would be as safe place for us," said Hedone. "Kore, you should come with us. There is no way Enyo or Deimos knows about the lower level."

"She can't," said Psyche. "Trust me on this, but Kore must go to the pomegranate grove. Come, Kore, I'll take you there myself."

"I'm going, too," Minthe declared. "It's my duty to protect her."

Psyche rolled her eyes, but allowed Minthe to join them. Eros went with Hedone and Hecate to the lower level while Phobos ran off to join Hades. The mansion was so quiet, and the very stillness of the air made it feel eerie to Kore.

Out back, Psyche led them to a cave. In the back of the cave was the grove. It wasn't very big. Only four trees, their branches hanging down with the large, red fruit, stood sentry around a stasis pod. Curious, Kore looked in the stasis pod. Inside was a pale woman with dark brown hair, wearing a simple black chiton. She recognized the woman from her visions with the seeds: Persephone.

"So, this is it," said Minthe. "We just wait here until the end?"

"No. I suggest we don't make this easy on Enyo or Deimos to find us," said Psyche. With a familiarity that shocked Kore, Psyche opened a hidden panel in the trees and inputted four codes. There was a rumbling sound, and Kore knew the cave was now closed.

"What if Hades dies?" asked Minthe. "Now we're stuck in here."

"We won't die." Psyche hefted her gun. "I can protect us if need be."

"There won't be a need, my friend." The stasis pod glowed and Persephone stood. She held out her hand to Kore. "It is time to end this."

Enyo glared around the welcome area and the vast open space. "This is not a good idea," she spat at Deimos.

"What are you talking about?"

Enyo gestured to the open field. "They can see us coming a mile away!"

Deimos shrugged. "It couldn't be helped. We didn't want them to get away, and forcing them to have only one option was our plan. Come on, we can start walking."

"And what if they shoot?"

"They're not expecting us. By the time they find out we jammed Hades' personal PortMat, it will be too late."

"What if they are expecting us? You said you thought Phobos overheard us, and we know he's chummy with Psyche and Hades."

Deimos sighed. "He won't betray me. Phobos is smarter than that."

A red laser beam shot out of a nearby wall and scanned the two of them. All of a sudden the room changed into a cavern with a large, rolling river. Shades appeared, all of them bloodied and grotesque. Deimos recognized a few as those who fell in battles by his hand.

"Welcome to the afterlife," snarled a bloodied soldier.

"Don't worry," said Deimos. "They aren't real. Nothing has changed. We're still in the same room. It's all a hologram."

At that moment, one of the Shades scratched Enyo's arm. She gasped, pulling her arm back and watched as the blood welled up in the cuts. She turned to Deimos. "It sure feels real!" Turning back, she aimed a shot at the soldier. It hit, but did no damage.

The soldier laughed. "You can't kill what is already dead!"

"Keep them occupied," Deimos demanded. "I'll find the origin of this hologram and destroy it."

Enyo fired again and turned to run. She may love bloodshed and the slaughter of her enemies, but only when she knew she'd win the fight. This was too much, even for her. The Shades were everywhere, swarming around her as she tried to escape.

In desperation, she headed into the water, only to feel it freeze cold around her ankles. More Shades were in the water, grasping at her, trying to pull her down and drown her.

"Deimos, hurry up!"

"I'm trying!" Enyo looked to see Deimos fighting off the Shades. Whenever he had a second to himself, he ran his hands over the walls, looking in vain for the source of the laser.

A hand shot up from the icy water and yanked Enyo down. Her cry was cut off as the water flowed over her. She struggled and managed to get back to her feet. Standing in front of her was a woman with dark skin and three scars on her face.

"Either you turn back and give up," the woman said,

"or we will make you join us."

Chapter Twenty-Six

Enyo ducked once more as the Shades reached out to grab her. The dark-skinned woman with the scars had identified herself as Odessa, and was acting as the leader of the Shades. Nothing Enyo did could get the Shades away from her. She couldn't hide in the water; it was too cold and choppy. If she tried to swim across, she knew she'd drown. Deimos' theory that this was all a hologram be damned! Enyo knew it all felt real and that made it real enough.

"Don't let her escape!" Odessa cried. "She had her chance. Now she'll pay with her life!"

"Deimos! Have you found it yet?" Enyo scrambled around another grouping of Shades. She tried to slash at them with her knife, but it did no good. It was like cutting air.

"Almost," came Deimos' strangled cry. Enyo managed to look where Deimos was scaling the wall. The Shades were pulling on his clothes and armor as he aimed his gun toward a craggy spot on the cavern wall.

Enyo slashed at another Shade and ran over to Deimos. The Shades grabbed her and pulled her away from the wall. She screamed as their claws ripped into her skin.

"You won't win," Enyo snarled as she dodged the claws of Odessa. "You're nothing more than pixels. It's my mind that keeps making me think this is real."

"You really think so? That's the beauty of the mind

– it can make anything feel real."

"What do you hope to achieve? Eventually, you'll fade. All of you will fade! You're nothing but a projection." Enyo kept her eyes on Odessa. The other Shades held back, waiting for some kind of signal.

Odessa smiled cruelly. "What I want is to keep you and Deimos busy. As you said, I'm just a hologram. But that's the beauty of it. Even if you destroy the machine, I can still return. I will never fade. You have a memory of me now, and I will live on there. Deimos remembers me. I'm part of his past that he wishes never happened. Too bad he's too much of a psycho to realize what it all means."

Deimos gave a cry and then the Shades sputtered and fizzled out. Deimos dropped from the wall and quickly shot out the remaining lasers. Almost immediately everything quieted down. The room was nothing more than an open space once more with the door on the far end. Deimos narrowed his eyes as he noticed a cave-like structure above the door, and he was sure he knows what would be waiting for them there.

"Those holograms sure pack a punch," growled Enyo. She wrapped a bandage around the very real gash in her arm. "I thought you said they really couldn't hurt us."

"I didn't think they could. It's all in the mind." Deimos motioned toward the door. "Come on. They've been alerted to our presence. We need to hurry."

As they crossed the open floor, Enyo said, "The one who was leading the Shades seemed to think she knew you."

Deimos snorted. "I knew many of those Shades. I sent them here myself. Why would she be different?"

"Do you remember anyone named Odessa?"

Deimos thought for a moment. "Did she have three scars on her face?" Enyo nodded and Deimos muttered a curse. "I remember her. Several years ago, she ensnared Phobos. He stopped being the brother I knew. Then he met Eros' pathetic scarred wife and continued to change."

"Phobos is starting to become a bother," said Enyo.

Deimos sighed and looked at his gun. "I fear it's time for him to find a new host."

It would be dangerous. Without a stasis chamber, forcing a Zyspadaden to change hosts could lead to the death of the Zyspadaden. So many of their brethren had fallen, culled so that the remaining Zyspadaden could keep their powers. Would the Station survive without Phobos?

Deimos shook his head. There was a chance Phobos would survive such an act. He could make it up maybe two levels and force himself in a new host. Or, there was the rumor about Hades having a stasis pod. If that was true, Phobos, who had been spending time with Hades, would know where to look. Deimos was sure Phobos would survive, and with a new host would come the chance to wipe clean all the personality changes. Phobos was the God of Fear, and Deimos needed him to be the bloodthirsty warrior once more.

Before they made it to the door, a large black shadow swooped down from over the door. Deimos, who had been expecting such an attack, pushed Enyo out of the way. Over them, Cerebos emerged from his perch. The massive three-headed dog growled down at them, thick ropes of drool slobbered over his jaws. This was no hologram. This was a real monster, standing before them.

"This is more like it," Enyo said. She took aim with her gun and fired.

Hecate jumped as she heard the sounds of blaster fire just outside of Tartarus. They made it further than she had hoped. Without thinking, she adjusted the Helm of Darkness and slipped unseen between the inhabitants of Tartarus. She quickly undid the chains that held Ixion to his wheel.

"Hades wants all of you to hide in the cave with the Titans," she whispered. "Hurry."

Ixion did not try to help any of the others, and Hecate hadn't expected him to. She moved on to the next tortured person and gave the same command. Quickly and quietly, the poor souls of Tartarus ran to safety. Just as the last left, the sounds of blaster fire stopped. There was a crashing noise and Hecate hoped they could repair the damage caused by Enyo and Deimos.

She hid behind Sisyphus' Boulder, watching the entrance. Phase three of Hades' plan was about to begin.

Enyo kicked the pile of metal parts and gears. The machine had been no match for her. Whoever thought Cerebos was dangerous never fought in a real war. It took only moments to figure out the dog's patterns. Swipe and bite, swipe and bite, it had been far too easy.

"Don't let your guard drop," said Deimos. "Beyond here, we are fully in Hades' territory."

"What do you think he'll have planned?"

Deimos shrugged. "This is already more than I

would have credited him. Everyone talks about him as if he were just sitting on his throne, twiddling his thumbs. Only Demeter thinks he's dangerous. He never struck me as a warrior, really. Did you see him? He's scrawny. I can break him like a twig. No, these traps have to be from Phobos."

"And what would Phobos do next?"

"I'm not sure. The old Phobos would keep the traps coming and try to push us into a corner. Knowing a little about the Underworld, I know we'll come across Tartarus. Maybe he'll send the tortured after us? Or unleash the Titans?"

Enyo snorted. "If he tries to send the tortured after us, we can just get them to change sides. After all, why fight for the man who has kept you locked up for centuries? Same with the Titans. I'm sure Cronus would love to exact his revenge on his captors."

Deimos nodded, looking thoughtful. "I think that would be a good idea. With Cronus by our side, we'll be able to take down Hades in no time. Possibly even Zeus. We could reshape the Station in our image." He smiled. "Picture it, Enyo. Only the best humans would be allowed to live. We'll have war and destruction and none of this coddling the mortals. Any who won't follow our laws will be sent down to the planet and we'll see if they can survive."

"Too bad you're married, Deimos. You'd be a man after my own heart."

"You flatter me, Enyo." Deimos looked around the craggy cavern. He could see the seats where the judges were supposed to sit and beyond that, the fields of

Tartarus. He knew that the Titans were nearby, but where?

"Does this seem odd to you," asked Enyo.

"What do you mean?"

"Where is everyone?" Deimos looked at her and then back to the fields. She was right! No one was around. Where was Ixion? Where was Sisyphus? Where was Tantalus? It was one thing to believe that Hades would ramp up the security, but to release all the tortured souls? Just what was he planning?

"Let's just find the Titans and get out of here," Deimos said. "I've got a bad feeling about this."

Hecate crouched down, even though there was no way Deimos or Enyo could see her while she wore the Helm of Darkness. She could see them searching for something, poking around every rock and tapping on the walls. They were too close to the Titans for Hecate's liking. The last thing she needed was them getting smart and freeing everyone. Taking on Deimos and Enyo would be hard enough without the added army of the inhabitants of Tartarus and the Titans.

She aimed her blaster toward the duo and fired a warning shot. Deimos and Enyo turned toward her, but couldn't find her. Alerted now, they started to walk away from the hidden entrance to the Titans' cave. She fired another shot and let the Helm of Darkness slip slightly as she ran away.

"There he goes!" She heard them chasing her. With a grim smile, she headed to the next phase of the plan.

Deimos and Enyo rushed after the figure. Only a slight ripple in the air let them know anyone else was around. Hades, Deimos decided, was indeed a coward, relaying on the Helm of Darkness to outwit his opponents instead of taking them head on. Nowhere in Deimos' inner thoughts did he realize he'd have done the same if he had the Helm of Darkness. His only thought on the artifact was that he'd take it as a prize.

Suddenly, the ripple faded and they lost track of the fleeing figure. Deimos and Enyo stopped, hoping to hear the sounds of footsteps or for Hades to make another mistake. Nothing. All was silent. Deimos quickly shot in the last spot he'd seen the ripple, but the shot hit the wall. There was no one standing there.

"Where did he go?" Enyo growled. "I swear, this is starting to be more trouble than it's worth. I should have asked for more money from Demeter."

"That really surprised me, you know," said Deimos, his bright eyes searching the shadows for the next trick.

"What did?"

"Doing this for money. I always pegged you as the ruthless 'I'll kill for free because I love it' type."

Enyo laughed. "Oh, I would have done this for free," she said. "However, it serves my little sense of irony. See, I'm not here to sweetly escort Kore back to her mother. I plan on dragging her corpse back, and to have Demeter pay me to kill her daughter was just too sweet."

Deimos frowned. "Demeter thinks you're killing Hades, not Kore. As much as I don't like my sister-in-law, killing her isn't the answer."

"Oh, but it will be glorious, Deimos. Just think:

Kore dies and the gods go to war. In all that chaos and bloodshed, we will rise as the new rulers and start our own golden age."

Deimos held back. While he would love to see an age filled with survival of the fittest and to take down the haughty gods, he wasn't thrilled with having it actually happen. Should they kill Kore, it would be all of Olympus after them. Their only hope would be to awaken the Titans, and they would have to find them after this whole debacle. Otherwise, he and Enyo might be seeking new hosts.

Or worse. It was not unheard of for gods who had long outlived their usefulness to be "recycled". The god Helios, God of the Sun, was destroyed and his powers given to Apollo. The same went for Hemera, Goddess of the Day. There used to be many Titans held captive, but without access to human hosts, they, too, had to fade or conserve their powers. The last time the Titans got free, roughly around the last time Zeus changed hosts, there were only thirteen left. So many of the minor deities listed in the humans' history were now swallowed by their more powerful brethren.

"Maybe we should hold off on the coup until after we have the Titans," Deimos suggested. He shivered slightly, remembering how he, himself, merged with the spirits of Alala, Goddess of the War Cry, Alastor, God of Blood Feuds and Vengeance, and Homados, God of the din in Battle. How many minor gods were left?

"Don't wimp out on me now, Deimos. We're so close to our prize, I can taste it."

"You are only close to your death!" The air around them felt electrified as a woman appeared before them.

She was a fearsome sight to behold. Her dark hair wild and her skin pale, her eyes were missing and only static could be seen. Her hands and feet seemed to disappear as her limbs went from ordinary to pure light. Crouching around her were the Shades of the lost, ghosts who, for whatever reason, never moved on.

"You're just another hologram," Deimos said. "Once I find how you're being produced, you're gone."

"Is that so?" The Spector laughed. "Oh, foolish Deimos, when was the last time you saw a hologram do this?" She raised one hand and sent a blast of pure energy his way. He dodged and noticed with horror that it destroyed a rock behind him.

"What are you?"

"I am Melinoe, Daughter of Persephone and Hades! You dare enter my father's realm and threaten my mother? I will not allow you to continue!"

"Nothing but a hologram," Deimos repeated. There had to be a trick to this.

"I am not a hologram," Melinoe said. "I am pure Zyspadaden. I do not exist in a host." She sent another wave of energy at them, causing Deimos and Enyo to scatter. "You have grown weak with your relying on the humans. I am pure and still as powerful as we once were."

"Then you know that Hades and Persephone aren't your real parents," said Enyo. "Why live this farce?"

"When I picked this goddess, I welcomed them as my parents. No matter the host, they are still themselves deep down. They have shown me love and treated me like I was real, though they themselves think I must be a hologram. Never once has Hades thought of me as less, nor has Persephone ever not called me her daughter. I have watched as they fought for me when the other gods would have pulled the plug. It is for them I will fight."

"I always thought Zeus was your father," said Deimos. "Didn't he trick Persephone and make her think she was sleeping with Hades?"

"Lies! I know my heritage!"

Deimos ducked behind another rock. He could find no crevice or crack in the walls where the hologram beams could be coming from. He didn't believe Melinoe. He'd seen the true form of the Zyspadaden and that was of golden light. Not some kind of static ghost.

"Distract her!" Enyo yelled. "I'll find the hologram origin point."

"Easier said than done," Deimos said. "They hide those things well."

Enyo scoffed. "I'd rather you get torn up by the Shades this time. Finding some silly little lens will be easy."

Deimos ignored her and took aim at Melinoe. He fired a shot and watched as the blast went through her. Her form split only slightly to allow the shot to go through and then healed immediately. She would not be an easy opponent.

"Do not think this will be as easy as it was to defeat the Shades in the Welcome Area," Melinoe warned. "I have more power than they do."

"What do you mean, 'power'?" Deimos sprinted from one covering to the next. One of the ghosts caught his leg and fell hard. He felt his head hit the ground and knew he'd be bruised when this was over.

"The Shades only have as much power as you give them. They are from your past, designed for you. I am real. My ghosts are what is left of our brothers and sisters after Zeus decided to downsize."

Deimos turned, aiming at the ghost on his leg. He stopped as Melinoe's words sank in. There, in front of him, was Homados, his hollow eyes focused on Deimos. The part of Deimos' power that came from dissolving Homados recognized its original soul and Deimos screamed as the power twitched inside him. It fought to free itself, to once more form a single god. He recognized the other ghosts who drew around him: Alala, Eupraxia (Goddess of Well Being), and Prioixis (God of Battlefield Pursuit, swallowed by Phobos). Their clawed hands reached out to him, and he knew they would tear him to pieces and draw his soul among them until Deimos was no more and they were alive.

"Stop this!" Phobos' voice rang out in the cavern. Instantly, the ghosts paused, turning to see who interrupted their fun. Deimos was never so happy to see his brother in all his life.

"Why are you interfering? They deserve this! They threatened Father and Mother!" Melinoe raged.

Phobos held his hands up to show he meant no harm. "I know that, Melinoe, but your mother and father would never want this to happen to Deimos. Don't forget, Deimos is now your uncle. He married Despoina."

"Despoina never cared for us," Melinoe said. "No matter how many times Mother invites her to visit or strives to be a friend when she's Above, Despoina always pushes Mother away. All because of some silly grudge brought on by Demeter."

"We can change that," Phobos said. "I'm sure that Deimos would love to help mend the strife in our family." He glanced over at his brother, a warning flashed in his eyes. "Won't you, Deimos?"

Scuttling back from the ghosts, Deimos said, "Yeah. I'll talk to Despoina."

"I can't promise that Despoina will fully accept Persephone, but I can promise we will work on it," Phobos said. "I know that Despoina feels like Demeter never pays her any attention, and she's right. Demeter has ignored all her children in favor of one, but," - this was directed toward Deimos - "it is not Persephone's fault. She was raised to think she was an only child. Each and every host that she's ever had has been delighted to learn she had siblings. If given the choice, Persephone would love to be friends with Despoina."

Enyo's face scrunched up. "We're here to get Kore, not Persephone."

Phobos smiled. "I think you're a little too late for that."

Chapter Twenty-Seven

Kore hesitantly took Persephone's hand. It was like touching a live wire and she gasped at the feel of raw power.

"You're a Zyspadaden" Kore said. She tried to pull her hand away, but Persephone held on tightly. Understanding dawned in Kore's eyes. "No! I don't want to change! I want to remain me!"

"It's all right, Kore," Persephone said. "I once thought like you. The thing is, you are me. The only way for this to end is for us to accept that."

"I don't want to change."

"It's not changing," said Psyche. "Kore, the goddess you were always meant to become was Persephone. That's why your mother never pushed you to finish the ceremony; she knew there was no goddess named Kore. Kore has always meant to become Persephone, Goddess of the Spring and Queen of the Underworld."

Kore looked into Persephone's dark eyes. "You're the one who will marry Hades? It's you he's really in love with?"

"It's complicated," said Persephone. She waved her hand and the room changed. It was no longer the pomegranate grove, but a lovely meadow. Kore knew this was not on the Station. There was just something pure about it; the way the sky looked or the sounds of the birds all pointed to this coming from a memory of a real place. Kore could see a group of women laughing and playing off to one side.

"Once upon a time, this was home. This is where our legends were created," Persephone said. "The humans of the first Earth were a mixing pot of cultures and beliefs. Even when they didn't know much of the world beyond their front door, they still sought to blend the various cultures around them. Sometimes, it was done peacefully and sometimes it wasn't."

"What does this have to do with Hades marrying you?"

"The one the humans called Persephone had a lot of names, depending on her office. Long, forgotten rituals point out that she was also called Kore, the maiden. There was a discussion when we rescued the humans on Earth Three, and it was decided to keep Persephone and Kore separate. However, that quickly fell apart when our two Zyspadaden merged. It was decided that Kore would be the daughter Demeter raised while Persephone was the final goddess."

Kore clamped her hands over her ears. "No! I refuse to take on a Zyspadaden. I'm Kore! I will always be Kore!"

"I fought it, too," said Persephone. The scene changed and Kore saw Persephone talking to another woman, one she recognized from the visions from the seeds. This was the previous Persephone. The vision shifted slightly, and Kore saw a long line of Persephone's meeting their new hosts. Some of the women were beautiful and some were average, some were tall and some were short, some fat and some skinny. She was surprised to see that a few were men.

"I thought you said Kore meant maiden."

Persephone smiled. "Mother has tried many tricks in the past to keep me out of Hades' grasp. She keeps forgetting that love always came first with us. The moment she picks her next Kore, Hades knows he must find a new host. He waits until I've gone into my stasis pod and then he lets his soul connect to the new Kore. Whoever Kore would find attractive, he picks. Inside, it's always him, just as inside, it will always be us."

"What will happen to me? To my body?"

"You'll still use it. I will reside in you."

Kore shook. "I can't. I'm too scared."

"If you won't, then I will!" Minthe pushed herself forward. They had forgotten about her.

"You can't be Persephone. You're Minthe and you already have a Zyspadaden soul," said Persephone.

"I don't care. I will be the one to marry Hades. I know he loves me, but if he can only marry Persephone, then I shall become her." Minthe shoved Kore out of the way. "I'd make a better queen, anyway. I know more about the real world than Kore, I can convince Demeter to stand down, and I am more experienced with management. Make me Persephone! I will bring the Underworld into a new golden age. I will break the mold on the whole idea of the Queen of the Underworld being a morose figure. Is that the life you want for Kore? A life filled with shadows where she'll never see her mother or the sun? I don't care. I have no parents to mourn me and I love the dark."

Persephone's eye twitched slightly. "You can't be me. I have long known I'd be with Kore. Hades has long known that Kore and I would one day become one. You are not queen material."

"Hades always knew," Kore whispered. "Did he ever love me?"

"Of course he did. I told you, love always came first. Hades loves you, Kore, for who you are. You won't lose any of yourself when you become me. You'll take on my name, my memories, but all your personality will still be there."

"He doesn't love you," Minthe said. "Hades loves me. All he sees when he looks at you is her!"

Kore looked over at Persephone. "What happens now?"

Persephone reached in the pocket of her chiton and held out a seed. "If you agree to become Persephone, you take the seed. It's a contract, really. By eating it, you agree to stay in the Underworld as Hades' wife for six months out of the year. You are the one that signals fall and winter."

Kore thought this over. She knew this was her destiny. Just as Hedone was born and raised to be the Goddess Hedone and Psyche was tested to become a goddess. Everyone was either born a goddess or made into one. Kore was born to be a goddess.

She reached out to take the seed when Minthe screamed. Kore looked up in time to see Minthe grab Psyche's gun. "You're not taking this from me!" Minthe cried. "I will be the one to marry Hades. I'll be the new Persephone! I am the one who deserves this."

"Minthe, you can't do this," Persephone said. "You already possess a Zyspadaden. If you try to become me, all you'll do is kill your host. I have a say in who I become."

"Give me the pomegranate seed," Minthe demanded.

Psyche and Persephone exchanged a glance and then Persephone held the seed out to Minthe.

"No," cried Kore. "You can't!"

"Finally! Everything I've ever wanted is finally mine," Minthe declared. She greedily swallowed the seed and looked expectantly at Persephone. Persephone crossed her arms.

"I told you nothing would happen," the Queen of the Underworld said.

"Why didn't it work? You should be dead and I should be the new queen."

Persephone sighed. "You just don't listen, do you, Minthe? You already have a Zyspadaden soul. For you, that was just a seed. It will only work with Kore."

"Then I guess she'll never be you," said Minthe. "I ate the seed."

"Do you really think that was the only pomegranate seed I'd carry," said Persephone.

Kore couldn't stop staring at Minthe. Of all the things the older woman had done, this was unforgivable. She had forgiven Minthe for treating her like a prisoner all her life. She moved on from the fact that Minthe was her mother's spy. She even forgave Minthe for her infatuation with Hades, knowing it was all from a love dart. But this! To try and take what was rightfully Kore's was just too much. Anger coursed through Kore's body. Everyone tried to control her life! Demeter kept her locked up and wanted her to stay a child forever. Minthe beat Kore down daily to keep her in a position under Minthe. Every little comment about how the gods were gloriously white and dark-skinned Kore would never be a goddess came flooding back.

"I won't let you," Kore said. Minthe turned to look at her, her expression making it clear that she didn't see Kore as a threat. "I won't let you take my place."

"There is nothing you can do, Kore. Just go back to Demeter like a good little girl," said Minthe.

"I don't think so." Kore surprised Minthe with a quick jab to the face. Minthe raised the gun to shoot Kore, but Psyche stepped in and grabbed her gun back. Before Minthe knew what was happening, Psyche shot Minthe in the hip, sending the other woman to the ground.

Psyche nodded to Persephone. "I think we can continue now. Minthe shouldn't be a problem anymore."

"You both will be in big trouble once Demeter learns about this!" Minthe swore.

Persephone held out another seed to Kore. "Only take this if you are sure," she said.

"What happens if I'm not sure?"

"I don't know,'" Persephone admitted. "I don't think there there's been a time when, after being offered the pomegranate seed, Kore didn't take it. I suppose I'd have to hold on to it until you are ready."

Hesitantly, Kore reached out and took the seed. Before she could change her mind, she popped it in her mouth and swallowed. The world tilted and Kore felt an explosion of light flared all around her. It wasn't painful, more like a sensation of the air pressing inward and then rushing out. She almost expected it to be in reverse as the memories of a thousand lifetimes came flooding over her.

She remembered the first time she met Hades, all the

first times. She remembered telling him goodbye as she went to the stasis pod. She remembered the arguments with Demeter about whether or not she loved Hades, and the sorrow she felt as her mother never believed her. She remembered living in the Underworld and lifetimes of happiness with her friends.

She blinked and noticed Psyche holding a body in her arms. The body was of a woman with dark hair, wearing a simple black chiton. There was something familiar about her, something sad.

"You're crying," said Psyche. She lifted the body and placed it in a stasis pod, but they all knew it was too late.

"I think I always cry at this point. It's the grief over seeing my previous host die. All her memories are now inside me, and I feel like I lost a true friend."

"I wish I can say I know that feeling. My previous hosts felt joy at seeing the new host helpless and dying. I remember the delight Lethe felt as she watched me suffer," said Psyche sadly.

"Maybe it will be different this time? You are different."

"Maybe."

Psyche watched as her friend reached into the stasis pod and, from a hidden compartment, pulled out a crown. Once it was in place, Persephone smiled. "Now, shall we go and stop this silly fighting in my kingdom?"

The fighting had resumed by the time Persephone and Psyche made their way out of the mansion. Enyo, enraged at the thought of not being able to exact her revenge or create a new world in her image, pushed past Melinoe and Phobos. With her gun ready, she made her way toward the mansion. Hades left his hiding spot to keep Enyo out of the mansion. By the time Persephone and Psyche came upon them, Enyo had Hades on his knees with her gun to his head. Phobos and Deimos were still fighting. Melinoe was nowhere to be seen.

"Now," said Enyo, "the real question is whether or not to kill you first. And, really, how does death work down here? I mean, this is the Underworld. Will you just reappear? Or is there an Underworld for the Underworld?"

"Let's find out, shall we?" Persephone stood at the entrance. Noticing that she didn't have a weapon, she quickly grabbed a vase off the table by the door in the foyer. Psyche shook her head and handed over her gun.

"Oh, you'll get yours, Kore," said Enyo.

Persephone smiled and pointed her gun. "It's Persephone, Queen of the Underworld," she said and pulled the trigger. Enyo managed to dodge the shot.

"No! It's not too late," Enyo sneered. "No one but us knows that. To everyone above, you're still Kore."

"What is your problem? Do you have any idea the trouble you'll cause if you kill Persephone," asked Psyche.

"I will cause a great war and reshape this station in my image," said Enyo. "All will remember me as a great warrior and not the goddess defeated by a little girl!"

Persephone rolled her eyes. "Is that what this is all about? I beat you in a stupid competition and now you're hellbent on destroying me? You have issues."

"You have no idea," said Phobos. He punched his brother and came over to join Persephone. "Enyo has always been very unstable. If there was a god of madness, Enyo would be it."

Enyo's gun wavered slightly. She realized that there were too many witnesses. She could kill her quarry, but now there was Psyche and Phobos to worry about. Not to mention the person with the Helm of Darkness. There was no way her dream of reshaping the station would ever come to fruition now.

Persephone leveled her gun on Enyo once more. "Stand down. You are hereby under arrest by order of myself. You dared to come here with the expressed intentions to kill the gods. I think you'll be lucky if Zeus merely locks you up for a few hundred years. Me, personally? I'd declare you obsolete."

Enyo growled, but knelt on the ground. Persephone, remembering the fight at Kore's Becoming Ceremony, did not take her eyes off Enyo as she instructed Phobos to tie the goddess up. As Phobos finished with Enyo, Minthe arrived, limping from where she had been shot.

"Good," said Persephone. "Now, let's all go up to see Zeus. I believe there is a wedding we must prepare for."

Chapter Twenty-Eight

The return to Olympus was both as glorious and as annoying as Persephone remembered. She missed the world above and the sun, but it was her mother's wailing that she found bothersome. The moment they exited the PortMat in Olympus, word spread to Demeter. The Goddess of Grain hurried to Zeus' throne room and was there mere seconds after Persephone.

"Oh, my darling Kore! I missed you so much!" Demeter wrapped her arms around her daughter. "There is nothing to fear. You're home now. I'll protect you from Hades."

"Mother, there is something you should know..."

"Hush! There will be time for all that talk later. You have to tell Zeus how horrible it was in the Underworld for you. I'm sure we can marry you off to Bion shortly. Or, if you prefer, to Apollo. Anything to keep Hades from touching you once more."

"I'm not marrying Bion."

"Of course not, Kore. Apollo would make a much better suitor for you. Remember his speech at your Becoming Ceremony? He's the sun, and all growing plants need the sun." Demeter beamed. "Oh, it's so good to have you home, Kore."

Persephone sighed. "It's good to be home, Mother, but there is something you really must know."

"It can wait." Demeter started to try and straighten Persephone's hair. She frowned and took the crown off and flung it in a corner. Hades, who had been waiting quietly, picked it up.

"Mother, I don't think it can wait," Persephone said.

At that moment, Hermes walked in the room. "Zeus will see you all now." They were led to a private office, and it seemed like every major, and a few minor, gods were in audience. Zeus and Hera sat at the head of a large conference table with the rest of the major pantheon flanking down the sides. Hegemon and Bion snuggled together in a corner, and Persephone was glad to know the dart's effects had worn off. Eros and Hedone ran up to hug Psyche when she entered the room. Ares barely acknowledged his sons, distancing himself from whatever mess this caused until he knew the score.

"Zeus. I got Kore back, with no help from you." Demeter clung to Persephone. "Tell him, daughter. Tell him how horrible it was in the Underworld and how much you missed your mother. Tell him about how Hades hurt you. Oh, my poor Kore, my darling flower, tell him how terrified you were and how you never wish to return to the Underworld again."

Zeus smiled and there was a twinkle in his eyes. "Yes, tell me all about your visit."

Persephone gently pulled back from her mother. "I rather enjoyed my visit to the Underworld. I'm sure you are all now aware of the results of my trip." She looked at her mother. "I am no longer Kore, Mother. I am Persephone."

Demeter recoiled. "No!" she cried in anguish. She rounded on Hades, who immediately shrank back. "You!

What did you do to my daughter? You defiler of the innocent!"

"You're giving me way too much credit, Demeter," Hades said. "I never once laid an inappropriate hand on Persephone. I merely asked her to marry me. She made the choice to embrace her destiny on her own." He smiled. "Speaking of which, I am in my rights to claim that my wife spends time with me throughout the year. Six months, to be exact."

Demeter now turned to Persephone. "You married him? How could you? My own daughter!"

"We're not married yet, but I do plan to rectify that soon. Father Zeus, with your permission, I'd like to marry Hades as soon as possible. There is a lot of work that needs to be done in the Underworld, and I'm sure Hades would appreciate the help."

"You can't," said Demeter. "It's not autumn yet. You cannot go back to the Underworld until summer has passed."

"She is going to need a honeymoon," Zeus said thoughtfully. "We can overlook that little rule for this one time."

"No, you can't!" Demeter stomped her foot. "Kore can't go back until summer is over. I don't want her to go back at all, but that's the rule. My daughter stays with me for another six months."

"A week, Mother. I'm asking for just a week," Persephone said. "After you sent Enyo and Deimos to fetch me, they made a mess of the Underworld. It isn't fair to leave my husband with the entire clean-up."

"I would think making Deimos and Enyo help with

the cleanup would be appropriate," Demeter huffed.

"Those two are not to ever set foot in my kingdom again," said Hades. He turned to Zeus. "I am willing to waive any punishment as long as I have your word that they will not enter the Underworld, under penalty of total annihilation."

"I will grant that." Zeus stood up, his blue eyes on Deimos and Enyo. "I'm very disappointed in you two. Gods are held in a higher standard. Going off half-cocked in the Underworld on a personal mission is not what we gods do. And to threaten to kill fellow gods..." Zeus shook his head. "In all my years, I've never known of another god to betray us the way you two have."

"It won't happen again," said Deimos. He looked down like a chastised puppy.

Enyo crossed her arms. "As if you wouldn't have done the same, Zeus. In fact, you have done the same. Didn't Cronos once rule the entire world? And you overthrew him and recreated the world in your image. What is wrong with us doing the same? The gods have become complacent and soft. We need a new age, and I am the best person to issue in the new age."

"You are wrong." Ares stood up. "Enyo, as much as I love war and my place in our society, I know it's not a good idea to rock the boat. Some war is good, but peace is also good. If we create a world in your image, the humans would all die within a month."

Athena looked surprised. "I never thought I'd hear those words coming from you, Ares."

Ares grumped. "Don't expect it too often. I agree we're all too coddled and wouldn't survive a real war, but

Enyo went too far."

Hera cleared her throat. "We can decide the punishment for Deimos and Enyo at a later date. Right now, I believe we have to finish with Hades and Persephone."

"Her name is Kore!" Demeter snapped.

"What more is there?" asked Zeus. "Kore ate the pomegranate seeds, she took on the Zyspadaden that is Persephone and has fully become the goddess."

"There is a wedding to plan," said Hera. Hearing these words, Demeter sat heavily in a chair, fanning herself.

The door to the conference room opened, and everyone looked surprised as Minthe limped in the room. Demeter jumped up and ran to her faithful servant.

"What happened to you?" Demeter cried.

"That evil Psyche shot me," Minthe cried. She turned to Zeus. "I demand justice! You know gods should not shed divine blood. I count as a goddess; I have a Zyspadaden soul. Psyche shed my blood without cause!"

Psyche snorted. "You were threatening Kore and trying to overtake Persephone. It was well within my right to prevent you from usurping the right of another goddess."

Zeus turned to Hera. "I'm going to let you handle this one, dear."

Hera frowned. "Oh, thank you darling. You're too kind." She turned back to Minthe and Psyche. "Minthe, everyone knew that it was Kore's destiny to be Persephone. No matter your reasoning, you should not have tried to become her. You have your own Zyspadden and your own destiny. It is against our laws to interfere in the destiny of another or try to steal their rightful place in the pantheon. For this, I am recommending you be put in a stasis pod until the next Kore comes around."

Minthe looked shocked. "You can't! I'm a faithful servant of Demeter. Only she may order such a thing. And she needs me! Without Kore around, I'm all she has left."

Hera merely looked at Demeter, who sighed. "As my queen wishes," Demeter said, "you will be placed in a stasis pod until I name my next daughter."

Minthe threw herself at Demeter's feet. "Please reconsider my Lady! I have served you faithfully for so many years and this is how it ends? All I did was think of you! If I became Persephone, you would still have Kore. It was the perfect solution! Please, Lady Demeter, reconsider and have mercy."

Demeter patted Minthe on the head. "Come now, let's get you fixed up. I would not have you suffer in your pod. Apollo, if you will help us?"

The sun god stood and bowed to his father before going to help Minthe up. As they headed out, Demeter leaned in close and whispered to Minthe and Apollo.

"Now, as for Psyche," said Hera, "you did still shoot a Zyspadaden soul-bound goddess, no matter how minor Minthe's position. Though you did only shoot her hip."

"I throw myself on your mercy, my queen," said Psyche.

Hera hummed slightly as she thought over the punishment. "Five years in the service of a mortal. I understand you have been secretly – and I use that word loosely – helping a mortal family for several years. I also understand they incurred the wrath of Demeter recently. I sentence you to live as a mortal among them for five years, and if you can soothe out whatever curse Demeter placed on them, do so."

Psyche nodded. "Thank you, my queen."

"And I do hope you learned your lesson," said Hera.

"I have, my queen."

Zeus looked amused. "Really? That's it? My love, sometimes I think you're too soft."

"Five years without the abilities of a goddess or to be able to fully feel your Zyspadaden soul will be torment," said Hera. "The normal punishment for shedding the blood of a divine being depends on their level, and frankly, Psyche shouldn't be punished as she was of higher rank. However, there has been a nasty trend of late with gods harming other gods. Can we not forget the incident nineteen or twenty years ago when Deimos and Enyo broke Eros in our very hallowed halls? You allowed them to go virtually free. Or, seven years ago, when Apollo challenged Aiode to a singing contest, and he practically beat the poor girl to death when he lost. I don't care if she was just going to be merged with Terpsichore as the Muse of Dance and Lyrical Poetry, the point remains that he spilled blood. And what was his punishment? He was under house arrest for a month."

Zeus shrugged. "What else can we do? I can't strip the major gods of their powers. We need to have Apollo, we need to have Ares, and we need to have Deimos and Enyo."

"We can stop coddling them. We may need Apollo,

but we don't need that Apollo. From now on, the punishments will fit the crime. I've been talking to Dikaiosyne, Nomos, and Astraea. As minor gods of justice, law, and righteousness, they have helped open my eyes to this trend. We used to be harsher on those who broke the laws, and now it's the equivalent of standing in the corner." Hera stood. "My husband, I want to create a council of judges for the gods. That way, our personal feelings will not interfere with the proper form of justice when a crime has been committed." Hera looked over at Psyche. "Sorry to say, it's going to start with you, Psyche. While I personally don't think you did any real harm, we need to start somewhere. May your next five years not be too horrific."

"If I may ask one favor, Hera," Psyche said. "I would like to stay long enough to see Persephone married."

"I'll allow that."

Zeus clapped his hands. "Wonderful. Let's get the wedding together if there are no more objections."

Epilogue

A week after her wedding, Persephone sat in the glorious mansion in the Underworld. Two stacks of reports sat in front of her: one for the issues caused by the early frost in the middle of summer and the other from what needs to be done in the Underworld. Hades, her loving husband, was currently out helping fix the broken hologram projector in the welcome area. His current host had been a mechanic with Hephaestus, and the knowledge stored in his memory came in handy. The inhabitants of Tartarus had been returned, along with a promise of a 'vacation' once a month. To ensure that they came back, Hephaestus issued special collars that each would wear. If they tried to remove them, they would be shocked into consciousness.

"Mother? You have a guest." Melinoe drifted into the room. Her looks now resembled a perfect blend of Persephone and Hades. She also de-aged to that of a child. Persephone thought it was vastly creepier to have an innocent child be followed by the ghosts of Zyspadaden past, which, she supposed, was Melinoe's intent.

Phobos walked in the room. On this day, he was not dressed in his normal armor. He wore a plain red peplos tunic that fell to his knees. The stubble on his chin gave evidence of his plans to regrow his beard. Either that, or he just hadn't shaved that morning. His wild hair was tamed in a thick ponytail at the nape of his neck.

"You wanted to see me?"

"Phobos, yes. Please have a seat." Persephone

waited until he sat before she said, "I've been doing a lot of thinking. Well, actually, now that I'm fully myself, I know my assumptions are true."

"I'm not following."

Persephone took a deep breath. "See, as Kore, I found out that Demeter wasn't my birth mother, but a woman named Odessa. I knew I heard that name before. Just before I accepted Persephone, it hit me. I heard her name from you. Do you remember? It was at Dionysus' party, and you said that I reminded you of a woman you knew named Odessa?"

"I remember." Phobos smiled. "You do remind me of her. I guess you being her daughter would explain that."

"Don't play games," said Persephone. "I know exactly who you are, Dad."

Phobos didn't look shocked. He nodded. "It wasn't really a secret, but I was told to never tell you. I was to treat you as if you were really Demeter's daughter."

"I know. Persephone, my past self, knew all about it. I remember my own crisis of identity when I found out about Demeter. I thought Hades would stop loving me if he knew what Demeter had done. I now know better. I have lifetimes of memories to tell me otherwise." She smiled. "But, none of my previous selves ever got to know their real father."

"I can't be your real father, Persephone. For the entire world, you are the daughter of Demeter and Zeus."

"Above world, I am that. Down here, I'd like to think of you as my father. You've had more of a hand in my life than Zeus. I don't want you to be a stranger."

Phobos sat back, tapping his fingers on the table. "I guess that means I'll be spending winters down here."

"You won't regret it. I happen to know that a lot of the mortals who reside here with families would be pleased to have self-defense classes. Enyo's attack really frightened them."

Phobos laughed. "Oh, now I get it. That's why you called me here. Not because I'm your father, but to get free lessons out of me. Sneaky."

"Who better to train them to take care of themselves than a god of war?"

"I'll do it." Phobos shook his head. "Times are changing. Everything is different now."

"Times have been changing for a while now."

Melinoe entered the room again. "Mother, you have another visitor." This time, instead of floating out, Melinoe went to Persephone and climbed up in her lap. The ghosts took stations around Persephone's chair, looking like macabre guards.

It was a good thing Melinoe was in Persephone's lap. When Minthe walked in the room, the Queen of the Underworld nearly jumped to her feet.

"What are you doing here? I thought Hera ordered you to be put in a stasis pod."

Phobos stood, reaching for the gun he wasn't wearing. "State your business and leave, Minthe."

"Minthe? Oh, you don't recognize me?" Minthe smiled and Persephone narrowed her eyes. There was something off about her mother's former servant. It was the subtle way Minthe held herself and how the mint-dyed hair was streaking with brown in some spots. At first glance, she certainly looked like Minthe, but now Persephone noticed that there were stalks of wheat sticking out of her hair and she was not in her normal light green clothing. She wore a wheat-yellow chiton and Demeter's jewelry.

"Mother?" Persephone couldn't believe her eyes.

"Yes," Demeter hissed. "This is what you've done, Kore. Your rebellious nature stabbed me so deeply; I had to move on to a new host. But I had to reward Minthe. After years of faithful service, I couldn't just let her lie there to rot. This is what we worked out. Her soul will wait for another girl worthy of being Minthe to come along, and I have a new body." Demeter looked down at her body in disgust. "Slightly used and I get echoes of Minthe's thoughts from time to time."

"Is this why you skipped my wedding?" asked Persephone. She had assumed Demeter stayed away because she was marrying Hades. This was just too disturbing to think of. While the Zyspadaden changed hosts often enough, they never swapped hosts with another.

"Correct. I needed a long time to recover. My poor soul just couldn't take it. I thought you would be my good daughter, Kore. I went over and over in my head what could have gone wrong. I did everything right! You were my obedient daughter for most of your life. Oh, fie! I know where I went wrong. I sent you to my enemies, thinking they would not turn you against me. Well, I won't have to worry about that next time. The next Kore will never leave her tower. She will not have to worry about her Becoming Ceremony or Hades. I will keep a closer eye on her. Just you watch! Your days of being disrespectful will come to an end!"

"You tried that already," said Persephone. "Actually, you tried that several times. I've had to either climb out of the tower and run away, or I'd see Hades from a distance and help him break in. It never worked, Mother. I'm meant to become Persephone and marry Hades. If I don't, we don't have winter, and without winter, we won't be able to grow all the crops."

"I'll pick a boy," Demeter crowed. "Hades can't marry a boy."

Persephone rolled her eyes. "Been there, done that."

"I won't let him win next time," Demeter said. "Kore, you have to return to me. You're my daughter. You know I get lonely without you. What kind of mother would I be if I didn't try to protect you?"

"I'm coming home in a week, Mother," said Persephone. "Really, it will be no time at all. You'll see. Before you know it, I'll be home and we'll be busy fixing this whole mess."

Demeter brightened up. "Of course we'll fix this whole mess. Oh, darling, I won't force you to stay married to Hades. Once you get home, we'll figure out how to make all this nastiness go away." Before Persephone could correct her, Demeter left.

Persephone groaned. "Oh, now it begins. Years and years of Mother trying to break up my marriage."

Phobos shrugged as he sat back down. "Well, times are changing. Maybe it won't be as bad this go-around?" He reached over and picked up one of the reports. "This isn't for here," he said. "This one is about growing food for the proposed mission to the planet."

"Yeah. I'm helping with that since Mother refused." She took the report back and let Melinoe slide down to the ground. She smiled. "Maybe it won't be that bad this time. After all, before Mother can find me a new host, I'll have a chance to see our people get off this Station. A whole new world is about to open up for us."

Character Pronunciation

All the character descriptions given are for the traditional Ancient Greek myths, unless they are an original character.

Aeacus – E/Kas

King of the island of Aegina, father of Peleus, Telmon, and Phocus, grandfather of the hero Achilles, one of the three judges of the Underworld.

Aidoneus – I/dawn/Us

Another name for Hades, one he uses in this novel to keep his true identity a secret.

Amphitrite – Ahm/frI/tea

Wife of Poseidon and a sea-goddess in her own right.

Aneriams/Levanti – Ann/Ear/E/Ams // Lee/Van/Tea

Little blue ant-like creatures that can be found around real flowers, their origins are unknown and possibly have been among the first aboard the Space Station.

Anteros – Ann/Tear/Os

Son of Aphrodite and Ares, God of Requited Love but he also is the avenger of those scorned by love, he has butterfly wings, in one myth, Eros refused to grow up until Anteros was born so they could be friends forever, part of the Erotos (Eros, Anteros, Himeros, and

Pothos).

Aphrodite –
Ah/Froh/Die/Tea

Daughter of Zeus and Dione (though some sources say she is the product of a disemboweled Uranus), Goddess of Love, Beauty, Pleasure, and Procreation, wife of Hephaestus but a lover of Ares, Poseidon, Hermes, and bunch of others, mother of many children, among them are Eros, Phobos, Deimos, Pothos, Anteros, Himeros, and the Graces.

Apollo – Ah/Paul/Oh

Son of Leto and Zeus, twin brother of Artemis, God of the Sun, Light, Music, Archery, Medicine, Prophecy, and Knowledge.

Ares – Air/eees

Son of Zeus and Hera, God of War (though the more blood lust part of it), lover of Aphrodite and father of Phobos and Deimos, and the Erotos (Eros and Anteros).

Artemis – Ar/tea/miss

Daughter of Zeus and Leto, Goddess of the Hunt, Childbirth, the Moon, and Archery, virgin goddess who punished men that trespassed on her property.

Cerberus – Ker/ber/us

The three-headed hound of Hades who guards the Underworld to keep the souls in, his name also means "spot". Seriously.

Charon – Kare/On

The ferryman who carries the souls of the newly deceased across the river Styx, but only if they have the coin to pay.

Chloris – Klor/Us

Minor goddess and personification of Spring

Chruse – Kroo/s

Wife of Theron, used to work in the Temple of Apollo, met Iona and befriended her, mother of a teenaged daughter also named Iona, twin sons named Telchine and Velbious, and a baby boy named Lykaios.

Deimos – Dee/Mohs

Son of Ares and Aphrodite, God of Dread and Terror, twin brother of Phobos.

Demeter – Deh/ME/Ter

Daughter of Cronus and Rhea, one myth states she started hating Hades while in the stomach of her father because he, as the eldest, did not save them, Goddess of Agriculture, Fertility, and Harvest, mother of Persephone, Despoina, Arion, and Plutus.

Despoina – Dez/Poy/Nah

Daughter of Demeter and Poseidon, known as "Mistress of the Horses", twin sister of Arion (a talking horse), also known as another name for Persephone according to some of the Mysteries (secret rituals) surrounding Demeter.

Dionysus – Dye/a/nI/sos

Son of Zeus and Semele, God of the Vine, Wine, Winemaking, Ritual Madness, Religious Ecstasy, and the Theatre, once brought Hephaestus back to Olympus drunk.

Enyo – I/no

Goddess of War, sometimes called the sister of Ares, the

daughter of Ares, or is identified as a female version of Ares, she doesn't appear to have any myths surrounding her and often plays just a minor role as a personification of bloodshed.

Eros – Ear/Os

Son of Aphrodite and Ares (though some myths have him much older and an original God of Love before being replaced by Aphrodite), God of Sexual Desire, Attraction, and Love, best known today as Cupid, husband of Psyche, part of the Erotos (Eros, Anteros, Himeros, and Pothos), father of Hedone.

Eileithyia – Eel/E/Thigh/Ya

Daughter of Zeus and Hera, Goddess of Childbirth, she shares this with Hera.

Flora – Fl/oh/rah

A Roman goddess of spring and flowers who made it in the novel because the author needed more goddesses of spring, Roman equivalent of Choris, has a myth where she becomes the lover of Zyphyrus.

Hecate – High/kah/tea

Goddess of Magic, Crossroads, Ghosts, and Necromancy, lives in the Underworld, mother of Circe, Scylla, and, on some occasions, Pan, was the goddess Medea prayed to the most.

Hades – Hay/Dees

Eldest son of Cronus and Rhea, brother to Zeus, Demeter, Poseidon, Hera, and Hestia, God of the Dead and Underworld, sometimes mixed in with Plutus, God of Wealth (Plutus and Hades became

Pluto in Roman mythology), because of this, he is technically also a fertility god, husband of Persephone.

Hedone – HE/doh/wn

Daughter of Eros and Psyche, Goddess of sensual pleasure, from her we get the word Hedonism.

Hegemone –
Hye/ge/mahn

Minor goddess who made plants bloom and fruit.

Hephaestus –
HE/Fess/Tus

Son of Zeus and Hera (though, some sources say Hera alone), brother of Ares, God of Fire, Metalworking, Forges, and Sculptures, husband of Aphrodite, known as the only ugly god among the beautifully perfect immortals.

Hera – Hair/ah

Middle daughter of Cronus and Rhea, Queen of the Gods, Wife of Zeus, Goddess of Marriage, Women, Childbirth, and Family, a very vengeful goddess whenever she could get her hands on any of Zeus' mistresses' children, mother of Ares, Hephaestus, Eris, Eileithyia, and Hebe, sometimes known as the mother of Enyo.

Hermes – Her/Mees

Son of Zeus and Maia (one of the Pleiades), God of Trade, Thieves, Travelers, Sports/Athletes, and Crossroads, father of Pan, known to be a trickster god.

Hestia – Heh/s/tea/ah

The eldest daughter of Cronus and Rhea,

Goddess of the Hearth, Home, Domesticity, Family, and the State, she was once part of the original Olympians but "retired" and handed her spot to Dionysus keeping the number of Olympians at twelve, she has no known consort or children.

Himeros – HE/mah/rose

Son of Aphrodite and Ares, brother to Eros, Pothos, and Anteros, God of sexual desire and unrequited love, often depicted with bows and arrows like Eros.

Hypnos – Hip/nos

God of Sleep, half-brother of Thanatos, Son of Nyx and Erebus, Father of Morpheus, Phobetor, and Phantasos.

Iona – Eye/owe/nah

1.   Iona Demarchis, youngest daughter of Hedyla and Metasis Demarchis of Tyrins, becomes Psyche and marries Eros, considered (at the moment) one of the ugliest goddesses due to scars and a near fatal mauling that occurred while she was still mortal.

2.   Iona, daughter of Theron and Chruse.

Ixion – Ik/Sigh/on

King of the Lapiths, possibly a son of Ares or Zeus, entered a feud with his father-in-law Deioneus or Eioneus, resulting in Ixion being punished in Tartarus on a burning wheel.

Kore – KOh/Ray

Daughter of Demeter and Zeus, another name for Persephone, her name means "Maiden" and is often used to refer to her pre-Hades.

Lykaios – Lie/kah/os

Youngest son of Theron and Chruse, cursed by Demeter after Chruse stopped Demeter from burning away Lykaios' mortality.

Melinoe – Mel/In/Oh/A

Daughter of Persephone (father rumored to either be Zeus or Hades), Goddess of Ghosts, Night, and Madness.

Minos – My/nose

King of Crete, son of Zeus and Europa, most famous for his labyrinth and Minotaur, later became a judge in the Underworld with his brother Rhadamanthys.

Minthe – Min/tha

Naiad of the river Cocytus who fell in love with Hades. In some myths, he was flattered by her attentions, drawing the ire of his wife, Persephone. Either Persephone or Demeter stomps Minthe into a plant (mint) for trying to seduce Hades (Persephone) or insulting Persephone (Demeter).

Odessa – Oh/Day/Sah

Parentage unknown, a devotee of Demeter, she is beloved by Phobos. Odessa becomes pregnant and is kidnapped by Demeter. She dies in childbirth and Demeter raises her daughter as Kore.

Pan – Pahn

Son of Hermes (many different mothers depending on the myth, including Aphrodite, Driope, and Hecate), God of the Wild, Shepherds, Flocks, and some association with Sexuality, from his name we get Panic.

Persephone –
Per/Sef/Phone/A

Daughter of Zeus and Demeter, wife of Hades, Goddess of the New Spring/Vegetation and Queen of the Underworld, if one wants a favor of Hades, they often sent prayers through Persephone to sweeten up her husband, mother of Melinoe (father might be Hades or Zeus).

Phobos – Foh/Bohs

Son of Aphrodite and Ares, God of Fear, twin brother of Deimos, while Deimos isn't mentioned in mythology, Phobos is mentioned briefly in Seven Against Thebes by Aeschylus.

Poseidon – Poh/sigh/Don

Middle son of Cronus and Rhea, God of the Sea, Earthquakes, Storms, and Horses, Husband of Amphitrite, Father of Theseus, Triton, and Atlas, lost a naming contest with Athena over the rights to name a new city (Athens), also fathered Despoina and Arion with Demeter.

Psyche – Syk/Key

A human princess who was too beautiful and angered Aphrodite, she eventually becomes the Goddess of the Soul/Mind, this story is the basic premise of famous fairy tales like Beauty and the Beast, mother of Hedone.

Rhadamanthus –
Rad/ah/Mahn/thas

Son of Zeus and Europa, brother to Minos, King of Crete and responsible for a few known legislative activities (such as self-defense), in some myths he's Hercules' stepfather later in life, sometimes the husband of Ariadne (daughter of Minos), one of the three judges of the Underworld.

Sisyphus – Sigh/e/Fuss

King of Corinth who was punished for being the first to kill his own kin. His punishment was to forever roll a large boulder uphill, only to have it roll back down before reaching the top. From him we get the word Sisyphean, meaning a task that is both laborious and futile.

Tantalus – Tan/tall/Os

Son of Zeus and Plouto (a nymph), possibly a King of Phrygia, attributed to being the husband of various wives in different versions of myths. Tantalus is most famous for his punishment in Tartarus. After being welcomed to Olympus to dine with the gods, Tantalus stole ambrosia and brought it back to the mortals. In another version, he's said to have killed his son, Pelops, and served him as the main course to the gods, with only Demeter eating the food because she was distracted over losing Persephone. In a lesser known myth, his crime was stealing a golden dog made by Hephaestus, or keeping the dog after a friend stole it. His punishment was to be placed in a pool of water up to his neck with a tree growing above him. He could never eat the fruit from the tree nor drink of the water in the pool.

Telchine – Tell/Kin/ah

Son of Theron and Chruse, twin brother of Valbious.

Telete – Tel/A/Tah

Daughter of Dionysus and

Nicaea, Goddess of the Initiation to the Bacchic Rites, associated with the nighttime festivities and ritual dancing and follows her father with her half-brother, Iacchus.

Theron – They/Ron

Parentage unknown, rumored to be the son of Apollo, a star athlete, married to Errita. After his wife's death, he remarries and moves to Eleusis, a level that is very devoted to Demeter. He becomes a farmer and leaves his athletic stardom behind.

Valbious – Val/BI/us

Son of Theron and Chruse, twin of Telchine.

Zeus – Zoos

Youngest child of Cronus and Rhea, King of the Gods, God of the Skies, Thunder/Lightning, Hospitality, Honor and Order, well-known for his playboy ways, has many children with many women, notably: Persephone (Demeter), Apollo and Artemis (Leto), Hermes (Maia), Athena (Metis), Dionysus (Semele), and Ares, Eileithyia, Hebe and Hephaestus (Hera).

Zephyrus – ZI/Fir/Us

Parentage unknown, one of the four major winds (Boreaus/North, Notus/South, Zephyrus/West, and Eurus/East), lover of Hyacinths (and accidentally killed him), some myths have him as the lover/husband of several women, including Iris, Goddess of the Rainbow, and Chloris, Goddess of Flowers.

Zyspadaden – Zis/pah/dah/den

The alien race that is responsible for the abilities and memories of the gods and goddesses on the station. Where they came from is still a mystery, but they helped the humans of Earth Three by creating several religiously-based space stations as religion appeared to be the main point of discontent at that time. The other space stations lost contact with one another, and it is unknown if only Space Station Olympus has survived. The Zyspadaden have been in their human hosts for so long, playing the parts of the gods, that they basically believe they are the gods.

About the Author

I have always wanted to be a writer. From the time I was around seven years old and took crayon to paper, I felt like it was my one true calling. I used to write (rather horribly) little stories for my family. A few years later, when attending summer camp, I was given another opportunity to put my creative muscles to good use. I wrote little five minute or so plays for some kids in the camp to perform. One of the counselors used to tape them and we'd have a little "movie" night with them. A year or so after that, I penned my first real play. It was called Underwater Friends, and I'm sure someone might still have a copy hidden away in some dusty attic. I really wish mine was still around. It was funny.

In high school, I finished my first draft of a novel, but never went beyond that. Writing was always my dream, but I thought being published was well beyond me. Goes to show what I know. I am now the proud author of the Space Station Olympus series, an on-going saga of Greek mythology in space, as well as some stand-alone novels.

A special thanks to all those who helped make this book possible. To my editor, Jeffrey Cunningham, whose wise suggestions helped steer this book in the right direction, and who I hope didn't run out of red ink correcting my mistakes. To my beta readers, Marcia, Maryia, and Jade, whose insight tackled problems that escaped my notice.

To all my readers, if I could bother you for a moment of your time now that you've completed reading Kore, and ask you for a small favor? Would you please consider writing an online review? For an indie writer such as myself, reviews are the best way I can learn how you feel about my work. I could never make it this far without you, and it is for you that I strive to make each book the best I can produce. If you enjoyed my story, please, tell your friends and leave a review to let me know how you feel. Thank you, from the bottom of my heart.

Upcoming Books

Forbidden Magic

Expected Release Date: November 2017

For as long as anyone could remember, the kingdoms of Fanarias and Anstaria have been at war. While there have been attempts at peace treaties, they never seem to truly achieve peace. When the next attempt happens in Anstarian Dione's lifetime, she hopes this will be the attempt that brings peace.

Raised the niece of a tavern owner and brought to the royal palace to be the companion to the princess, Dione does not hope for a very adventurous life. Married at the age of fourteen to an elderly duke and widowed by nineteen, she wishes to settle down in the country home left to her and spend her days in solitude. But, when the prince of Fanarias decides to claim her as his bride, her quiet plans fall apart and her protector since birth, Prince Klaus of Anstaria, quickly marries her to another at the cost of angering Fanarias.

What happens next will always be described as the Dark Age. A deadly plague whips through Anstaria, killing many of the people. On the heels of the plague comes a sudden blossoming of Hex in the people of Anstaria. Hex (magic) had been outlawed for centuries with the fate being death. Dione's brother, who is acting as king while their father mourns, knows something must be done to save his people. But how does one fight Hex when no one is allowed to use it.

Then, the unthinkable happens. Dione falls ill from the plague. With her death surely at hand, Prince Klaus makes one final decision regarding Dione's fate. He sends her to live with her betrothed in the hopes that he gets her out of Anstaria and to safety.

The forces of Fanarias won't just let Dione go. Her carriage is attacked on the way out of Anstaria. Still fevered by the plague, Dione preforms magic in front of her enemy. Now he has her. Her beloved hates Hex almost as much as the entire kingdom of Anstaria and Dione is a Hex hag. The enemy offers to help her, in exchange for information. She can either be their spy, or risk revealing her magic to the man she loves.

Lykaios

Expected Release Date: November 2018

"You will lose the one you love to Hades, just as I've lost mine!"

The words of Demeter cursed Lykaios when he was just a baby. His whole family was forced to move in secret after his father, Theron, found himself between fighting gods twice in his life. Fearful that he'd lose his family, Lykaios spent every day with them as if it were the last, wanting to keep his memories happy. He grew to become a fantastic musician, but never traveled.

That is, until a call went out for men and women to help settle the planet below the station. Lykaios only went because Eurydice, a golden helper of Hephaestus, was going. Wanting to impress the sour woman, Lykaios boarded the ship Oceanus to the planet and set his own story into motion. He is not the only one who wants Eurydice's hand, but he may be the only one brave enough to face down Hades for her.